CHOICES

To Diana

Hope you enjoy the

story

Best Wishes

Robert Sterling

2013

CHOICES

ROBERT STIRLING

Library of Congress Control Number: 2013902826
ISBN: Hardcover   978-1-4797-9561-1
                 Softcover   978-1-4797-9560-4
                 Ebook   978-1-4797-9562-8

This book was printed in the United States of America.

Rev. date: 03/15/2013

To order additional copies of this book, contact:
Xlibris Corporation
1-888-795-4274
www.Xlibris.com
Orders@Xlibris.com
129230

PROLOGUE

Roger Abbott was dreaming. In his mind, he went back to that horrifying day when he lost the most precious thing in his life: his wife, Anna.

He could still see the car skid into the ditch, still hear his wife's screams. Was there no relief from the raw, tormenting pain?

CHAPTER ONE

Roger Abbott loved Nova Scotia winters and was living a childhood dream as he skimmed over the sheer ice of Dartmouth's Lake Micmac. He felt a cold February breeze sting his face and heard the scrape of the runners and the flapping of the yellow sail as the iceboat glided effortlessly over the ice.

Unaware that she was not alone, Janice Peterson was just ahead, practicing her figure skating jumps. She suddenly appeared before Roger's boat.

"Hey, you on the ice, get out of the way. I can't stop!" Roger frantically yelled over the roar of the wind as the pine iceboat bore down on the young woman. She was wearing a pale ski suit, so was almost invisible on the gray surface of the lake. It appeared the woman was not even aware he was about to run her down. "Look out!"

Frantically, he pulled on the silk airfoil sail, trying to slow down the craft. With a sharp tug on the tension control, he hoped to avoid a collision with the skater a few yards in front of him. As Roger struggled for control, he knew it would be a miracle if he missed her.

As this was playing out, the woman fell. She had been doing some sort of jump when the boat with the bright yellow sail had suddenly appeared around the bend in the shoreline. She always enjoyed skating and practicing her easier figure skating jumps just as the sun came up in the early morning. Since the accident, she had to be careful. Janice had thought she was the only one on the lake at this hour.

On this day, she was wrong.

It looked like she was going to pay the price for her inattention to what was happening around her. As she was concentrating on her technique, she was blissfully unaware of her surroundings. Today, she was also reflecting on the support her mother always gave her when she was skating. She missed her desperately. Out of the corner of her eye, she saw the iceboat slowly change direction to the right of her. It would miss her, but it would be alarmingly close.

Janice watched the boat turn and saw the wind catch the yellow sail, then she stared in dismay as the boat began to tip to one side. She saw the wind push the boat over until the man was thrown to the ice.

Roger felt the boat tip, and in slow motion, it capsized. He was thrown roughly to the ice. Its hard surface knocked the wind out of him. As a final insult, the sail settled over him like a silken shroud. Catching his breath, and scrambling to his feet, he rubbed the wet seat of his denim jeans and skated across the ice toward the woman. Even from this distance, he could tell that she was favoring her right leg.

His blade hit a crack, and he almost fell as he approached a beautiful young woman. She looked to be about his age and had long lustrous blonde hair and a heart-shaped face. That face was fighting back tears as she limped toward him.

"Why don't you watch what you're doing? I could have run you over. What were you trying to do anyway?" Roger looked from her strained, pain-filled face to her sore ankle. He softened his tone of voice. "You're hurt."

"I'm sorry. I get so involved in my skating that I sometimes lose tract of my surroundings. Like just now." She looked down at her foot. "My ankle is killing me. Could you help me home? I live over there." She pointed toward the shore behind them to a large beige-colored home that faced the lake. She studied his face, the firm jaw, then the red-and-white winter jacket, and faded jeans. His eyes bored into hers. "I thought I was alone today. My name's Janice Peterson. I've seen your iceboat on the lake before. Do you live around here, Mr.—?"

"Roger Abbott. No. I'm staying with my uncle while my home is being repaired. I'm a police officer and live about eighty miles away in Avonvale. It's about two hours from here. I'll help you any way I can. By the looks of that ankle, we need to get you to a doctor."

"Thank you for your concern. My father is a doctor, so I should be okay if you'll just help me home."

He felt strangely off balance being so close to Janice. It almost seemed that an invisible current passed between them. Since the feeling was fleeting, he chose to ignore it. He was not interested in any kind of a relationship with a woman right now. His heart was still too raw from the loss of his wife.

They were not the only ones near the lake this early in the morning. The two of them had no idea that two men were watching from the shelter of some nearby trees. Actually, it was Janice they were interested in. From their hiding place, they had seen the whole incident involving the iceboat. After a few minutes' observation, they disappeared.

Roger succeeded in getting Janice to the oak dock that jutted into the lake near her home. The wind blew around them, sending up little swirls of snow that stung their faces. It seemed to stimulate all his nerve endings. Helping her up onto the pier, he hopped up beside her and reached for her hand.

She winced as she landed on the dock. "Thank you. It's just a step to the house. I should be able to manage now. You best go see to your boat. I hope it's not wrecked."

"The boat will be fine. I wouldn't think of dumping you here. Is anyone home?" He looked up at the huge structure, noting large windows, a wide glass-enclosed patio, and tall trees.

As Janice unlocked the back basement door, they could hear voices raised in anger somewhere above them. He tried to make out what was being said as he sat on the bench and removed his skates.

"It sounds like Dad and my Uncle Boyd are arguing again," she sighed.

"Do they fight often?" He knew it wasn't any of his business, unless it turned out to be illegal, but he was concerned. He didn't stop to analyze too closely if it might be because of the beautiful woman beside him.

"Uncle Boyd is trying to get Dad to give him some money to help his small trucking company. He's been pressuring him for months now." She wondered what else he wanted from her father. She sounded disgusted with her uncle's attitude. She looked up as her father and two other men descended some steps off to the left of them. Janice managed a faint smile as her father came into view.

Roger observed that the doctor was in his late forties or early fifties and was well dressed, with a self-assured attitude. He decided he liked Dr. Peterson. Two others followed the good doctor. The man behind him looked like Janice's father, so had to be the uncle. The second man was slightly younger, with blonde hair and startling blue eyes. He felt the hairs on the back of his neck stand up. There was something about this uncle that he didn't like. Besides being tall and imposing, the man exuded an air of arrogance. The other man had a scar down the left cheek. Roger sensed that he was dangerous, as was this Boyd Peterson.

"Janice, you're back. How was the—" He stopped in midsentence when he noticed his daughter limping. "What happened out there? Who is the young man with you, honey?"

"This is Roger Abbott, Father. I twisted my ankle when I fell. He was iceboating and gave me assistance. I think it's sprained. I guess my skating will have to be put on hold—" At this point her breath caught, and Roger felt a shaft of guilt pierce him. "Roger, my father, Frank Peterson. My Uncle Boyd is with him. The other man is an associate, Peter Boyce. Uncle Boyd has a trucking company in Avonvale." As she made the official introductions, Roger could pick up the slight tremor in her voice, the startled look. It looked like he was not the only one to have a strong disliking for this duo.

"Nice to meet you both," he managed to acknowledge. Actually, he was not pleased to meet either one of them. Not one to make snap judgments, he sensed this man could be dangerous if crossed. He saw that Boyd Peterson made no move to shake his extended hand. Nor did the other younger man. He let his hand fall back to his side. That little lack on the men's part was telling. Roger assessed Boyd. He was tall, probably six foot or taller, with a high forehead, a hawkish nose, and very cold eyes. Those eyes were also making an assessment of him. Straightening up, he looked right at him, refusing to be intimidated. A second later, Boyd looked away, and the impasse was over.

"I think I remember you from somewhere," Boyd probed. "You live around here?" He seemed entirely too interested in finding out where he lived.

"I live across the lake with my Uncle George. I just happened to be in the right place at the right time to help Janice here." He motioned to her as she sat on a small chair. "I iceboat on the lake during the winter."

"Probably that's where I've seen you. Remember what I said, Frank. I need that money!"

As the two of them passed, Boyd gave him a searching look. He had never felt such a strong instant dislike for a man before. Not much sense in worrying about it since one chance encounter didn't prove anything.

"I must be going too," Roger said, reluctantly. "I hope your ankle isn't too bad. Nice to meet you, Dr. Peterson."

"Thank you for helping my daughter. Maybe we'll meet again sometime." He extended his hand and gave Roger a hearty handshake.

As Roger grabbed the doctor's hand, he felt the warmth and firmness of the clasp. Again, he was impressed that this man was honorable and would be a good friend. His dark eyes were kind and revealed compassion. He suspected Frank Peterson was a very good doctor. The bifocals perched on his long straight nose gave him an aura of a man of culture. His astute observations revealed this when he shook the man's hand. He took a quick look at the room they were in. It was some sort of family room, complete with pool table and a large flat-screen TV off to one side. A beautiful stone fireplace stood at the far end of the room. He admired the man's taste.

"You're welcome. The pleasure is all mine, I assure you, sir. I'm sorry we had to meet on such trying circumstances." He turned to address Janice, who had removed her skates and was rubbing her sore ankle. "If your daughter is agreeable, I'd like to see her again." He couldn't believe he actually said that out loud. He was supposed to be mourning the loss of his wife, not looking forward to seeing Janice Peterson.

No matter how beautiful the woman was.

"I guess you'll have to ask her, son. If you do see her, you have to promise me you won't tire her. I'd like to stay and chat with you two, but I've got to go see a patient at the hospital." He leaned over and gave his daughter a quick kiss on the forehead. After helping her remove her other skate, he grabbed a bandage from nearby. Quickly, he bound up the sore ankle. "I'll see about getting you a pair of crutches, Janice. After the other accident, you really should have it seen. I'll talk to Dr. Abbass at the hospital." Grabbing a briefcase, Frank Peterson went back upstairs. Roger heard the door shut a minute later.

They were alone in the house.

"Well, would you be interested in showing me a bit about this skating technique of yours? And what is the other accident your father mentioned?" He looked at her with questions in his eyes. He wondered if he dared ask her about the strong reaction she had shown when her uncle had appeared. Not being shy about asking questions, he decided to chance it. "I couldn't help noticing how you reacted to your uncle earlier. I see you dislike him as much as I do."

"You're very observant. I don't skate much anymore. About twelve years ago, I had a bad spill during practice. My leg was badly broken, and my ankle was sprained. That ended skating in competitions. I still like to skate for recreation on the lake whenever I can. I also get to coach some kids at the local rink, where I really enjoy showing them the ins and outs of skating. If you would be interested, I can give you a book on figure skating that might be of help," she offered. "Now, about my reaction to my uncle. It was him, but it was also Peter Boyce. He and I used to go together, until I found out he was using drugs. It doesn't surprise me he hooked up with my uncle. They're a lot alike."

"Oh. I see it's still a sore point with you. And I'm grateful you didn't mention that I almost hit you." He replied with a feeling of relief evident in his voice, and then added, "Where's this book of yours?"

Janice hobbled over to the bookcase on the far wall and withdrew a dark blue hard-covered manual. She handed it to him, "Enjoy it. Take as long as you want. I know it wasn't your fault you almost hit me. Sometimes the skating takes so much concentration that I forget what's around me. And thanks for your concern about my relationship with Peter. I'll survive." Roger felt the jolt go through his system when her hand brushed his. The soft touch seemed to bring all his senses to life. He had thought his heart had closed down after Anna's death.

Apparently he had been wrong!

"I look forward to seeing you again. Maybe on the lake." Where did that thought come from? He hoped they could meet in a more conventional way, however. He put on his skates, making a quick exit before any more unwanted feelings started in the pit of his stomach.

"If we do meet on the lake, I'll be sure to stay away from your boat. Maybe we can go skating together." She wasn't interested in any more encounters with his iceboat, but she managed to let him know she was interested. The strained look on her face told him that she was in a lot of pain.

Looking over his shoulder, he saw Janice standing by the patio door, watching as he made his way down to the lake. The wind blew into his face, sending wisps of snow around his head. The snow wet his face, stinging his cheeks. The image of her face in the window stayed with him as he skated across the smooth surface of the lake.

Roger found the overturned iceboat where he left it. Bending down, he grabbed the mast and lifted the sail. Once the boat was upright, he jumped in and let the sail catch the wind. It was awesome out here on the lake, just him against nature. He steered the boat toward the far shore where his car and trailer waited. The chance encounter with the beautiful blonde girl hung in the back of his mind, much like an image seen through the fog. The other image that refused to go away was the hard face of Boyd Peterson. Something about that face was familiar, but the identity stayed just outside his consciousness.

While Roger was enjoying a quick sail across Lake Micmac, the object of his thoughts was talking to one of his suppliers on his cell phone as he drove toward Avonvale. He headed along a narrow country road toward the coast. As he drew near a turn, he could hear the surf crashing against the base of the cliff. Pulling off the road, he stopped and exited the car. Ahead of Boyd Peterson was a small island, just offshore. It sat about a half a mile away and looked to be about a half mile wide, and maybe a mile long. It, along with Sober Island, lay just at the entrance to Sheet Harbour, guarding the channel. Boyd knew the island was deserted now. Years ago, a family lived in the small house he could just make out through the thick trees. The red-topped structure was automated now. That fact could work to his advantage. Boyd smiled at the possibilities that lay hidden in the trees, just offshore. A stiff breeze blew toward him, ruffling his sandy colored hair.

He turned his fur collar up as he made his way along a narrow path toward a thicket of trees. As an opening appeared in the trees, a large Cape Cod-style home materialized. Boyd unlocked the heavy red oak door and disappeared inside. Approaching a large book shelf, he pushed a button on the side of the unit and the shelves moved to one side. The exposed wall revealed a narrow door cut into the Gyprock. Opening the creaky old door, he entered a dark damp passageway. Oil lamps cast an eerie light along the gently sloping tunnel that had been used years ago by rumrunners. As he made his way down the steps, he could hear the sound of the surf in the distance.

Once at the bottom, he approached a few men from the U. S. who waited nearby on the windswept sand. A small skiff had been pulled up on land. Boyd saw the small boat, the larger craft anchored just offshore.

He needed more capital. He was losing money to some rivals in New Brunswick. He knew his brother had lots of the stuff, he, being a well-known heart surgeon. Boyd always was of the opinion that family should share. And he felt that his brother should hand over his share of their father's inheritance money. He was entitled to his share of it, and he still couldn't understand why his father had left it all to his brother. Despite his hard crust, that snub hurt him.

He would get the funds one way or another.

But he would get them.

A large black car followed Roger along Prince Albert Road as he made his way to his uncle's place. Not expecting someone to be interested in him, he ignored the car behind him. As he pulled on to his uncle's street, the vehicle continued toward the overpass. Backing up to the garage, he prepared to put the iceboat away. He pushed the trailer into a small blue garage that sported a basketball hoop as well as a small loft. With a squeal of wheels, he pushed the vehicle into the open space. It was hard going. He forgot just how heavy the boat was. As he passed the door, he flipped a switch, revealing a row of shelves on one side, a row of shelves at the back, and a long scarred work counter that ran the full length of the building. It was here that he spent his off hours working on his boat. Also in the open space, his uncle's old antique car sat on blocks, ready for restoration.

"Uncle, I'm home." Roger opened the side door and bounded up the short steps that led to the kitchen of his uncle's house. Entering a cheery yellow kitchen, he saw his uncle George sitting at an oak table, reading a newspaper.

"Have a good time with that boat of yours, son?" His uncle looked up, raising bushy eyebrows. His eyeglasses were perched precariously on the end of his nose. He often could be found here, reading his newspaper.

Roger felt a momentary twinge of resentment. Why did his uncle still think of him as a boy? He was twenty-seven years old, had been married, and he was a police officer in the nearby town of Avonvale. From his uncle's stage in life, he probably was still a boy. He smiled then at the kindly man, realizing it was a term of endearment, no more.

"She worked like a charm, Uncle." His mind replayed the chance encounter with Janice Peterson. "I even met a girl." His voice held a note of excitement as he went on to explain about his adventures on the lake. The faint twinge of attraction was still in the back of his mind, just out of reach. He noticed his uncle's amused expression. "What's so funny, Uncle?"

"Sounds like you literally fell for the girl, eh?"

"Well, it turned out to be a rather pleasant accident."

"So what's the appeal of sailing over a sheet of ice on a pair of blades in nothing but a tiny wooden box? Unless it's a new way you young people have come up with so you can meet girls. I'd rather have a boat that sails in the water. Ice is for drinks and skating. I like to be in control of where I'm going." Here, he raised his bushy eyebrows.

"It's fun, Uncle. And you have more control than you think. Maybe, I'll take you out for a spin. I've named her the *Snow Queen*. It was invigorating."

"I'll pass on the trip. It's the spinning I'm worried about. She sounds like she could be a royal pain, or could cause some." With that his uncle gave him one of his questioning looks, and then went back to reading the newspaper. "Supper will be at five o'clock. Fish." He looked lovingly at the young man who had become like a son to him. He and his wife had agreed to look after Roger after his parents had been killed in a plane crash when he was only five. It had turned out to be a blessing for all of them. Now, it was just the two of them.

"Okay, see you later. I'm going to look at a book I borrowed from Janice Peterson today. It's about figure skating."

At his uncle's amused expression, he left through the side door, running up a flight of steps that clung to the side of the old garage. Opening the beige door, he was flooded with a sense of deja vu when he entered the small bed-sitting room. It was the same color, a pale green, with flowered curtains at the windows. The perfect colors to brighten a person's day. Throwing himself on the loveseat, he opened the book and began to read about the world of figure skating. He thought of the many times had he done this very same thing when he was younger when he had come to live with his father's brother.

Roger found himself suddenly revisiting the chance encounter with the beautiful Janice Peterson. If he was into the philosophy that everything was destined to happen as it did, he would say that it was fate. He could picture her lovely face, the pinched expression as she tried to hide her pain. The ice around his deadened heart began to crack just a little. Maybe he would get another chance to meet her.

Maybe the fates would work in his favor.

The fates, as they were called, indeed worked in Roger Abbott's favor a couple of days later. Taking a short skate on the ice, he approached the spot where he had almost hit Janice. Skating up to the area, he noticed a smudge of blue lying crumpled on the sheen of ice. Coming to a quick stop, he saw that it was a toque. Janice's toque. It was partially covered with snow, but he recognized it. Roger smiled as he suddenly realized this was his opportunity to see Janice again.

He still had a week of vacation, and he planned on using that time to his advantage. He didn't stop to think of the possibility he could be hurt again. He only knew that something about the woman touched him. They had a common thread in their lives.

That thread was for now just out of reach, somewhere in space.

While he was daydreaming about Janice, she was sitting on a wine-colored wing chair, looking at the framed photo of her father, mother, and her. As she focused on the picture of them hugging in front of a skating rink, she felt tears fill her eyes. Despite the fact that it had been four years, she still really missed her mom. They had been very close. Louise Peterson had been her friend and confidant. She had also been there to give her moral support when she had the accident during skating practice. That accident ended her professional skating career. Now, she reflected on the other accident that had taken her mother's life. She thought about that winter day on a highway just outside Dartmouth. In her mind's eye, she saw the car skid, sliding into the side of a car that had been coming toward them. She had tried vainly to regain some control of her Honda, but it was too late!

Her mother did not survive the crash, while she suffered a broken leg and lacerations. That had further added to the end of her skating career. There had been another accident that day. A car had gone over an embankment about a half mile from where she was. She had no way of knowing that that event would be the common thread that would connect her to Roger Abbott.

She was so absorbed in the past, of connecting with her deceased mother, that she didn't hear the tap at the back door. The visitor rapped louder on the steel. Janice looked up and saw a man's shadow in the window. She suddenly found herself smiling when she recognized the man as Roger Abbott. There was no mistaking the tall form, the dark hair. Her heart skipped a beat.

"Roger, come in. It's nice to see you again," she called as she unlocked the door. A sudden lightness seemed to touch her deep down in her soul at the thought of seeing him again. "Why are you here this time of day?"

Roger appeared in the mudroom, sat, and removed his skates. Tossing them on the floor with a loud thud, he padded into the family room where Janice had moved to the comfort of the wing chair.

Something was obviously wrong.

She appeared to be upset about something, because even at this distance, he could make out the sad expression on her face. "Is something wrong, Janice?" He noticed a framed photo in her right hand. A hand that was trembling ever so slightly.

"I'm all right. It's just that sometimes I see this picture, and I realize how much I miss my mother. Even after four years. She was my biggest fan when I skated."

"What happened to her? I wondered why she wasn't around the other day." He noticed the quiver in her soft voice. "If you don't feel like talking about it, that's okay."

Maybe he shouldn't have asked the question.

He looked closer at the photo that had to be her as a child, with her mother and father. It had been taken several years ago by the look of Frank Peterson's hair color. It was tinged with white now. He let his gaze go to Janice's tear-stained face.

Janice looked directly into Roger's eyes, and his heart stopped beating for a second. There was that invisible thread between them again. He also saw the tears standing in her eyes. Those tears nearly undid him. Wasn't he the one who wasn't going to get involved in a relationship again?

Roger felt something deep inside him move in response to the lovely young woman in front of him, despite that resolution he had made.

"She was killed in a car accident four years ago. I can't seem to let go of the guilt, even after all this time. It's my fault she died, Roger! I was driving the car." She ended on a sob. "It happened early in December, just outside the city. The roads were slippery, and I was trying to get home after a visit with friends." She was surprised at how easily the words slipped out.

"I don't believe it's your fault. You did all you could to avoid an accident. You've got to let go of the guilt or it will eat you up. I know what it's like. My wife, Anna, was killed in a car crash the same year. Just outside Dartmouth. I slid on some ice, and the car slid over an embankment." Looking down at the old photo, he noticed the skating attire. Determined to lighten the moment, he changed the subject. "I see you were interested in skating when you were a little girl."

Strangely, he felt some of the burden lift from his shoulders as he was able to tell Janice, even though he had only known her for a few days. What was the word called? Karma? Somehow, it seemed that he had known Janice Peterson a lot longer.

"I think I learned to skate before I could walk. As a teen, I entered competitions and was quite good. I even won a silver medal. The accident I told you about ended my skating career." She decided to change the subject. "Now, about the accident outside Dartmouth. Thank you for being so understanding just now." She looked oddly at him then, and he wondered what was on her mind. A few tears slid down her face, and she brushed them away with the back of her hand. Janice's eyes widened, and then an expression of disbelief crossed her face. "It was you in that car I saw, wasn't it? Did it happen near an overpass?"

"I'm sorry you lost an opportunity to have a skating career. That must have been tough. Were you in a car accident in the same place that December morning?" The truth suddenly dawned on him that this tragedy was the thread that had linked them together. The image of the accident scene was so clear now; his car sliding toward the bank, and the loud crash as the other two cars collided about a half mile away from him. Intuition now told him that one of the other cars belonged to Janice. "If I believed in fate, I'd say that we were put there by a force greater than ourselves. It's unbelievable that we ended up at the same place at the same time, but in different accidents."

"I wouldn't say that it was fate, but it sure is an unusual coincidence. Who would have thought that we would meet in another accident on the lake?" Her face showed compassion as she realized the great loss they both had suffered. Something passed between the two of them that was much like a current. Janice had never felt such a strong feeling for a man. Though she never married, she had had some fairly serious relationships; they just never ended up going beyond the casual.

"This brings me to the reason for my unplanned stop." He reached into his jacket pocket, producing her blue toque. "Thought you might want this." Looking over his shoulder, he pointed to the family room. "You really have a beautiful home, Janice. And the toque was just an excuse to see you again."

"Oh, my toque. I had forgotten all about it. You didn't have to make a special trip to return it. I have lots of other ones." She looked pleased at the small gesture on his part to return the hat. "And I appreciate you returning the hat. I was sort of hoping we would run into each other again too. Sorry about the pun."

"There's another reason for my visit. And you are right, it was a very unusual coincidence." He gazed into her violet-colored eyes, and time seemed to stop. His heart did a strange flip-flop in his chest. "Maybe we could go out sometime. I could take you out for a ride in the iceboat. That's if you would be interested," he finished, wondering at his feeble attempt at seeing her, and also wondering why he felt so much like a schoolboy on his first date. This had never happened with him and Anna. He had known her for such a short time; just six months. Not enough time to know someone. Not enough time to start a family of your own.

"I still can't believe we were so close together, but in completely different accidents. It was uncanny how we were in the same place at the same time."

While Roger was worried about a budding relationship with Janice Peterson, her Uncle Boyd was concerned about a shipment that had just arrived off the coast. It had been brought ashore near the old lighthouse. He had paid the suppliers, opting to hide the stuff with a shipment of textiles ready for transport to Ontario. His small transport firm made a perfect cover to ship things out of the province unnoticed. His associates, who were the eyes and ears of the streets, were always waiting for new drugs to sell to the addicts on the streets of the big cities. They also reported on activities of rival groups.

CHAPTER TWO

Boyd closed up his storage building and walked down the snow-covered path to the shore. The bank was shallow here and allowed for easy access to the crescent beach that was tucked into a small cove. His firm was near the old highway that curved along the coast and connected Avonvale to other parts on Nova Scotia. A small cluster of trees behind the business hid the old farmhouse that he lived in and used for easier, unnoticed access to the beach below. As yet, the island off shore was not being used, but Boyd had ideas for the house. It would make a perfect base of operation. The power was still on, it was secluded and even better, the citizens of the surrounding towns wouldn't bother him.

Guess there was something to be said about superstition.

Stories of a ghost on the island kept nosey people away. Just the way he wanted it. And to make the stories more believable, he decided to set up some special effects.

Another rather effective plan involved his girlfriend Sara. She worked in the kitchen in the hospital in Halifax. Hospitals used drugs.

Drugs he would like to get to add to his stash for sale to those who wanted them. Sara would be very useful in obtaining those drugs. A sinister grin crossed Boyd's weathered face. It was the smile of a person who never gave in to emotion; was always in control. If he couldn't control his foes, he got nervous.

There was one person he didn't like and wouldn't mind meeting again sometime. Despite the fact that his men had tailed the young man several times, they hadn't learned much about him. They had followed him to the Eastern Shore, but had lost him in the Ship Harbour area. It was almost as if the man knew he was being followed. He still couldn't put a finger on where else beside the lake that he had seen Roger Abbott.

Obviously, it hadn't been recently, or he would have remembered the young man. The undercurrent of dislike between the two of them was hard to ignore. The face hovered just on the perimeter of his mind, and it was driving him crazy. Finally, the annoying thought faded.

Boyd saw the small aluminum boat still pulled up on the beach. As he approached it, he heard a vessel's motor off to the entrance to the harbor. A small fishing boat with the name *Maggie Mae* on the bow moved slowly passed him. No one on board noticed him there, so he pushed off into the stream. After pulling the rope attached to the small outboard motor, it finally caught. A small puff of bluish smoke drifted up from the Evinrude engine. He could smell the oily odor of the cloud as it drifted over him. He made a face. Outboard motors were such distasteful things. Turning his collar up against the stiff breeze, he headed for the island that was less than a mile away. The cold air stung his face, mist flew over the bow, and the small craft pitched as she headed against the incoming tide.

He could make out the tall white pillar of the lighthouse on the far end of the island. Despite the fact there was still snow on the ground, it had melted enough that the path was negotiable. That was what he was counting on, so he could check out the place.

He had to convince his brother that he needed extra cash for his transfer business. Of course, he wasn't saying what he would be transferring!

Thinking of his girlfriend, Sara Martin, he smiled. She was beautiful, in a classic way, but he was interested in her for what he could get out of her. He made sure she had the impression that he liked her. It was amusing that the thirty-five-year-old seemed to really like him. That should make her more easily motivated to help him.

Finally, the boat approached a tiny dock. The narrow finger of oak stuck out on the lee side of the island. Boyd threw the heaving line, catching a drum that sat near the end of the planking. Killing the motor, he jumped on the wooden platform and secured the skiff. Once she was tied off, he started off along a narrow path through the woods toward the outbuildings in the distance. The crisp snow was up to his ankles, but he had on good hiking boots.

A feeling of anticipation coursed through him as he approached the weathered farmhouse that sat about thirty feet away from the massive tower of the Spooner's Island lighthouse. He could see the gully at the back of the old house that led down to a small beach. That beach would let him land on the island unobserved. This was going to be perfect for landing drugs. He had to admit, it was tailor-made for him. The only concern was working with the tides.

While Boyd was off exploring Spooner' Island, his girlfriend Sara was trying to relax in the old farmhouse that sat near the cliff. She was in the yard watching the boats entering Sheet Harbour. She could hear the putt putt of the small motors twenty feet below as the craft sailed passed her. The wind was cold and ruffled her brown hair. With a sigh, she turned away, and then made her way back to the warmth and security of the old house. She still didn't understand what Boyd wanted to do on the windswept rock. Turning her back on the ocean, she opened the old creaky door, disappearing into the dark interior of the house. A growing feeling of love for Boyd flooded through Sara, making her realize that she would go to the ends of the earth with him. Even to getting him drugs, if necessary. Despite the fact she was a grown woman, she was still ignorant of the world in which Boyd lived. She ignored the faint warning in her heart about what the future might hold. She also ignored the faint shadow of pain from her past. The past was the past, and it didn't relate to things happening to her now. Did it?

Back in Dartmouth, Roger and Janice continued to visit and get better acquainted. They found that they had some similar interests. Both enjoyed skating, and both of them had suffered a great loss four years ago. "I still can't believe that you and I were in two separate accidents at the same time, only a mile apart. Our spirits must have connected. It seems that we have known each other ages." Janice looked at him with those big compassionate eyes.

"Maybe we're what they call kindred spirits, Janice," he observed, reflecting on the way they met one another. "Can I ask you a personal question? You can say yes or no, and I promise I'll go along with your answer." Roger crossed his fingers, hoping she would agree to go out with him. There was still a week and a half of his vacation to explore a possible relationship with her. His heart was on the line, it felt a bit like walking on a tightrope with no net underneath.

"If you're asking me to go out on a date, the answer is yes. I'd like to see you again. As long as I don't have to go near that iceboat of yours." Here, she gave a quick laugh. "You intrigue me, Roger Abbott. Would you be interested in going to a movie day after tomorrow, on a Friday? Last day off until next Friday. Maybe even better, we can watch a movie at home. It would probably be easier on my ankle." She looked expectantly at him with a faint smile curving her lips. "If that sounds a bit too intimate, my sister and her kids will be there too. They can be our chaperones. Is that okay with you?"

"That would work. Maybe I can help take that frown off your face." He gave her an encouraging smile. It seemed he was smiling a lot more the last few days. The reason was the woman right in front of him. He couldn't seem to look away from her lovely face. Deep, expressive eyes stared back at him, her nose was straight, with a liberal sprinkling of freckles across it. Silken strands of hair framed that face, and he had to resist the urge to run his hands through the long golden tresses.

As they continued to discuss the coming date, they heard the front door upstairs open and close. By the sounds that drifted down to them, it appeared Janice's father had just got home. The moment was a little like having cold water splashed in ones face.

"Hello, Janice, are you home, honey?" Frank yelled down the stairs to them. "Would you be up to having your sister come over for supper?"

"That would be great, Father. Is Betty coming alone, or will she have the kids with her? It's been a while since I've seen Amy and Ben," she answered as her father appeared at the foot of the stairs. Maybe she would be able to concentrate on the children and forget her swollen ankle. Betty was a nurse's assistant, so would be able to tell her how serious the sprain was. "You brought some crutches." She rose to greet him as he strode across the thick carpet. That carpet looked thick enough that you could probably walk across it in your bare feet.

'don't get up. Stay there and rest your foot." Frank noticed Roger sitting in the chair near his daughter. "I see you have company. Nice to meet you again Mr. Abbott." He extended his right hand to give Roger a hearty handshake. "To what do we owe this visit? Although I think I have a pretty good idea why you're here." At this point he looked at his daughter, and then at Roger, who grinned and even winked at Janice.

"I found her hat and brought it back, then we started talking. I always had the impression we had met somewhere before. That we had a connection." Again his mind pictured the accident that had taken his wife's life as well as her mother's. Why was it that they always seemed to meet because of some sort of accident? Janice looked up at him, and there was that invisible thread that joined them. Its intensity scared him. Anything that involved his heart called for a great deal of caution. Even if he pursued seeing Janice, it was only going to be a casual friendship, nothing more.

Now, if he could just convince his heart of that promise.

"What is this connection you two seem to have? Believe me, I'm very aware that you have something in common with Janice. You seem to be a very passionate young man. My daughter said you were a police officer. Do you belong to the local police force in the city?" He brought the crutches over to where his daughter sat and then laid them against the side of the wing chair. "Here's something to make getting around a bit easier."

"Thanks, Dad. Roger was telling me about an interesting coincidence that brought the two of us together about four years ago. We both lost someone we loved." She gave Roger a look of sympathy, hers eyes shone with unshed tears.

"I work for the Avonvale force, sir, just outside Sheet Harbour. I graduated from a maritime academy, and then was posted in Halifax. It didn't work out, so I transferred." He looked rather unhappy at relating that part of his life. Frank saw the fleeting emotion pass across the young man's face. "I enjoy it in Avonvale, have even purchased a small house near the highway. Maybe someday I'll start a family." He offered Janice's father the chair so he could sit near his daughter.

"Now, what is this coincidence Janice alluded to? It sounds like it has had a big impact on both your lives. I know when I lost my wife, it really shook my faith. Janice and I have had to dig deep to sustain our faith in God. We never stopped believing. Friends and a good minister have helped us cope. And God, of course."

"Of course."

Roger knew he sounded cynical, even a bit bitter, when he thought how Anna had died. He had no use for a God who took loved ones away and left a big hole in place of love. Looking at Janice, he marveled that she had not let the loss of her mom make her bitter. It just proved she had a strong faith and was a better person than he was. Her face seemed to shine from within as she gazed with love at her father. Even a blind man could tell that they had a strong bond, probably made more close by the recent loss of her mother.

All his loss had done was make him bitter, afraid to give his heart to anyone else.

"Are you all right, son? You look like you've seen a ghost." Frank Peterson looked with compassion at his stricken expression.

"Sorry, I was just thinking about my dead wife, Anna. She was killed in an auto accident about four years ago, just outside Dartmouth. It still hurts. It seems Janice and I lost someone at the same time and on the same stretch of highway." There, he had said it. Their compassion touched the dark place in his soul, bringing in a welcome light.

Frank gave him a curious look as the truth dawned on him. He gave a low whistle, and then placed a comforting hand on his arm. "So that's what Janice had been hinting at. They say the Lord works in mysterious ways. Maybe this was a way to bring the two of you together. I know it's been very hard for you, son. If you need to talk, I'll make myself available. And, believe it or not, the pain will gradually go away. Here's my cell number."

With that, he scribbled a number on a slip of paper that he pulled from his attaché case. After handing it to Roger, he turned to his daughter. "Your sister, Betty, will probably come for supper. She's bringing Chinese food. The kids love it, and I know you would live on it if you had a choice." He smiled lovingly at the camaraderie between them. She was so much like her mother; in temperament, looks, and even the same colored eyes. A deep violet color.

"Thank you, sir. I may take you up on that offer. I really must be going, or else Uncle George will be worried about me." He turned to Janice, a lazy smile spreading across his face. "I'll see you on Friday, Janice."

"Bring a big bag of popcorn. The movie of the night is *Madagascar*. Do you like animated movies, Roger?"

"Sounds good to me. I'm easy. I'll let myself out. Nice to see you again, Mr. Peterson." Roger moved to the mudroom and put on his hockey skates. With a wave to her, he opened the door and slipped out into the cool March afternoon.

A quick walk and he was once again on the lake. Swiftly, he skated the width of the lake to come ashore near his parked 2005 Chevy Malibu. He happened to look toward a clump of trees that clung to the edge of the lake. Two men stood near the trees, obviously in the process of making an exchange of some sort. One of them turned slightly, giving Roger a clear view of his face. His breath caught when he recognized the man.

It was Boyd Peterson.

Moving out of sight, he kicked off his skates, donned sneakers, and then headed for his uncle's place on Wyndcrest Drive. He was still thinking about his visit with Janice Peterson, or he would have noticed the large sedan tailgating him. As he slowed to pull onto his street, the car pulled around to pass. The Lincoln Town Car was so close, he could feel the whoosh as it slid by him. It had been close enough that he could make out two scratches along the front fender. He also noticed the car had tinted windows, and it had no license plate. Strange. Chalking it up to an impatient driver, he pulled his sedan into the driveway. Again, he thought about the strange encounter at the lake. What was Boyd Peterson doing hiding behind some bushes? And what was in the package the other man passed him? There wasn't much he could do about it, but the images clung stubbornly to the edge of his mind. The encounter with the Town Car was forgotten.

"Hi, Uncle. Hope you had a good day."

"Supper's ready in a hour, son. Did you have a good visit with that girlfriend of yours?" He gave his nephew a knowing look. Apparently he was of the opinion that some sort of romance was blossoming between the two of them.

"I had a great visit with Janice, Uncle. And no, there's no romance. We are just friends. I have a date with her next Friday." Now why did he mention he had a date with her? Roger hoped to correct his uncle's mistaken idea of his love interests. "I have to do some research on the Internet for a while. I'll be there in time. Wouldn't miss your famous fishcakes for all the money in the world."

"Okay, if you say so." His uncle gave him a questioning look then winked. "Mark my words, someday you'll find love again, Roger." George turned and went back inside the small house, while Roger ran up the steps and quickly unlocked the oak door. His uncle's words about finding love echoed in his mind.

CHAPTER THREE

Stepping inside, he flipped the light on. He wondered what he would find as he searched the Internet.

Approaching the small desk that sat near the window, he looked out over the driveway. With a sigh, he turned away and sat at the pine workstation. After turning on the computer, he waited for the screen desktop to appear. It was a picture of a sailing vessel. Using the mouse, he positioned the cursor to log on to the internet. Roger found the Web site for the local paper and scrolled down to find news items that were news four years ago. It seems that anything that happened near the death of his wife was only a blur.

Something was pushing him to look in the news archives in the hope of finding the identity of who Boyd Peterson really was. He was sure he had seen him in the past.

A small icon appeared on the left side of the page indicating the year; 2008. The year Anna was killed in the car accident! Memories flooded his mind.

Roger felt the sudden stinging in his eyes as he recalled the events of that December morning. His eyes were drawn to the insert on page two that told of the two accidents on highway 101. He scrolled down to the next couple of pages and found himself staring at a black-and-white photo of none other than the infamous Boyd Peterson. A low whistle escaped his lips as he remembered where he had seen the man before.

"So that's where I know you from. Now what have you been up to that has made the headlines?" He quickly read of a drug cartel that had been operating in the area. He remembered then that Boyd and a couple of his men were allegedly involved in this drug cartel. An investigation followed where he was helping with the gathering of information when Anna was killed. He tried to go back to work after the funeral, but he couldn't put it behind him. Distracted as he was, he missed a lot of clues that could have led to the arrest of Boyd Peterson. Because of his inexperience and grief, he had let a drug lord and his men get away. Shortly after that, he had transferred to Avonvale's force. He had gotten a good recommendation from his staff sergeant who had stated that he had good instincts and would make a good cop. However, he needed to separate personal feelings from his work.

"Maybe I'll get a second chance to make things right." Roger knew that meant he would have to keep a close watch on Boyd to see if he was doing anything that could be considered suspicious. And he would have to do it without making Boyd aware of him. Also to be considered was the caution he would need so he would not be accused of harassment. Closing down the Internet, he shut his computer off and prepared to go into his uncle's kitchen for supper. Bursting into the kitchen, he nearly scared his uncle who was just getting ready to set the plates on the birch table that sat against the far wall. Delicious aromas of fishcakes filled the small room. He thought of the many meals he had eaten in this very spot, prompting him to smile affectionately at his beloved uncle.

Later in the evening, the two of them had a spirited game of chess at the table in the den. His uncle was an accomplished chess player, giving a triumphant *Checkmate* before he had even formulated a plan of attack. Well, it just proved his uncle George was still sharp.

"Well, son, it's getting late. I think I'll read for a while then settle down for the night."

"Thanks for a wonderful meal. Uncle, do you find it hard being here alone so much after Aunt Becky died?"

"It's not so bad. You sure keep things interesting around here, always did. It was a real godsend that you were sent into our lives, Roger. Your Aunt Becky and I never had children of our own. You were just like a son to us."

Roger looked with love at the wrinkled kindly face of his uncle. The old gentleman had the face of one who still believed in God and in the good things of life. He looked up to him, he realized then, always had since he was a young boy. "Thank you, Uncle, for everything. I think I'll head off to the loft to do some work then head to bed."

"Sweet dreams, Roger. I have a pretty good idea who you might be dreaming about." His uncle's eyes seem to have a pensive look in them, hinting at what he thought about Roger and Janice.

"See you in the morning. Maybe I'll take you iceboating with me," he said with a hint of challenge in his voice.

"Think I'll pass on the iceboat adventure. Probably I'll just stay here and enjoy listening to a good symphony by Beethoven or Schubert. Nothing like a good piece of classical music to brighten a dull day."

"Okay. I'll pass on the long-hair music, though. Give me a good rock and roll song any day." His lighthearted bantering with his uncle was something he always enjoyed. Feelings about his choice of music and his uncle's choice were a frequent source of discussion between the two of them. Reluctantly, he left through the side door, making his way to the steps that climbed the side of the garage. That garage held his iceboat as well as an old 1937 Ford that his uncle was trying to restore. Apparently, it was an old car he had owned and wanted to put back into shape. His uncle must have some money because it wasn't cheap to restore an old vintage automobile. Unlocking the brass lock, he moved into the small bed-sitting room. Cheerful yellows, earthly colors, and a polished wood floor made this a very welcoming place to come home to. Roger liked it much better than the blue bedroom back in the house.

The loft was basically one room, with a small bath on the right. A knee wall separated the living room from where his bed was. Nestled into the far corner, it sported a very old handmade quilt as well as pale green sheets. A small window interrupted the wall facing him. It looked out on the neighbor's yard. He loved it. It was his and always would be a place he could come home to. That was something he really appreciated. Putting his CD player on, he selected a CD by one of his favorite groups, ABBA. Despite the selection of new artists with their rock, hip-hop, and alternative music, he still preferred the old songs from the '70s and '80s. Soon, strains of "Waterloo" filled the room, and he relaxed in the old wing chair near the main window.

That evening on Spooner's Island, Boyd Peterson began exploring the old house that sat at the end of a meadow, perhaps thirty feet from the lighthouse. He was impressed by the sheer height of that structure. It was a good fifty feet high. Made of whitewashed stone, it sat on the edge of a high bluff. It had warned ships for a hundred years of the dangerous shoals. As interesting as the lighthouse was, his attention remained on the farmhouse. It was a weathered gray clapboard, very much in need of a coat of paint. Perfect for his uses, and the trees around the place hid it from the mainland.

Boyd checked the rusted brass doorknob. The weather had turned the metal a dull green. While twisting the knob, he pushed the door open with an accompanying creak of well-rusted hinges. Stepping over the threshold, he found himself in a small living room. "This place has potential." Dust covered everything; most of the furniture was covered with dull white sheets, giving the place a rather ghostly appearance. The floor was made of old tongue and groove boards and was still in pretty good condition. Some of the boards were loose and creaked when he stepped on them. He knew the place had been vacant since the early '60s when the government had automated all the province's lighthouses. Because of the lighthouse, the power was still on, so the house had some heat.

Boyd made his way through this room. A kitchen with a pantry was located off to one side. "This is perfect. Nice and private." This pantry would be used to prepare drugs for street use. Near the small room, the bathroom was located, complete with an old claw-foot bathtub as well as a sink. The white porcelain was chipped from age and many uses. The small oval mirror over the sink was dirty, and a crack was evident along one side of it. Outside the bathroom, he found a narrow set of steps leading to the upstairs. Creaks echoed through the place as he made his way up those steps. The boards were loose in spots, so he held onto the handrail as he made his way to the second floor. The whole place was covered in dust and huge cobwebs. He took a quick look around then made his way downstairs. "We'll have to fix some of the steps, but it could work."

This place would serve him well.

Once he was back outside, he found that the wind had picked up, making it colder. He turned the collar of his winter jacket up against the biting wind. A quick trek across the yard took him to a small shed near the lighthouse. Inside the red door, he found the mechanism that worked the air-powered foghorn. Looking out over the bank, he could see the entrance to Sheet Harbour about twenty feet below. Waves sent their whitened spray against the rocks at the base of the cliff. If he was careful, he could work from here undetected for quite a while. Pulling out his cell phone, he called one of his dealers in the city.

Anyone seeing Boyd would have caught just a glimpse of a satisfied smile cross his face. Reluctantly, he made his way toward the narrow path that led back to the dock where his small skiff was secured.

Unaware of the events in Avonvale and still on vacation, Roger continued to enjoy his CD of Gordon Lightfoot. The man could sure touch your heart with his poignant ballads. He even sang along with a few of the more familiar pieces. It had been a day since his game with his uncle, and he was looking forward to a rematch. Since he'd been practicing, maybe he could win this time. After getting a drink of orange soda from the small fridge near the bathroom, he made his way over to the window overlooking the driveway. Pulling back the green curtain, he saw his car, Braemar Drive, and beyond that the wide gray expanse of the lake. By the way the ice was turning black, his iceboating days were numbered. Sitting at the small desk near the window, he flipped open his laptop. When the screen turned blue, and then the background picture of the tropical beach appeared, he logged on to his novel.

For the next hour, Roger worked on his mystery novel. The words seemed to pour out of him. And by the time he was done for the night, he had written about ten more pages. A sense of satisfaction settled over him.

At ten in the evening, he decided to call it a night and turned off everything, while he quickly undressed by his bed. Pulling the curtains across the darkened glass of his window, he crawled under the covers.

Roger was tired, so sleep seemed to claim him almost as soon as his head hit the pillow. He found he was dreaming, a dream that he had experienced many times in the past couple of years. Cars appeared in front of him, his and two others about a mile away. The road was slippery, driving was slow, and he worried about skidding. His car hit a patch of ice, heading for the embankment near the overpass. He saw himself trying to correct the skid then heard his wife scream as the Chevy plowed through the snow, slipping into the deep recess of the ditch. The sedan turned over and blackness blotted out the world.

When he came to, he found himself looking at Janice Peterson's face, mixing with the fading image of his wife, Anna!

How had that happened?

And what did it mean? Where did Janice fit in his life?

While he was trying to figure that out, he woke up.

Sleep eluded him now, and he quickly sat up in bed. Pushing back the covers, he went to freshen up after this strange dream.

Janice's day had gone much smoother. She had explained why Roger had stopped by, and then had enjoyed a wonderful supper with her sister Betty and her two children, eight-year-old Amy, and her five-year-old brother, Ben. She loved her niece and nephew dearly. Later, they had talked about her meeting Roger Abbott. Betty had wise advice to give her about affairs of the heart. She always appreciated her older sister's counsel. The other counsel that she knew she needed was advice from the Lord. Whether a relationship developed between them or not, only time would tell. She sensed Roger was interested, but she also sensed that something held him back. She knew he still was in love with his deceased wife.

And it was hard to compete with a ghost!

"Will you be here with me on our date, sis?" Janice suggested they have a group date. She still felt very unsure of herself around Roger.

"If you think that will help. You're old enough now that you don't need a chaperone, Janice. If you feel safer with me there then I'll keep an eye on him."

"I know. And thanks for the sisterly support. I'll call him and let him know you and the kids will be here. With my bad ankle, I can't go very far. By the look of the lake, the ice is starting to break up, so Roger won't be able to use his iceboat. After my near run-in with it, I don't really care if I ever see the thing again."

"What is it with you two that you always seem to be meeting in some sort of accident?"

"I was wondering the same thing, sis. Hopefully, we can break that trend. Otherwise, one of us is going to end up in traction."

Both of them had a good-hearted laugh over it. It helped when you could see the humorous side of life. Sometimes it took a real effort to be positive about life, especially when it handed you a left hook.

Friday finally arrived. It was his last day of vacation, as well as Janice's last day off until next week. Janice was on her way home when she sensed that someone was following her. When she looked in her rear view mirror, whatever it was had disappeared. Shrugging, she tried to forget about it.

Back at Uncle George's place, George grinned at his nephew. "Have a good time. Have you got enough popcorn there?" His uncle eyed the huge tub of popcorn clutched in his nephew's right arm. "Did I hear her sister and her kids are going to be there too? She must think you need a chaperone." He raised his bushy eyebrows in question. Roger could see the look of amusement in his uncle's eyes. He seemed to be having a good time with this latest development. "What movie are you seeing?"

"*Madagascar*. I hear it's quite funny. Gotta go, it's almost 7:00 p.m."

"I never got anything out of those animated movies. Enjoy your evening, son. I think I'll watch the news and turn in early. If you want, you can put your car in the garage. There should be enough room."

"Okay, I just might do that. See you, Uncle." He gave his uncle a quick hug then headed out to his red Malibu. The March air was cool, hinting at the possibility of snow. He backed out of the driveway and headed along Prince Albert Road to the overpass. Going under the roundabout, he headed along the highway and the turn off for the Micmac Mall. Here, he turned to Lakecrest Court where Janice lived. As he approached the large brown house, he felt the fluttering in his chest and the sudden attack of sweaty palms.

Was he really as nervous as he used to be back in high school?

The thought made him laugh. Looking over at the popcorn, secured among a blanket on the front seat, he slowed down and stopped in front of the estate. The house had pillars across the front well-manicured plants and a stone walkway. A large bow window faced him. Bright lights shone from between dark heavy drapes.

Clutching the tub under his arm, Roger walked up and knocked on the dark steel door. It sounded hollow as he clapped the brass door knocker against its base. A scurry of feet could be heard just inside the door then it was swung open. A woman with short blonde hair stood in front of him. She smiled, inviting him inside. She was slim, probably a bit older than Janice, and wore blue jeans and a blue blouse. Slightly behind the sister were two young children. They both eyed him with curiosity and maybe a hint of wariness. He could see that uncertainty in their eyes.

"You must be Roger. Welcome. Please come in out of the cold. You can hang your coat here." At this point, she gestured to a hall closet just to his right. Opening the birch door, he hung up his black winter jacket. "Janice is downstairs. She still finds it hard to maneuver up the steps. It's going to be a couple of weeks yet, but she's convinced she can manage work next week."

"She said she worked at a dentist's office."

"She does. She also couches kids with their skating at the local arena. We'll see. She can be pretty stubborn sometimes. My name is Betty, and these two ragamuffins are Amy and Ben." Betty moved to one side and motioned her children to come forward. Amy was the most interested in him and gave him a good unflinching stare. She managed a shy smile which didn't quite reach her eyes. She put her small right hand out to shake his hand.

Roger thought about that last bit of information about Janice as he took her hand. The small fingers clutched his then she looked away. She was the exact image of her mother, right down to the hazel eyes. His smile seemed to relax her somewhat, and she gave him a bigger smile this time.

"My name is Roger Abbott, and I'm here to see the movie with you and your Aunt Janice. We've been seeing each other. I guess you could call this a date."

"I've never been on a date. I don't trust boys. Most of them do gross stuff. But you sure are handsome. No wonder, Aunt Janice wants to go on a date with you. Did you bring popcorn?" Amy eyed the bucket he had set on the small table near the door.

"Yeah. Do you like popcorn, Amy? I even put butter on it. How about if we get some bowls so we can divide it up?" At this point, he gestured toward the inner parts of the massive home. This place was so big, three of his uncle's houses would probably fit inside it. "So you think I'm handsome, do you?"

"I heard Aunt Janice say that she thought you were handsome too." The child smiled up at him, her honesty and innocence written on her face. Her freckles stood out on a pert, slightly upturned nose, her blonde hair hugged the side of her head.

"And what else did your Aunt Janice say?"

"She said you were sad because someone you loved had died." Amy looked at him with a slight frown showing on her face.

"Amy, what did I tell you about eavesdropping on other people's conversations?" Her mother, Betty, interrupted her poignant question about his wife. He wondered just how much the child had overheard.

"Sorry, Mom. Eavesdropping, that means listening to something you're not supposed to, right?"

"Right. I think you owe Mr. Abbott an apology, honey."

At this point, Roger spoke up. "That's not necessary. I'm sure Amy is sorry. And I did ask her. No real damage done." He looked at the child, noting the contrite expression on her oval face. It seemed that she got the message.

"I couldn't help it, Mom. You guys were talking pretty loud."

Betty cleared her throat and amended her punishment, "Well, in that case, I guess we were just as much at fault as you were, Amy. Still, it is not a good idea to repeat something unless you're sure it won't hurt a person's feelings."

"I'll try to remember, Mom."

"Let's let Mr. Abbott get settled so we can all enjoy the movie with your Aunt Janice." Betty gently lead the Ben and Amy toward the stairway that lead to the downstairs family room.

"So you don't like boys, Amy?" He wondered how she got along with her younger brother. They seemed to be comfortable around each other, but a few minutes probably wouldn't tell too much. And he wasn't the best authority on childhood behavior as he was an only child.

Amy looked up at him, giving him one of her charming smiles. He was a sucker for those doelike eyes too.

"Most boys are really gross. The other day, Peter Miller brought his pet garter snake to school. The teacher took him by the ear to the principal's office. He got in trouble and had to let the snake go outside. Then yesterday, Brad tried to put a worm down Jody Carmicheal's back. She kicked him." She looked totally disgusted with the boys in her class. "He was limping for the rest of the day."

Roger glanced around the house as they drew closer to the oak banister. His quick appraisal revealed a long living room, plush brown chairs, a couch by the bay window, as well as mahogany coffee tables set up near the chairs. A small office alcove was set into the wall near the far end of the room. It held a computer as well as a row of books. Moonlight was evident outside a large set of patio doors. Shifting his attention back to those near him, he addressed Amy again. He wondered if she approved of any boys. He smiled when he thought of the boys in her class.

"Not all boys are like that. You'll find a boy you like someday. So do you have any favorite rock stars that you like? What kind of music do you like?"

"Justin Bieber is nice, and his music is so cool. I have a lot of his CDs."

"I like him too." Ben spoke up for the first time. Roger noted the youngster seemed quite shy. Just the opposite of his very bubbly sister.

"Justin is a real favorite around here. I have to admit, I like to listen to him too."

"You can call me Roger." He ventured. "Since we're going to get to know each other better, I'd feel more comfortable with Roger. And I don't mind them talking. They're actually quite charming, Betty."

"Okay, Roger it is. Ben, Amy, do you have the drinks with you? And thank you for your comment about the children. They're both pretty special."

The four of them moved down to the landing then into the cozy family room where Janice was setting up the DVD player to show the movie on a large flat-screen television. As he made his way to the flowered couch, his eyes locked with hers, and again, time seemed to stop. He was so absorbed, he almost dropped the popcorn. Once the movie was running, he found himself completely enjoying the antics of the animated animals. He had never considered the fact that a fantasy movie might actually be enjoyable. However, he was also very aware of Janice nearby.

"This isn't bad. I can see the resemblance to real people in some of those characters." Roger observed. Looking down, he saw that Amy had changed positions with her brother so she could sit next to him. At this point in the film, he had a good laugh over some of the antics of the zoo animals.

She leaned closer to him and whispered, "The lion looks something like our principal, Mr. Hastings." The girl giggled at the image that was presented.

"Amy, he's not that bad," her mother commented, although she did have to smile at the picture portrayed by the girls comment.

"It's true, Mom. He really does look like a lion with a bushy mane."

"Maybe you're right, I had never thought of it that way before. I guess we all could resemble one of those animals, Amy. Which one would you like to be?"

"I'd be the monkey. He gets to swing in the trees."

Both Janice and Betty glanced over at him. He failed to catch the flash of understanding that passed between them as they observed his reaction to the film.

"Are you having fun, Mr. Abbott? Which animal would you want to be?" Amy whispered in his ear.

"Yes, as a matter of fact, I am. If I had a choice, I'd be the giraffe." He was surprised by his own admission.

She giggled at his candid admission about the giraffe then she looked thoughtfully at him, "I'm glad you're having fun. Now you won't be sad anymore."

If only things could be that simple.

CHAPTER FOUR

Later that evening, a couple of drugstores in Avonvale were held up after closure. Closed circuit television cameras picked up the image of two people, both dressed in dark clothes and ski masks. It was obvious from the height of the pair that one of them was a slim woman.

They were quick, knowing exactly what drugs they wanted to steal. The Avonvale police force scoured the area for clues, but other than the camera images and some tire tracks, there was not much to go on.

After Roger left, Betty had a heart-to-heart talk with Janice about a certain handsome policeman. The evening had gone pretty well, although Janice sensed that Roger was a bit uncomfortable with Amy snuggled up next to him.

It was quite obvious to the two women that Amy Richards had a king-sized crush on Roger. She didn't usually warm up to strangers that easily. Perhaps she had sensed his vulnerability, and in her youth, had responded to his inner feelings. It was also obvious that Roger was scared of his feelings. He did seem to enjoy the kids even though he had just met them.

"What do you think of him, sis?" Janice was anxious to have her sister's opinion. She had good instincts about affairs of the heart.

"I think he feels something for you, Janice. Didn't you pick up on the way he slid these sly little looks at you? I think he was watching you more than the movie. Roger is a nice guy, but I think you should still take my advice and be very careful with your heart. He's still mourning his dead wife, but from what I've seen, he's fighting it. He also seemed to interact well with the kids, especially Amy." Betty looked at her sister, theirs eyes met, and Janice leaned over and gave her a hug.

They looked over at the chairs sitting near the massive stone fireplace. With a cheery fire in the hearth, the room had become warm and cozy. Both of Betty's children were lying on the plush carpet, side by side. Ben was absorbed in an ultra-large coloring book. Crayons lay in colorful disarray on the floor around him. Amy was on her back, headphones plugged in her ears. It didn't take much of a guess as to who she was listening to. Her smile of contentment said it all.

"Two guesses who she's listening to, Janice. It's a wonder she doesn't have the CD worn out by now."

"Probably Justin Bieber. I have to admit, he is kind of cute. A little young for me, though," Janice observed with a wistful sigh.

"You're kidding, right?"

"Of course, I'm kidding. If you want my humble opinion, I think Justin may have just been replaced by Roger Abbott."

Betty looked at her eight-year-old-going-on-twenty-year-old daughter, and smiled." I've noticed that she does seem to cling to him. If you could have seen her face as they watched the movie together. She adores him."

"She's at an age when she needs a man for a role model. She also thinks Roger is handsome. Since Roy is away, she has obviously transferred those feelings to Roger. When is he expected home, Betty?"

"In about six months. His letters say where he is, but not much else. I worry about him being over there in Afghanistan. Only my prayers have made this bearable. You never get used to the loneliness of being married to two partners; your spouse and the Armed Forces."

"I've been praying for his safe return as well as for you, sis." Janice gave her sister a quick embrace, then the two women joined the kids by the fire.

"Okay, you two, it's nine o'clock. Time we headed for home. Both of you need to get to bed." She reached down and gave Amy a gentle shake then helped Ben gather up his crayons.

It had been an enjoyable and a revealing evening.

Roger regretfully took his leave after the movie was over. He sensed the two sisters would have a good candid talk after he left. He knew the subject too: him. Pulling into his uncle's driveway, he cut the engine and hopped out of the car. After a quick search of his pocket, he found the key to the side door. A welcome light was on in the kitchen when he opened the door.

"Uncle, are you awake? Where are you?"

A muffled voice came from the direction of the living room. "I'm in the living room, watching the news."

"Well, I'm off to the loft. Sweet dreams, Uncle." Roger gave him a quick hug then headed out into the kitchen.

Snagging a couple of sodas from the fridge, he pulled on his coat and headed out into the still night. It was a beautiful evening, with a clear sky filled with thousands of stars. Roger sprinted up the stairs and stopped on the landing. The dark shadow of the lake caught the lights from the street, making the open water shimmer like a million sparkling diamonds. Reluctantly, he turned away and unlocked the heavy oak door.

A flip of the light switch bathed the room in a soft warm light. Hanging his coat on the hook near the door, he placed the pop in the fridge and headed to the small bathroom located at the end of his flat. The clock on the counter in the kitchenette said it was after ten. Time to turn in. He wondered if he would dream tonight. In recent weeks his dreams seemed to be changing in their direction.

Once he had his striped pajamas on, Roger pulled back the green bedsheets and climbed beneath the covers. As his head hit the pillow, he smiled as his thoughts turned to his visit with the Petersons. He even chuckled when he recalled the comments made by eight-year-old Amy, Betty's charming daughter. Tired from the day's events, his eyes grew heavy and his breathing became shallow, and he fell into a fitful sleep.

Just as on several nights in the past couple of weeks, he started dreaming. First, he was in a car sliding toward a deep ditch. Snow sprayed all around the car as it plunged over the edge of the road. A scream made him look at his wife, Anna. His blood froze when he saw the image of her injured body thrown against the dash. He felt the pain of his own injuries as he was slammed into the steering wheel. He had broken ribs as well as lacerations. Sirens echoed in his head as the paramedics rushed to their aid.

The clear picture of the hospital appeared in his mind's eye and then he was standing with his uncle in the cold by a granite tombstone. Anna's name was engraved in white in the front of that stone. Tears flowed freely down his cheeks and he buried his face in his Uncle George's fleece jacket. The dream began to evolve into the faint face of his wife, mingling with another face. He opened a heavy door and stepped out into the winter afternoon. Anna's face appeared in a haze in front of him for a second then disappeared in a cloud of smoke. The next image to stand in front of

Roger was that of Janice Peterson. Smiling at him, she opened her arms, beckoning to him to take that first step toward her.

That step scared him to death because it meant leaving Anna behind!

Could he make his feet move toward her, or was he going to remain paralyzed in the experiences of the past? Of course, anything is possible in the world of dreams, and this one was no different. Roger was standing at the entrance to a church he didn't recognize.

Janice Peterson was standing on the top step.

And she was wearing a long white wedding dress.

What did it mean?

Who was Janice waiting for? Was it him?

As he awoke in the dream, he also woke up to find his pajamas wet as in his previous visions. Trying to remember the events in his mind's eye, he crawled out of bed and went to splash water on his face. A change of clothes was also in order. After slipping into a pair of clean pajamas, he decided to sit on the couch. Sleep eluded him until early in the morning when he finally fell into a deep sleep.

This time there was no dream.

After Betty and her children left for home, Amy seemed to talk nonstop about Roger. She definitely had a bad case of hero worship. The fact that he wore a uniform added to his appeal as well.

Betty got the two of them ready for bed then read Ben a bedtime story. It was a must that he have a story before settling down for the night. This night, he wanted to hear the story about the pirates who roamed the Atlantic in the early days of the nation. Boys and pirates seemed to go together, much like peanut butter and jam in a sandwich. Amy was busy changing the clothes on her collection of Barbie dolls. She looked up as her mother bent down to talk to her.

"Okay, honey, time to settle down." Betty moved to hug her daughter then drew back the flowered sheets. As she knelt next to the flannel bedding, she gazed very intently into her mother's eyes.

Quietly Amy whispered, "Mom, do you think Mr. Abbott had a good time tonight? Does he like Aunt Janice? He sure looked at her a lot."

"Yes, I do think he had fun tonight. You made him feel better, sweetie. You could pray for him when you say your prayers. I'm sure that would help because God loves Mr. Abbott too. And yes, I think he likes your aunt Janice."

"That's a great idea, Mom. God always answers our prayers. I know he made Aunt Janice and you feel better after your mother went back to heaven. I think I'll pray that God will bring Mr. Abbott a new wife so he won't be so unhappy."

Betty was at a loss for words. Her daughter's fervent desire for Roger Abbott to find happiness touched her, and she had a sudden burning in her eyes.

"Dear Heavenly Father, I'm grateful for my mom, for a warm bed, for good food. I'm grateful for my computer that does really neat things. I'm grateful for cool teachers at school, for friends to play with at recess, and even for the rain. I am grateful for my brother, although sometimes he bugs me." Amy's voice grew softer as she began to pray for those in her life that she loved. "Please bless Mommy. And Daddy in Afghanistan. I guess it would be okay if you blessed my brother, Ben. And please, don't forget to bless Aunt Janice and Roger, eh, I mean Mr. Abbott. Help him to be happy and find a wife. In Jesus's name, amen."

"Amen. Sweet dreams, Amy. That was a very sincere prayer. I know Mr. Abbott would appreciate your prayers on his behalf. And your father would sure appreciate your prayers for him." She smiled at her success in saying such long, adult names. Clearly, Betty was touched by her eight-year-old daughter's worry about a virtual stranger's welfare. It just added to her confirmation that her child was very special.

Betty tucked Amy under the covers then bent to give her a last hug. Straightening, she reached for the Mickey Mouse lamp on the nightstand, plunging the pink-colored bedroom into darkness. She stopped at the door and looked back in love at her child already asleep on the plump pillow. Leaving the door slightly ajar, she made her way back to the living room, to watch the late news. It had been a very busy and enjoyable evening for all of them. Thinking of Janice, she knew she had enjoyed herself too.

Saturday slipped by, and finally, it was Sunday again. Roger stirred and turned to face the fleeting rays of sun that shone through his window. It looked like it was a glorious day. Noting the clock stated the time as being around 8:00 a.m., he hopped from bed and went to freshen up. Suspecting that his uncle would have breakfast on already, he hastened his pace.

Before Roger was even dressed, he heard a knock at his door. Throwing on a blue terry cloth robe, he went to answer it. "Uncle. I was just coming in. I guess I overslept a bit."

His uncle stepped into the small room and gazed at the décor. "No problem, son. Breakfast is on. I want to attend church this morning. I've missed the past couple of weeks. I think I might take the old Kia. She needs to have a good run. It's been a while since I have been in here. You've done wonders fixing the place up. You always liked this spot. It gave you a place for some privacy."

"Thanks. I guess I won't be spending much time here once the house is ready in another couple of months. I'm having the kitchen modernized." He glanced wistfully at the small loft that had been his home for about half of his life. It would be hard to leave behind.

"Just remember, you're always welcome to stay anytime you want a place to crash."

"I'll remember, Uncle. Just wait for a minute and I'll be right with you."

Roger reached for his clothes, slipping into brown cords, a green sweater, and sneakers. Grabbing his coat and keys, he motioned for his uncle to lead the way into the house. The morning was crisp, with a late April sun warming the land. It was hard to believe, but spring was almost here, things would turn green once more, and his iceboating would be forgotten until next winter.

He wondered if his uncle George would expect him to go to church with him. He hoped not, he was not really in the frame of mind to worship. It would make him feel like a hypocrite.

The two of them had a good talk at the small breakfast table a minute later about Roger going back to work, and how the house was progressing. It was a comfortable subject right up until his uncle asked, "Want to come to church with me this morning? It might do you good to have a heart-to-heart talk with the Lord. He always listens to us."

"I don't think so, Uncle. I don't have much use for God these days. Maybe I'll think differently someday," Roger stated flatly. He was starting to feel uncomfortable and pressured by his uncle's question about Sunday worship. And he really didn't have anything to say to God anyway.

Or did he?

"You don't need to be afraid of him. I think it would help settle your mind about a few things." Here, he looked up at his nephew, indicating that he knew all too well just what was bothering him. Compassion and understanding was very evident in the dark eyes.

"Well, okay, maybe I will go with you. I still don't think it will do any good, though."

"Good. I'll get my keys and we'll head out. The church is just a couple of blocks away."

"Meet you outside." He made a quick exit, waiting for his uncle in the driveway.

Once outside, he noted that a cool breeze blew off the lake and birds sang in the trees nearby, giving one a sense that all was well in the universe. Even with the nice day, Roger still felt that turmoil inside of him. Something was missing from his life, something that hung in his subconscious, just out of reach.

The trip to the church off Prince Albert Road took about ten minutes. The old blue Kia worked well, except for a rather noisy muffler, accompanied by the jolt from worn shocks. His uncle pulled into the parking lot of St. James Church. It was on a short dead end street.

"Well, we're here, son. I'll introduce you to the minister after the service."

"Looks like a lot of people here. He must be a good speaker to draw such a big crowd." Roger took note of the large group of parishioners gathering near the entrance. There was quite a variety of ages and social backgrounds present. Despite his misgivings, he was impressed.

The two of them hung their coats on hangers near the entrance then proceeded into the main part of the church. Stain glass windows ran along both sides of the interior, sending rays of colored light into the room. It was breathtaking. Roger had forgotten how spiritual it made him feel when he was in one of these old Gothic churches. He still didn't feel like sitting up front with his uncle. He let the older man make his way to the front pew, while he sat at the back. From here, he could make a quick exit if he got too uncomfortable. Slinking down in the wooden pew, he tried to make himself as invisible as possible. He soon forgot about his original plan when he looked around the church.

There were several families sitting to his right, as well as two dark-suited men. Both of them gave him a quick stare then looked toward the front of the church. As he glanced around the room, his eyes came to rest on a blonde woman about six rows in front of him. Something about her looked familiar. When she turned, he almost caught his breath. She was familiar, all right. It was Janice Peterson with her father. Next to them, he caught sight of Betty and her two children. Unknown to him, the two men in suits he had seen were also looking at Janice.

Talk about it being a small world.

As the first strains of the opening hymn "How Great Thou Art" began from the small pipe organ, he picked up the green-colored hymnbook. Singing was something he had always enjoyed, so the notes came quite naturally to him. Forgetting that he was supposed to be as inconspicuous as possible, he sang with gusto. His deep baritone voice was heard above some of the other more timid singers, and more than one person turned to give him an approving smile. He had the grace to smile back and even blush a little at all the attention.

One of the members of the congregation that turned to look at him was Amy, Betty's daughter. Roger saw her lean over to whisper something to her mother then she slid out of the pew, making her way to where he sat. So much for making a quick escape. He smiled at her as she slid into the seat.

"Hi, Mr. Abbott. Can I sit next to you? I promise I'll be really quiet so you can hear the minister." Amy moved closer until she was sitting right next to him. She looked up at him, hoping he would be agreeable.

"Sure. As long as your mother's okay with you being here, you can stay for as long as you like. I didn't know you came to this church."

"Yeah, we've come here for a while now. Mom says the preacher gives a really good sermon. I guess he does, I can understand him. I have a really nice Sunday school teacher too."

"Good, I'm glad you can enjoy your teacher. That makes a difference when you're learning. I guess we should be quiet because the minister is about to start his sermon."

The two of them listened intently as the white-frocked minister made his way to the brass pulpit. The man appeared to be in his sixties, balding, with glasses perched on the end of a long straight nose. The faint sound of paper rustling came to him as the heavy book was opened. Flipping through a large leather-bound Bible, he began to read. He had a firm commanding voice.

"Welcome, everyone. I hope you will find that the words I will speak to you today will be of help and touch your souls. As you listen today, I pray you will be able to use the lessons portrayed in the pages of the Holy Bible to your own lives. Beginning in the book of Matthew 11:28-30, we read, 'Come unto me all ye that labor and are heavy laden, and I will give you rest.' We learn from these passages that the Lord is always there to help lift our burdens and our cares."

As the preacher proceeded with his lecture to all those seated in front of him, Roger found himself sitting straighter in his pew. The words spoken touched an empty place in his soul. Despite his resolve not to get emotional about anything, Roger felt hot tears sting his eyes. He blinked then he felt those tears slide silently down his cheeks.

The tears may have been silent, but they were not unseen.

CHAPTER FIVE

Amy had been listening to the message too, but she had also been watching Roger. She had seen the tears glistening in his hazel eyes then watched as those tears ran down his cheeks.

"Are you sad, Mr. Abbott? How come you're crying? Did something the minister said make you unhappy?"

Amy whispered to him, concern evident in the soft voice. She looked directly into his tear-stained face. His left hand rested on the pew, and he felt her small hand cover his. Her compassion touched his wounded heart.

"I'm not really sad, just thinking about some things that have made me cry. The minister's message has good advice, Amy. If I can follow what he says, maybe I'll be able to move on with my life again."

He tried to explain the feelings he had, but doubted an eight-year-old could fully understand affairs of the heart. He barely understood it himself, despite his twenty-seven years.

"Oh, you mean because your wife went back to live with God? I know you'll see her again. Mommy told me that she and Aunt Janice will see her mom again. That's a long way off. Maybe you can fall in love with my aunt then get married. You always look really happy when you're with her." Amy had comforting words for him, and her remarks about Janice left him speechless.

He was dumbfounded by the poignant comment about moving on in a new relationship with Janice Peterson.

Could he shake off the memories of the past with God's help?

He'd have to have a heart-to-heart talk with that minister. From the tone of his voice, he obviously had great faith in God. A warm feeling seemed to settle over him, much like a blanket, erasing some of the darkness from his heart.

As the closing hymn was announced, he grabbed the hymnbook, letting Amy look on as he sang the words to the familiar song, "Abide with Me This Eventide "Amy sang loudly next to him, her clear childlike voice touching him. She had a nice voice for a little girl.

After the final benediction was pronounced, people began to rise and move to the exit. Amy grabbed his arm, drawing him toward her mother and Janice. If he didn't know better, he would have had the impression Amy was trying to get the two of them together. He wasn't sure if that was a good idea.

Roger noted that Janice was still limping a bit, but it was obvious that her ankle was almost healed. Boy, was he happy about that.

"Well, hello. I didn't expect to see you inside a church, especially after what you told me the other day," Janice observed, evidently surprised by his appearance at the service. "Although I am glad to see you here. What changed your mind, Roger?"

"I decided to come, partly for my uncle, partly because I need to clear my mind about some things."

Janice knew what things he hinted at. She was inwardly happy for his decision because it meant he was trying to make changes in his life. Those changes meant that just maybe, they'd have a chance. She was just going to start down the aisle when a man in a dark suit jostled her. He gave her a good hard stare before turning away to leave the church. She felt a little stab of fear when she looked into his eyes. Eyes that were hard and very cold. He didn't seem to belong in a church.

"How are you, Roger? It's nice to see you here. By the looks of things, there's someone else who is glad you came." Betty gazed down fondly at her daughter, who apparently only had eyes for Roger. She knew she loved her dad, but she also knew the girl missed having a male figure around.

"I'm glad I came, contrary to the way I felt earlier. Guess I was wrong. I've been wrong about a lot of things. Amy, here, has helped me with some of the questions I asked." He felt the child's small hand clutch his.

"Mr. Abbott said he really enjoyed the service. He can sing real good, Mom, "Amy interjected. She looked up at Roger as they made their way toward the entrance of the old church.

"I'm glad he enjoyed the meeting, Amy. And his singing is very good. But it's okay, we know what you mean. We should get you to the hall for your Sunday school class. We'll be back in a half hour to pick you up, how's that?"

"That's cool, Mom. Oh, there's Becky. She helps me with my lessons sometimes." Amy quickly let go of Roger's hand, then raced off to join her friend at the door.

"Looks like I've been replaced." Roger laughed good-naturedly. "I'm glad she's making new friends. She deserves all the friends she can get." He made his way to Janice, a smile spreading across his face. This was turning out to be a better day than he had even hoped for.

"So you enjoyed the service?" Janice asked as the two of them watched Amy leave with her friend. The rude man who had brushed past her was forgotten. Her father joined them a minute later, and the interlude was lost. She was happy he had decided to come.

"I really have a lot to think about. I need to talk to the minister, so if you'll excuse me, I will be back in a few minutes." Roger gave Frank Peterson a hearty handshake then made his way to the entrance, where the preacher was shaking hands with his flock. His uncle was already talking to the kindly gentleman, so he'd wait until he got an opportunity to speak his mind.

"Oh, there you are, my boy. Did you enjoy the meeting?" His uncle gave him a shrewd look, noticing the puffy eyes and the softness in his nephew's face. It was very obvious to him that something had touched Roger's heart today. That made George Abbott very happy.

"The preacher here is very convincing." Roger walked up and was introduced to Rev. Peter Jennings by his uncle.

"Glad to meet you. I'm Roger Abbott. I came with my uncle."

"It was touch-and-go for a while, but Roger finally decided to humor me." Uncle George smiled at him then looked at Reverend Jennings.

"No matter the reason, I'm glad you came." He looked intently into Roger's tear-stained face as if waiting for him to say something more. "Is there something I can help you with? Your uncle told me you have suffered a terrible loss and that it has been weighing heavily on your mind."

The visible compassion in the preacher's face was the catalyst Roger needed to ask for help. It was a small step, a painful one, but it was a step nevertheless. He decided to take the plunge before he lost his nerve.

"I was wondering if I could talk to you about how I can move past the guilt I feel. Could we set up a time through the week where we could discuss this?"

"That would be fine, Mr. Abbott. How would next Tuesday night be?"

"Okay, I'll make myself available. I'm willing to do whatever is needed to turn things around."

"I'll look forward to seeing you at the church." The Reverend gave Roger a hearty handshake then turned to greet another parishioner.

Roger's heart felt lighter, more released from pain at the thought of telling about his ordeal. Hearing a rustle near him, he turned and looked into Janice's deep violet eyes. Eyes that spoke of her growing feelings for him. She was pleased that he was going to get some counseling. It had worked for her, she knew it would work for Roger too, if he let it. She knew the minister was a very good listener, and a man of faith.

He gave her arm a gentle squeeze then turned to address her father who was hovering just off to one side.

"I was wondering if I could talk to you for a few minutes, sir? It won't take very long. It's about your brother, Boyd."

"What about my brother? Is he in some kind of trouble again? We're not that close, but even so, I do worry about him. I don't see him very often."

Roger drew Frank Peterson off to one side and explained his suspicions and concerns. Frank said he was being pressured to give Boyd a $40,000 transfer to prop up his company. He was also concerned about his brother's lack of emotion, even bordering on ruthlessness. The one thing he kept to himself involved the use of his medical expertise to treat Boyd's men without notifying the authorities.

Roger listened to all these admissions by Frank, inwardly wondering if the change was caused by the use of drugs. Janice came up behind them and the impromptu interview was over. However, it raised some alarm bells in Roger's mind. He was even more determined to keep an eye on Boyd Peterson. He would have to be discreet, so he didn't alert Boyd he was watching.

While Roger was worrying about keeping a discreet eye on Boyd, Boyd had troubles of his own. A couple of shipments that left for New Brunswick had been waylaid between Avonvale and the New Brunswick border. The trucks had been searched and the hidden drugs taken. His men were also roughed up. Someone in his company was working for a rival drug cartel. Losing these drugs made Boyd very angry. Like all his dealings, he felt very uneasy when he was not in complete control.

Boyd stared at the wall of his office for a few minutes then in a fit of anger, he picked up a paperweight and threw it at the far wall. The heavy glass pitted the blue-colored Gyprock wall then crashed to the floor. Moving to the door, he gave it a kick with his foot then went back to look through the invoices stacked on his oak desk. Paper rustled as he looked for the bill of lading that indicated the shipment that was stolen by his adversaries in New Brunswick.

This drug shipment would mean the loss of several thousand dollars. At this rate, he would go bankrupt. He wasn't going to give up, and he was prepared to use force if necessary. Reaching for the dusty black telephone on his scarred desk, he dialed one of his contacts for some support.

Once he hung up, he reached in the side drawer of his desk, closing his fingers around the small automatic pistol he kept there for emergencies. Pulling the black metal gun from its hiding place, he held it up, a feeling of determination on his hardened face. No matter what the obstacles, he was going to win this war. Weapons just might help him win it. If the others wanted a fight, they would get a fight.

Boyd pushed back the black office chair then he moved to the door. A quick stride took him to his supervisor, Jason Cox.

"Jason, contact them in Truro, tell them we'll get another shipment to them and not to go with the group from across the border. I won't lose this deal."

"Got it, boss. Should we have someone ride shotgun next time?"

"Good idea. The shipment will be ready in another day or so."

With that curt statement, Boyd crossed the cement floor and disappeared through the metal door leading to the front parking lot. He needed to go for a walk to clear his head. Maybe he'd take a quick run down the gut to the beach. He could plan his next method of attack. A hint of a smile appeared on his weathered face.

He would make sure the trucks had someone on board to protect them against the opposing drug cartel. While he thought about this, he thought again about the young man he had met at his brother's house. Vague memories that he had seen him before continued to hang just outside his thoughts. With a shrug, he let the persistent thoughts fade away. He probably would never see the young man again anyway. He wondered how his men at the church made out. They were positioned to watch Janice's movements.

Boyd gazed at the distant island, just offshore. In the coming weeks, he was going to use it for expanding his business. He also wondered how Sara was doing. She had done well the past couple of weeks, and so far, he was very pleased with her. He was anxious to convert the hard drugs for street use. By the time the boys in blue figured it all out, he would have the money he needed and would move on.

"Good luck, guys. You'll never catch me." Boyd taunted. He pulled his cell phone out of his pocket, dialing Sara. Time for plan B.

"Sara here. Can I help you?"

"How are you doing? Any more leads on getting your hands on some OxyContin? I know some people who would kill to get some of that stuff."

"I've got a lead on where I could get some. Possibly at the hospital."

"Be careful. I don't want any loose ends. I'll talk to you later tonight." Boyd signed off, not giving Sara time to say goodbye. She was hurt that he was often so coarse around her. Her only explanation was that Boyd was anxious about his shipping business. She had heard about the hijacked trucks.

Sara was worried about him, so overlooked Boyd's little missteps as well the times he was inconsiderate of her feelings. He came over and gave her a quick kiss. Despite his being inconsiderate at times, she was still in love with him. As long as she was with him, she was happy.

Love may have been blind in Sara Martin's case, but that potent emotion was just beginning to bloom with Roger and Janice. Spring was well under way, the ice was all melted, and the two of them were anxious to see where their relationship would go.

It was late April and Roger was back at work again. He was back to twelve-hour shifts, with four days off. He hoped he would get an opportunity to see Janice. Also on the agenda was his meeting with Reverend Jennings for counseling for his nightmares. He found himself actually whistling as he went about his daily activities. He also asked his uncle if he could borrow his Bible. He had a lot of catching up to do.

"You can read it anytime you want, son. If you'll wait just a minute, I think I can let you have your aunt's old Bible. She would want you to have it, I'm sure."

"Thanks. I promise I'll take good care of it." Roger reached for his uncle's extended arm, retrieving the old black Bible. "I will be in the living room, reading. Let me know when supper's ready, Uncle."

"Take all the time you need. Supper will be ready at 5:00 p.m. We're having chicken sandwiches and salad."

Roger gave his uncle a hug then moved into the pale yellow living room. It was his favorite room, with a comfortable flowered couch, an oval rug in the center of the room, and a stone fireplace at the far end. Plunking himself down on the old couch, he opened the Bible.

His visits to Reverend Jennings were starting to help him let go of the misty images from his past. They no longer held him captive. For the first time, he felt free, free from the awful weight, and free to pursue his growing relationship with Janice Peterson.

He almost felt like laughing out loud. However, a dark shadow hovered just on the edge of his thoughts. He didn't stop to analyze the meaning of that shadow. It resembled a storm cloud hovering on the distant horizon.

He jumped when he felt his uncle's hand on his arm.

"Sorry to startle you, but I think I'll turn in early tonight."

"Thanks. Good night, Uncle. I'm going to take a quick trip down to the Breamar Drive Superstore before they close then I'll head off to the loft. I'll be up early for work so I'll try not to wake you up. I am kind of glad to be back to work again."

"Promise me that you'll be careful when you're on duty." He looked thoughtfully at Roger

"I'll be careful, I promise, Uncle."

He made his way to the side door, letting himself out. Shutting the heavy door, he enjoyed the cool evening. He had to be up early for the two-hour long drive to Avonvale where he worked, so reluctantly, he tore himself away from the scene in front of him. He made his way to the waiting Chevy, grabbing his keys from his pocket in the process. In only minutes, he was in the large grocery store. Grabbing a cart, he started down the canned food aisle. He was in a bit of a hurry to get his shopping done, so wasn't as aware of the other shoppers as he should have been. As he came to the end of the long aisle, he pulled around the turn.

Crash!

"Why don't you watch out where you're going?" Roger growled as he felt the jolt go up his arms. He looked up into the startled expression on the face of Janice Peterson. "Janice, what are you doing here?"

"Apparently, the same thing you are. I was just about to say something mean when I realized it was you. Why do we always seem to be meeting in some sort of accident, Roger? Hope we can break this trend, or one of us will end up in the hospital."

"Yeah, I know. How is the skating and counseling going? It must be awkward without ice to skate on."

"It can be. I'm using the rink. I love teaching the little ones to skate. It makes me feel like I'm making a difference. Some of them are showing real potential. Any leads on the drug cartel? Are you still watching my uncle, Roger?" The two of them moved their carts off to one side to let the other shoppers go by. Some gave them a quick once over as they passed.

"I've been watching his business. So far, nothing out of the ordinary. I did see someone go out to Spooner's Island the other day, but I don't know if it was one of his men, or a member of the Coast Guard. He must have money because I saw a Cadillac as well as a Lincoln Town Car. Anyway, I don't trust him, Janice."

CHAPTER SIX

"Sorry I scared you. Well, I guess we'd better get our shopping done. I'm off to work tomorrow. It's going to be an early day."

"Just to let you know, I don't trust Uncle Boyd either. I'm positive he wants Dad's money for something illegal."

"I've been thinking about that too. Be careful, okay? Nice seeing you again."

"You too." She watched as he headed down the next aisle. Her heart did a strange little flip-flop at the sight of him. She was unaware that she was being watched from the next aisle over. As she headed for the checkout with her groceries, two men fell into step behind her. While she watched Roger go through the checkout, she waited for her turn. She felt that strange light-headedness at the sight of him. Swinging around, she gave the men a quick smile.

They didn't smile back.

Both were dressed in jeans, with shirts and ties. By their appearance, they looked like college students. Her time to pay approached, so she put the handful of groceries on the black conveyor belt. The men were forgotten as she prepared to pay for her purchases.

Once she was outside, she made her way to her small car. She was almost to the driver's door, when she heard a scuffling sound behind her. As Janice turned, someone grabbed her left arm. She recognized the two men who had been behind her at the checkout. "Who are you? What do you want? Let me go, you're hurting my arm."

"We have orders to take you with us. Who we are isn't important. If you cooperate, no one will get hurt." The man who held her had a calm voice, but it held a thinly veiled threat. His hard cold eyes frightened her.

She quickly assessed the situation. Two against one.

Not the best odds.

What was she going to do? There was no way she was going to go along with this plan to abduct her. Trying to think on her feet, she formulated a plan of attack. She thought of the course she had taken about six months ago on self-defense. If she was going to escape, she had only minutes to make a move. As the man moved to grab her, she brought her foot down on his instep. She heard his gasp as her high heel found its mark. When he loosened his grip on her, the other, older man reached for her.

Before he was able to grab her, someone shouted, "Leave the lady alone or I'll call the cops!"

With their plans exposed, the two men took off, running among the parked cars.

With a wave of thanks to the man who had rescued her she quickly ran to the safety of the grocery store. Despite the fact she was out of harm's way, she was scared. Who wanted her badly enough to kidnap her?

Once she settled down enough to ask someone to call the police, she thought about her abandoned groceries. With a grim shake of her head, she wondered about the importance of a few groceries at a time like this. She also went to a pay phone and called Roger. While she sat in the lobby, her hands began to shake slightly. So much for her quick trip to the grocery store.

The police arrived, took a statement from her then looked outside by her car. After they got a statement from the old gentleman who had thwarted the kidnapping, they left. The only satisfaction she got out of the whole ordeal was the knowledge that she had given both of them something to remember her by.

Roger finished his shopping then headed back to the loft with his groceries. He had missed seeing Janice in trouble by mere minutes. Unaware of the situation back at the grocery store, he put things away and got ready for bed. When the phone rang, he sprang to answer it. When Janice related her near kidnapping, his temper flared. He forgot about everything else as he ran to his car. In only minutes he was at her side, comforting her. She must have been rattled because he could feel her trembling as he held her. After a half hour, he walked with her to her car, making sure she was safe inside. She assured him, "Roger, really, I'll be fine. I just need to go home and unwind."

"If you're sure. Call me later, okay?" He gave her a tender kiss on the cheek then he reluctantly headed for his own place.

The encounter with Janice replayed itself in his mind as he lay back on the pillow about an hour later. Who would want to kidnap her?

The sun was just coming up. The whole world was bathed in the golden glow of a spectacular sunrise. Roger could see the pink stain on the placid waters of the lake. Now that it was May, it was starting to warm up, giving the city the decree of warmer days ahead. Finally, he tore his gaze away from the lake and went inside to have breakfast.

"Uncle, what are you doing up at this hour?"

"Couldn't sleep. Thought I'd get an early start on the day."

"It seemed pretty quiet last night. I slept like a log." He decided to keep the little incident at the grocery store to himself for now.

"Well, I kept thinking about your aunt last night. Sometimes I really miss her. If you need to talk about Anna, just let me know. I feel like going for a walk this morning."

"I'm off to work. Still working on the drugstore robberies. It's a baffling case. No clues to use. The thieves were very careful."

"Sounds like they were professionals, son."

The two men had a quick breakfast then Roger bade his uncle goodbye. Retrieving his car keys from his pocket, he crawled behind the wheel of his red Chevy. He backed out of the driveway then headed for the highway that would take him to the Eastern Shore and the town of Avonvale. He kept replaying the incident with Janice and her near-abduction. Once he arrived at the police station, he was assigned his regular companion. Together, the two officers were to continue the investigation of the drugstore robberies. Whoever was guilty, they were fast and very efficient in their routine. In and out in a matter of minutes. They had left very few clues for them to examine.

While Roger was involved in the drugstore robberies, the drug scene hit close to home with Betty Richard's family. The incident involved Amy, her eight-year-old daughter.

Amy left home at 8:30 a.m. School was just around the corner, so with Ben in tow, she skipped down the sidewalk toward the red brick school house. The sun was up, a cool breeze fluttered around her flowered skirt. She loved spring. Once in the schoolyard, Ben went in with the younger kids, while Amy waited in the yard. Off to one side, near the back of the building, she saw a man sitting on the cracked stone wall that ran the length of the property. She still had about five minutes until she would be ushered inside, so she decided to see who was waiting in the shadows. A vague thought told her she should not go too close to the stranger, but curiosity got the better of her. The fact that danger could be present never entered the eight-year-old's mind.

Approaching a scruffy looking man, Amy noticed that he was probably in his late teens. The teen's dark hair was unkempt and long. He had a hard look in his eyes, and he hadn't shaved in several days. A quick look at his dirty denim jacket and faded jeans told Amy he might be a street person. For the first time, she felt a stab of fear. She was still far enough away that he didn't notice her.

As Amy watched, the young man took his jacket off and rolled up the right sleeve of his shirt. His arm was pockmarked with puncture holes. Quickly, he positioned a syringe and injected something into his arm. He looked up just then and Amy froze.

"What are you looking at? Why don't you beat it, kid, before I do something to you that you won't like. Maybe a little of this stuff will fix you up." The man looked very angry, and he raised his arm as if to threaten the girl in front of him with the half-empty syringe.

"Why are you putting a needle in your arm? Do you have to take drugs for a disease or something?" Amy continued to stare at the syringe in the man's hand. "How come you have all those marks in your arm?"

"Yeah, that's it. I have a disease and have to use drugs." He let out a loud bark of laughter. "If you're not gone in ten seconds—"

At that moment, Amy heard her teacher calling the students to class. She turned and ran back to the safety of the other students gathered at the door. Once they were inside, she approached her teacher.

"Mrs. Lewis, guess what I saw outside in the yard?"

Her teacher, a stout middle-aged woman, looked down at the child. "What did you see, Amy?" She knew Amy was very inquisitive, so she assumed the girl probably saw a garter snake in the grass near the wall. Her eyes widened in consternation at the answer she received.

"While I was waiting, I saw a man sitting on the wall. He had a needle stuck in his arm. There were all kinds of marks on his arm too."

"Did you approach him?"

"Yes. He wasn't very happy to see me. I think he might be a drug user, Mrs. Lewis."

"You must never go near strangers, Amy. This man sounds like a drug addict. He might be dangerous."

"Oh. Am I in trouble? I've never seen a drug addict before. Would he really hurt me, Mrs. Lewis?"

"No, you're not in trouble, but please, in the future, tell an adult if you see someone like this. An addict is a person who takes drugs when he doesn't have to. He can't stop, so he needs help, and, yes, he might harm you."

She looked thoughtful for a moment then she looked up at her teacher. "Maybe if I prayed for him, he would be able to stop doing it."

"It couldn't hurt. Meantime, we need to get you in to your class, Amy."

Amy, along with the rest of the class, made their way to their classroom. Once the principal checked the yard and found the young man had gone, the incident was forgotten. There were other more pressing problems to take care of.

For Amy, as she listened to the teacher explain some math procedures, her mind kept replaying the encounter with the drug user. She was going to have to ask her mother to explain more about drug use. For her, the world just got a lot more complicated. Amy had lost something that day.

Innocence.

Despite the engrossing lesson, Amy kept thinking about the young man with the needle that she saw outside. The encounter left a feeling of unease in the young girl's mind. Finally, the recess bell sounded its loud clang, proclaiming freedom for the students. Boys and girls scraped chairs against the tile floor, grabbed backpacks, and made their way outside.

It was a beautiful day. The late May sun hinted at hotter days to come. Amy and her best friends, Sara and Lisa, made their way around the corner to the shady side of the school. Amy half-expected to see the scruffy young man still there, sitting on the rock wall. She was visibly relieved when she saw that he was gone.

"Wow, Amy, did you really see a man with a needle in his arm here?" Sara asked, her hazel eyes round with wonder. "I'd be so scared."

"How did you know about that?" Amy addressed her friend. She had forgotten that some of the other students had been nearby.

"We saw you talking to him. I wouldn't have the courage to talk to a stranger. My mom would be cross if I did, anyway." Sara declared solemnly.

"Come on, you guys. Recess will be over soon and I want a game of Double Dutch." Lisa waited impatiently for her two friends to grab the long red skipping rope.

With the discussion about the drug addict over, the girls went to join their friend for a spirited game of Double Dutch.

While Amy had her first experience with the world of drug users, many teens around Avonvale were being pressured by the pushers to use drugs. Marijuana seemed to be the drug of choice for the pushers. Often, they would introduce the harder drugs as well. Unfortunately, a lot of young people succumbed to the lure for that first high.

The month of May passed quickly as did the month of June. Roger Abbott and his companion, Detective Butler, were still trying to sort through the mystery of the drugstore robberies. There was not much to go on. It was frustrating, and more than once, Roger felt like hitting his fist against the wall. This was the part of his job he disliked the most. The waiting.

On the plus side, his guilt over the loss of his wife has disappeared.

He always looked forward to his visits with Janice. By now, they both had forgotten her experience at the Superstore. Quite often in May and June, she would be at the local rink. He, along with Betty, would sit in the bleachers and watch as Janice interacted with the children. A talented skater, she would show them the basic methods used to do figure skating. When their eyes met, he smiled at her, aware of just a hint of sadness in her eyes. It was a shame, her injury had brought an end to her own dreams. He knew that at times it was hard for her, living her dreams through these girls. But true to her nature, she never let it get the best of her. His admiration for her courage and grace went up even higher. His heart was telling him that he had serious feelings for her. It didn't matter what they were doing, just as long as they were together. He admired her patience with Amy and the other children she was teaching. They obviously adored her, were always willing to imitate her skating techniques.

On this last day of June, Roger made his way to his red Chevy, preparing for the hour-and-a-half-long drive to work. His trip was made without incident, and he pulled into the police department's gravel parking lot. The tires made a crunching sound as he drove into the yard.

After attending the briefing with the other officers, he was assigned to work with Peter Butler. Detective Butler was about thirty years old, had an infectious smile, and very expressive hazel eyes. At six four, he was a tower of a man who always commanded respect. The uniform helped give him an authoritative air. Peter and Roger had become good friends, and both had good instincts. They made their way to the waiting cruiser, a white Ford sedan with a red-and-blue light bar resting on the white roof. The department's crest and the words "Avonvale Police" were printed on the side of the car. A couple of small dents on the front fender reminded Roger of the encounter with a rather violent offender they had arrested the other day.

"Guess we're back to looking for the proverbial needle in the haystack," Roger stated cryptically. "We need a break. Surely, someone will make a mistake and give us a lead."

"Patience, my friend. It's my experience that sooner or later, they get careless and will leave us some clues." Peter gave Roger a wan smile, one that was meant to reassure him. "Let's head over to Maple Street and see if we can find any new clues."

"Good idea. You drive, while I check the computer for any updates."

Once the two of them were seated, with seat belts fastened, Roger logged on to the computer. While he scanned the information that came up on the small screen, Peter drove to the latest pharmacy to be held up.

As they drove along Shore Drive, Roger gave Peterson's Trucking a quick glance. Trucks moved in and out of the gravel parking lot, and at the warehouse, men loaded other trucks. He wondered just what Boyd Peterson shipped in those trucks. He also noticed the expensive luxury sedans parked off to one side. Somehow, they seemed out of place here. The trucking lot gave way to a cliff, with a gradually sloping bank where people could launch small boats. A few seagulls wheeled overhead, their sharp cries to each other blending in with the soft breeze that blew.

As they turned inland, Roger was again impressed with the beauty of this small town. It had quiet tree-lined streets, lots of places for people to get out and enjoy the sun as well as the lure of the sea only a stone's throw away. He felt blessed for belonging to the community. People were friendly and caring and more than willing to share.

As the police cruiser turned into the small gravel parking lot, Roger observed the red brick building in front of them. Flemings Pharmacy proclaimed its name in bright red lettering on a white background. Awnings gave the entrance a welcoming appearance. Colorful displays were set up in the windows to entice people to come inside. The only thing that was out of place was the boarded up front window to the right of the main door. Plywood covered the opening and glass still littered the sidewalk that ran along the front of the complex. Thieves had stolen a large quantity of prescription drugs last night while the community slept. These drugs would be easy to sell to those interested in a quick high. Yellow police tape was stretched along the front of the building.

Taking some equipment from the trunk of the car, the two officers searched the area near the window for some sign of carelessness on the part of the criminals.

"They were smart to bypass the alarm system. Obviously, they're not amateurs. Possibly they left behind some clothing fragments on the glass. You got the camera, Roger?"

"Right here. Let's take a look at the window area. Peter, you check the lot for footprints or tire prints. Maybe we'll get lucky."

"We're due for a break." Butler made his way to the edge of the gravel parking lot in hopes of finding some footprints. The sun shone brightly, birds chirped in the nearby trees, and a gentle breeze ruffled Roger's sandy hair. Little droplets of moisture broke out on his brow as he joined his colleague by the edge of the lot. Despite the situation, Roger smiled at his friend.

"Looks like there's a muddy spot, right here." Roger joined the other officer near a small patch of wet earth. It offered a slim hope for a clue.

"Take a look, Roger." Peter Butler moved to one side, exposing the muddy grassy area next to the gray gravel. He looked closer, his trained eye hoping to spot anything out of place. For a few minutes nothing showed up then Roger gave a shout of triumph. "Bingo." Just to the left of where he was standing, he could make out the faint indentation caused by two people's footprints. Along with the footprints, he could see the tire tracks near the thick scrub of grass.

"I think we just got the clue we needed." Roger grabbed the camera, snapping a couple of close up shots of the depressions in the soil. He also taped off the area with police tape. "We should probably make a cast of the tire tread as well."

"Couldn't hurt. By the looks of these prints, I'd say we have a man and a woman. Peter took a second look at the smaller set of prints, which were slightly more than half the size of the man's tracks. "They probably never noticed the wet spot in the dark. I think the pharmacist said they have a closed circuit security camera under the eaves at the front of the store. Maybe it picked up some images." Before they examined the surveillance video, the area was secured with orange police tape.

For the next hour, they looked at frame after frame from the camera. Just the normal comings and goings of customers. Toward the end of the tape, they saw two shadowy figures approach the darkened building. A security light came on, catching the two in the glare of the light. They quickly turned away, but not before the image showed a tall man, along with a short slim woman. Both wore black jeans and sweatshirts. Gray masks covered their faces. The image showed the man grab a bat from the trunk of the car. A quick swing of the bat achieved the desired results, giving them access to the interior of the store.

"Not very original, but it got the job done," Peter commented. "I'd sure like to get access to that bat. Too bad the license plate's covered with dirt."

"Maybe they left some prints in the store. Apparently, they only took certain drugs," Roger observed, thinking perhaps this might help their cause.

Both men went back into the store to check for fingerprints on the counters. Their procedures took most of the day, so Roger had little time to reflect on his growing feelings for Janice. It was probably just as well, because she could be quite a distraction for him. By supper, they were finished, had gathered the data needed, and then headed back to police headquarters.

Roger finished his report then headed for the parking lot to the waiting cruiser. The rest of the day was mostly uneventful. The two officers had a bit of excitement when they caught a teen in the act of shoplifting from a computer store. Roger felt bad for the young man, but he needed to realize that he had broken the law. He was lucky this year. July 1 was a holiday, and he was off for the three days following as well. Slipping behind the wheel, he started the car and pulled out to the highway. A magnificent sunset was just starting to cast its orange hues across the darkening sky. Clouds scurried overhead, tinted with the soft shades of pink and mauve. Roger felt almost at peace as he observed nature's art at its best.

Traffic began to grow heavier as he drew closer to the city of Dartmouth. After an hour, he pulled into the side street off Prince Albert Road. His uncle was out front waiting for him on the front porch.

"How was your day, Roger? Catch any criminals today?"

"Just a teen for shoplifting. Spent most of the day looking for clues in the latest drugstore robbery. We're making progress. I worry that these drugs will turn up on the street. We have a few people we're watching.

Hopefully, they'll make a slip and give us the evidence we need to arrest them."

"Don't concern yourself, my boy. I know sooner or later you'll get the break you need. Sorry to hear about that young man. I'll be praying for you."

"Me too, Uncle. Thanks for the prayers. I appreciate it. The flower garden looks nice. Guess you inherited Grandmother's green thumb. I can't even grow weeds. What's for supper?"

"How does take-out sound? Maybe pizza. I really don't feel like slaving over a hot oven tonight. Tell you what. I'll pay. Are you going out with your girlfriend tonight?"

CHAPTER SEVEN

"Sounds good to me. Alex's Pizza is just around the corner. You like the works? And just for the record, Janice is not my girlfriend."

"Everything except mushrooms. Your aunt was always trying to sneak them into supper. It got to be a running joke with us. I still miss her, Roger." George had that wistful look in his face that he always got when thinking about his late wife. "And I think Janice would be just who you need in your life. You're too young to shut yourself off from life, son."

"I know you miss her. It's the same for me with Anna. Thanks to a good minister's counsel, as well as some guidance from above, I think I'll survive."

Roger gave his uncle a quick nod then reached into his car for something to write on. A few jots with the pen, and he had their order written down.

"Be back in a flash, Uncle. And you don't have to be matchmaker. I'm fine, really." Now if he could just convince his heart of that. He turned to slide behind the wheel of his Chevy, and he took a quick glance at the man who had been his father and mother this past few years. His uncle George was just getting ready to go back inside the house.

Pulling into the newly paved lot of Alex's Pizza, he noted that as usual, the joint was crowded. He suspected he'd have a wait tonight. Slamming the car door, he made his way to the wide aluminum door with its blue awning overhead.

Once inside, he took his place in the long line of customers at the striped red-and-white counter. Rock music blared from a stereo hidden somewhere above in the recesses of the ceiling. A popular Beach Boys song caught his attention and he began to hum along. Several patrons seated at tables off to one side turned to look at him. He smiled back rather sheepishly. The lure of popular music always made him feel like singing along.

As he let his gaze sweep the place, he noticed a blonde woman standing in front of the man next to him. She turned slightly and he caught his breath.

His heart did a funny little dance at the sight of Janice Peterson. The evening just got a whole lot brighter.

"Good evening, Janice. I guess we have the same idea for supper. Can't go wrong, though. These guys make the best pizza in the city. Actually, it's rather convenient that we met here. Would you like to be my date tomorrow night?" As far as Roger was concerned, they didn't need to worry about fireworks. Every time they met lately, there had been a different kind of fireworks. He was feeling them right now. From the flushed look on Janice's face, she was too.

They were so caught up in staring into each other's eyes that the store and the people near them dropped away. Several moments slipped by.

"Hey, man. Could you two stop making doe eyes at each other long enough to place your order? Like, some of us want to eat tonight," the tall teen with the baggy jeans gave them a big toothy grin. Both Janice and Roger broke apart, totally embarrassed by the young man's comment.

"Sorry. This always happens when I see her." Roger whispered. The moment passed, but it had revealed just how potent their feelings were. "Someday you'll be in the same position I am." He gave the youth a knowing smile.

With a shrug, the young man said, "I don't think so. You guys must be really into each other in a big way."

Another teen swung around to talk to Janice. The girl, who was making quite a scene herself with her bright pink hair, put in her two cents' worth.

"Don't you listen to Tom. He's just jealous because he doesn't have a girlfriend. From the way your eyes were locked, I'd say you two have it bad. Still, it's not a good idea to keep these hungry guys from their pizza. Right now they're more concerned with their stomachs."

"Roger and I have something really special. Sometimes we get so caught up in the moment that we forget where we are. Sorry about that." Janice quickly apologized to the teen with the pink spiky hairdo then added, "My boyfriend's right. Someday you'll know how we feel."

Roger regained his voice and added with a wry smile. "Wouldn't want to keep them from their pizza. Why don't you two go ahead. We're not in any hurry." He made a quick bow to motion the two boys forward.

"Thanks man. This place has the best pizza and donairs in town. You should try the pizza with the works. It's totally awesome. And I'm not in any hurry to get that deer in the headlights look that you two have. Life is too much fun to get tied down." This comment came from a long-haired youth named Jed.

The clerk at the counter had been watching the exchange and added. "I wish one of you would step up. The pizza's not getting any warmer. Okay, who's first, the young lovers, or the teens with the fluorescent hair?"

The two of them were still flustered as they finally stepped up to the bright red counter. Quickly, they placed their orders with the clerk. The encounter of a moment ago hung in the back of their minds. They smiled at the comments about not being involved with anyone. The teens were still too young to know what was important in life.

At the same time, as Roger and Janice were placing their orders for supper, Janice's father, Frank, was preparing to leave the hospital after a long and very trying day. Things had not gone well for Dr. Peterson. He had encountered a rather rude student doctor who figured he knew everything. Despite his counsel, the young man remained defiant. Then around noon, one of his patients succumbed to complications from open-heart surgery.

Frank always took the deaths of his patients hard. Equally as difficult was the talk and counsel he had to give to the grieving relatives. Seeking some peace from the ordeal, he slipped into the hospital chapel for a few minutes silent reflection.

Finally, Frank grabbed his suit jacket and headed out the front doors toward the staff parking lot.

His day was to get a lot more complicated.

It was a warm evening, birds chirped in a chorus in the nearby trees, and he heard someone's dog barking in the distance.

As he approached his silver Lexus, he pushed the open button on his black remote unit. The car's orange sidelights flashed, and the horn beeped twice. Frank had just reached the car and was about to open the door when he heard a car's tires crunching on the gravel next to him.

He turned, coming face-to-face with his brother Boyd. "What are you doing here, Boyd? How did you know I'd be off work now?"

"I know more about your comings and goings than you think, brother. Seems to me you were going to give me some much-needed money. I'm here to collect."

"I don't recall saying that I would give you that much money. If I did, the bank would question why I withdrew such a large amount. Why don't you take out a loan?"

"I figure family should share, Frank. I know you've got lots of the green stuff. Besides that very lucrative career, Father left you most of the money from his fortune. I'm here to collect my part of it. And I might need your help with an associate of mine who was injured the other day. I want to avoid questions at the hospital. And don't try and put me off again. This time it won't work, big brother." Boyd's voice had a hard edge to it, and as he gestured with his right arm, Frank looked down.

His face paled when he saw the small black handgun in Boyd's right hand.

"So now you're playing with guns? Why the secrecy about a hurt friend?"

"I'm not playing. Believe me, this is not a toy. If you cross me, you'll find out just how real it is!" Boyd sneered at him. His face turned to stone, and he grabbed his brother's arm, gesturing for him to move toward his black Cadillac. "Let's go. We're going to take a little ride in my car. First, you need to be blindfolded. I don't need the cops snooping around my place. Don't ask questions about my medical requests. You're safer that way."

Boyd reached into his pocket. He withdrew a checkered bandana. He removed Frank's glasses and told him to put them in his pocket. Coming up behind his brother, he placed the bandana over his head and covered his eyes.

"Can you see. Frank?

"No. I still don't see why you have to go through all these theatrics." Frank felt fear for the first time as he realized that his brother was quite serious. He began to come to the sad conclusion that he really didn't know him at all. The gap between them just got a whole lot wider. He thought back to the many times his father had ignored Boyd. Even as a boy, he had been combative.

"Humor me, okay. It's quite necessary, I assure you. Get in!"

Boyd quickly moved to the driver's side and slid behind the wheel. Frank sat staring straight ahead, his blindfold rendering him sightless. He tried to settle his frayed nerves, offering a silent prayer for help. He was unsure of what Boyd was capable of, but in his present state of mind, he knew he would have to do all in his power to stay on his good side. For the first time, he wondered if his brother had a good side.

As the car pulled out of the lot, mingling with the traffic, Frank tried to remember sounds and how many turns they made. He heard the usual car sounds. Horns blared, a siren sounded nearby, and he heard the traffic signal chirp. He heard the pitch of the tires change beneath them. They seemed to have a hollow sound, and he realized they were just starting up the slope to the MacDonald Bridge. They stopped several times in heavy traffic then finally they stopped to drop the fare in the booth.

"Nothing to say, Frank? Hope you enjoy the ride." With that sarcastic comment, Boyd gave him a jab with the automatic, just to remind him. He kept the gun low enough that no one outside would notice anything amiss. "Just in case you forget, I have the control here."

"Believe me, Boyd, I haven't forgotten."

"Just be patient. Why don't you think about a good way to convince your bank to give you that forty thousand dollars."

"Forty thousand! I thought you said you needed thirty thousand dollars" Frank turned toward his brother as he turned a corner. "I'll do what I can to help your friend."

"Thank you. Now, about the money, the price just went up. Every time you stall, Frank, the cost will get higher."

"That's robbery!" Frank protested the twisted logic that his brother was using.

Boyd gave a loud bark of laughter "Robbery. You're a good one to talk. I don't recall you offering to share that inheritance with me. Seems to me that brothers ought to share." Boyd's voice held an edge of bitterness and hatred. "So it's time to balance the accounts, you might say."

"What if I refuse to go along with this scheme of yours, Boyd?"

"I've thought about that possibility." Boyd turned to look at his brother, a look of pure loathing crossing his tanned face. "In that event, my men will deal with that beautiful daughter of yours, Janice. They have been watching her, and if you should try and get out of this deal, my men will deal with her." He glanced at Frank to see if his threat had registered with him.

Frank's face went a deathly white at the mention of his daughter. "You wouldn't dare do anything to her!"

"No? Do you want to test that theory? Why not make things easier for everyone, just pass over the money." Boyd was losing patience with his brother's reluctance. He just might grab the girl anyway for a little insurance. When he recalled how she had foiled his men, he saw red. It appeared she was very resourceful. If it came down to taking the girl, he would do it himself.

Frank didn't answer his brother, much to Boyd's annoyance. He didn't like being ignored.

They continued along the coast out of the cities. Frank could hear the roar of the ocean and smell the salt air as they got closer to their destination. A few minutes later, Boyd braked hard, throwing Frank forward in his seat.

"We're here." Boyd pulled into a gravel parking lot.

Frank felt the sedan slow, heard the crunch of gravel beneath them, and then the car stopped. He heard his brother jump from the car and come around to his side. The door was wrenched open and Boyd growled. "Okay, Frank, get out."

Frank was hauled roughly to his feet. With Boyd behind him, he was pushed toward a long aluminum building. With his brother giving directions, he was able to stumble toward the long shed. Boyd grabbed him, bringing him up short near a red metal door. He quickly opened the door and shoved his brother inside. Frank stumbled over the threshold, falling heavily on his right arm. The cement floor was cold and dirty. His hands sustained several scrapes as he pitched forward. The smell of oil mixed with the other smells in the large warehouse. He struggled to get to his feet while his brother laughed at his misfortune.

"Come on, Frank. Straight ahead to the backroom. Just feel the wall till you come to the door." Boyd was eager to get the money transferred, so he wasn't inclined to have much compassion for his brother's discomfort. On the contrary, he seemed to get some enjoyment out of his sibling's inability to see. Control was the important thing. All else was just something to complicate life.

"When can I take this blindfold off? Is it really necessary to leave it on all this time?"

"Patience. You can remove it as soon as we are in the back office. I want to be sure you don't have anything that will identify where we are. Remember what I said. If the cops come snooping around here, and I find out you went to the cops, you can kiss that daughter of yours goodbye!" Boyd snapped at his brother.

Frank still couldn't see his brother, but he could sense the deep hurt he was trying to cover up. Despite his harsh tone, Frank heard an underlying feeling of being alone seep into his brother's voice. For the first time, he wondered if Boyd had got some of their father's inheritance, would it have made any difference in his attitude and choices. Unfortunately, it was too late now for what ifs.

Boyd came up behind his brother, ripping the bandana from his eyes. Frank blinked several times as his eyes were exposed to the glare of the office overhead light. As his eyes finally adjusted to the light, he noted a small office about 10x10 with dull blue walls. Several file cabinets stood against the far wall, while a scarred oak desk sat to his right. The desk held a phone, a computer printer, and a black laptop computer. Frank could see the initials HP on the cover.

"Sit down, Frank. We need to make a little transfer to my company account." Boyd whispered in his ear. He could almost taste the money.

"I'll see what I can do. Like I said, the bank may not let me transfer such a large amount of money." Frank silently prayed the bank would allow the transfer to go through.

Taking the black swivel chair, he drew himself up to the desk. Once he had flipped the computer lid open, he turned the unit on. The machine beeped once then the screen turned a bright blue. Once the icons appeared on the screen, Frank logged on the Internet and typed in the bank's Web site letters. After a minute, the bank's page came up with the prompt about what you wish to do. He typed in his account number and the type of account he had. Turning to Boyd he asked." What's your account number, Boyd?"

Boyd pulled the drawer open and withdrew a large company check book. "This should be what you want. I hope you don't have any problems." He looked on as his brother initiated the transfer.

Frank took a quick look at his formerly clean blue suit. The material was wrinkled and smudged with dirt from the warehouse floor. He also had some nasty scratches on his hands from his fall on the rough cement. He watched as the on line banking link connected to his bank. In about two minutes, he had the answer as to whether or not they could get the go ahead with the money transfer.

The answer was what he expected.

No!

He glanced up at his brother, noting the hard expression. Both of them saw the blue square in the center of the screen with the red letters that said, "Access Denied."

"I told you, Boyd. It says I need to go to the bank, sign a form stating my income will support this transfer then you have to sign as the other party."

"How long does that take? I really don't need a lot of hassles right now. Remember what I said about your daughter still stands, Frank."

"What is it that has you needing so much money right away? Why do you need to use guns, unless you are involved in something that's illegal. Is it illegal, Boyd?"

Boyd didn't answer right away, but when he did, he had a hard bitter edge to his voice. "You ask too many questions. Better that you not know too much. It'll keep you and your daughter safer."

Frank thought about the very real possibility that his brother was up to his ears in the drug business. Suddenly he felt a wave of longing go through him. Longing for happier times for the two of them, before life got complicated. For the wish that their father hadn't played favorites when they were younger.

"I won't be able to get to the bank until Tuesday." He closed down the Web site then shut off the computer.

"That will have to do. But don't take too long, or I might have to take some insurance," Boyd added, hinting at something Frank would rather not think about. "Come on. I have someone here who needs a little medical attention." He pushed his brother into another room, indicating a young man sitting on a wooden chair. "Jamie here cut his arm. He needs to be stitched up. Since you're a doctor, you're elected."

For the next half hour, Frank used the medical supplies on the desk to stitch up the young man's arm. By the look of the wound, it appeared the youth had been in a fight. Noting his brother's scowl, he didn't ask questions.

Boyd reached for the bandana, putting it over his eyes, rendering him sightless as before. He gave his brother a push toward the door. "Watch the doorstep, Frank. We wouldn't want you to fall and mess up that expensive suit of yours." Sarcasm laced his voice.

He walked in the direction his brother told him to, and finally, he bumped into the car. He heard Boyd open the car door then he was pushed down into the seat. He heard him move around then the other door opened. After a minute, he heard the engine start.

Boyd quickly pulled out on the highway that lead back to the cities. With the dirty bandana over his eyes, Frank could only hear sounds and feel the vibration of the tires beneath them. It seemed they had arrived at their destination because his brother slowed down then pulled into a parking lot. The car stopped and Boyd leaned over his brother. "Okay, end of the line. You can find your way home from here. Remember, you've got three days to make an appointment to transfer that money."

"I haven't forgotten, believe me." Frank jumped out of the car seconds before his brother started to pull away. He heard the squeal of tires as he pushed the accelerator down. Frank ripped the smelly bandana off and glanced around him. He was standing in the lower parking lot of the Micmac Mall. Just below him, he could make out the outline of his home showing through the trees. With a slight limp, he made his way across the lot toward his house. Janice was probably getting worried about him, considering it was close to 8:00 p.m.

Frank made his way down the bank to the access road then to the entrance to his subdivision. In a matter of minutes he was at his door. He saw a slight movement off to his left. The drapes were pulled back, and he saw his daughter staring at him through the living room window.

Before he had a chance to pull the keys from his pocket, the door was swung open and Janice stood in the opening. Her face registered a look of concern when she saw his unkempt appearance.

"Dad, what happened? Why are you so late for supper?" She surveyed his rumpled dirty suit, then she saw the scratched hands. "Were you in an accident?" Janice was shocked by the vision of her father as he moved past her into the house.

"Sorry I worried you, honey. I had a little run-in with your uncle Boyd a couple of hours ago." Frank sounded tired and moved to sit down on the sofa.

"What do you mean you had a run-in with uncle Boyd? What did he want with you? Did it have something to do with his demand for cash? That's it, isn't it? Wait here. I have to take the wash out of the dryer."

Janice quickly disappeared downstairs. He heard the dryer door slam a minute later. He quickly phoned Aunt Audrey in Falmouth with a plan he had been forming in his mind. He was quite certain that his brother didn't know where Aunt Audrey lived. He wasn't one to keep in contact with family members. While he was sad for the emotional disconnect, in this case, it would work in their favor.

As Frank thought about the events of the evening, Janice reappeared with a drink in her hand. Her father tried to relax on the plump couch. His arm hurt, and his hands were badly scratched and bloody. A slight rustle alerted him to his daughter's presence. He must have dozed off because she managed to sneak up on him unnoticed. She set the drink on the end table. She reached for a bottle and some cotton swabs she had brought.

"Just relax, Dad. Let me see your hands." She lifted his right arm, applying alcohol to the injured flesh. She heard her father's sharp intake of breath as the liquid was rubbed over his skin. "You've got some bad cuts. This should keep them from getting infected."

"That hurts. What is this stuff, anyway?" Frank attempted to pull his hand away.

"It's alcohol. Honestly, you'd think I was killing you. Men are such cowards around medical treatments." She laughed at the irony of that statement. Her father was a heart surgeon. He probably saw blood on a regular basis in the hospital.

"Well, you know what they say. Doctors make the worst patients."

"I believe it. Now, what did Uncle Boyd want that made him rough you up?"

"He came to collect the money I said I'd give him. We went to his place outside Dartmouth. I don't know where it is, but I tripped and scratched my hands. I have to meet with him in a couple of days at the bank to transfer the money." Her father sounded exhausted by the ordeal, and Janice's heart went out to him. She still would like to know exactly what happened.

"Why is he so desperate? It's about drugs, isn't it? She came and sat next to him on the flowered sofa. "I've noticed an increase in drug activity the last couple of months. I bet Uncle Boyd is behind it."

Frank sighed, "You're probably right. He wants the money to finance something illegal. Probably drugs. There's no proof, so he can't be charged."

"We can still report him for abducting you, and holding you at gunpoint. There's a law against holding a person against their will." She looked intently into her father's face, noting the gold flecks in his eyes. They always appeared that way when he was upset about something.

"That may be, but I'm not going to do anything other than give him the money." His voice held a note of resignation to it.

Janice sat up, anger drawing her lips into a thin line. "Why not? You can't let him off the hook that easily, Father."

He knew when she used *Father* that way, she was very angry. He didn't blame her, but with the threat against her, his hands were tied.

"I didn't tell you the whole story. Boyd has had this house watched for the past couple of weeks. He said if I, or anyone else goes to the cops, your life will be in danger. The threat is very real, believe me, honey."

Janice sprang to her feet, making her way to the large bay window. Pulling back the heavy curtain, she peered out into the darkness. The streetlights illuminated parts of the area in light circles beneath thin poles. Houses had their outside lights on, and the moon cast a glow over the trees. As she looked up the street, she saw the dark outline of a large sedan. It sat against the curb about three houses up. Something about the car looked familiar and she tried to recall if she had seen it before. Letting the curtain fall back, she turned to her father.

"There's a car about three houses up. Might not mean anything." Despite the denial, Janice sensed the car meant danger. She thought about the attempt to kidnap her earlier, realizing that her father was telling the truth.

"That means they've been watching you. Have you ever felt like you were being followed?"

"I recall one day I did think someone was following me, but figured I was mistaken when I didn't see anything."

Frank took his daughter's hands in his. "Honey, I've thought about this ever since Boyd released me. I've got to get you out of harm's way. We're going to throw them off the trail. If the transfer doesn't go through, my brother will hit the roof." He didn't add the part about Boyd wanting him to doctor wounded men.

Janice began to feel the first stab of fear. Fear of the unknown, fear of what her uncle Boyd might do to them if he didn't get his money. She mentally amended that. Her father's money. His brother didn't deserve it. "What are you planning on doing, Dad?"

"We're going to play a little game of charades. Switch places. You and Betty look enough alike that we can fool them. Especially under the cover of darkness." Frank rose and made his way to the black hands-free phone that sat on the end table. Picking it up with tender fingers, he dialed his daughter Betty. His face lit up, telling Janice that one of the children must have answered.

"Ben, hi. Could you be a good boy and put your mom on the phone?"

Frank smiled into the phone, obviously amused by the young boy's comments. "Betty. Could you come over here right away? Yes, bring the kids with you. We have a little problem that needs your help. Great. See you in the next half hour." He hung up and gave Janice a slight smile. It didn't quite reach his eyes, but it meant he was feeling more positive about the situation.

"They will be here shortly. Now, we need to get a change of clothes for your sister. Can you put your hair up like she does? Do you remember your Aunt Audrey in Windsor? I think the last time you saw her, you were about seven."

"Isn't she the relative who has sixteen cats, collects Smurfs, and has no running water in her house?" Janice wasn't impressed by the thoughts of spending time at her Aunt Audrey's house. The woman was a bit eccentric.

"She's the one. She's not that bad, and she has fixed the house so it has running water. As far as I know, she doesn't have a house full of cats anymore. She'll love you like you were her own, Janice. She will also make sure you are kept safe. She has a rifle and she knows how to use it. Her son also lives nearby."

"Who is she, Annie Oakley or something?" She couldn't picture the old girl handling a rifle. "Does she even remember me?" Janice sounded doubtful about the whole idea.

"I talked to her when you were downstairs finishing the laundry. She said she would love to see you again. She also said you could stay for as long as you like. Audrey lives alone in that old house, so she is probably pretty lonely, Janice." She heard her father's chuckle then he crossed to her side.

"What's so funny? It's about Aunt Audrey, isn't it?"

"Actually, it's interesting you should mention Annie Oakley. When she was younger, she did some acting at the local theatre in Windsor. She actually played the part of Annie Oakley." Frank thought the choice of words his daughter used was quite humorous.

"It figures. I hope she still knows how to use that rifle." Janice heard a car stop out front, so she moved to part the heavy drapes that blocked the view of the street. Her quick glance told her that Betty had just pulled up in front of the house. "Sis is here. She has the kids with her." She watched as her sister and Ben and Amy jumped from the blue Mazda. As she moved to answer the door, a sharp tap echoed through the house.

"Come in, you guys. What a lovely evening." Janice took a glance past her sister's shoulder, admiring the warmth of the late June night.

"What's the emergency that has us here at this hour of the night?" Betty moved into the living room, guiding her tired children to the couch. She gave Janice a quick appraisal, noting the hairdo that resembled her own. "Are we changing places because Janice needs to be protected?" Betty's assessment was dead-on. Her father gave a solemn nod.

As he filled Betty in on the events of the past day, he heard her soft gasp when he mentioned that Janice was in danger. "I always thought Uncle Boyd was bad news. I suppose he's involved in the drug trade. That's what he wants the money for, isn't it? What's the plan to protect Janice, Dad?"

"Yes, it is. So you two can change outfits, since you both are about the same build. Betty, you can take Janice's car and go to the mall. We'll wait until the car leaves to follow you. Janice, we need to let your work know that you had an emergency and had to go stay with a family member. We'll let them know first thing tomorrow." At this point Frank moved to the window and looked out. "They're still there, waiting for Janice to leave."

The children had been quiet to this point. Ben was playing with his crayons on the plush carpet, while Amy was looking at a fashion magazine. Both of them yawned several times as they tried to stay awake.

"Grandpa, how come we have to pretend we are somebody else? Is Aunt Janice in trouble?" She threw down the book, moving to stand in front of him.

"Amy, honey, your aunt has someone bad threatening her, so we have to hide her. We are going to make believe that your mother is her sister. Can you keep a secret? This is a really important one."

Betty moved to give her daughter a big hug. "I love you so much, Amy. I need you to do everything your grandfather says, so we can protect your aunt."

CHAPTER EIGHT

"I love you too, Mom. It's Uncle Boyd who's threatening Aunt Janice, isn't it?" She looked into her mother's eyes.

"Yes, honey, it is. Your uncle Boyd is a bad man. We must stay away from him. He sells drugs to kids." Betty gave her daughter a reassuring hug. She thought suddenly of the incident when Amy saw the drug addict at school and had an even greater resolve to help her sister. This was very personal.

Speaking of Boyd, he was taking possession of a Cape Island boat at Sheet Harbour. He had borrowed it from a friend who worked with him at the transfer company. Boyd jumped aboard the *Bay Boy* and released the ropes that held her fast to the dock. The evening was warm and the breeze cool, the type of night that would be perfect for a stroll along the seashore. Boyd didn't notice as he was in a hurry to get to Spooner's Island to check on his marijuana plants. The small green-hulled boat sputtered to life. A plume of bluish smoke drifted from the short silver smokestack. As Boyd headed toward the island, he reflected on his good fortune in using the island. He found out that the house was wired into the same circuitry as the lighthouse. Since the town wasn't monitoring the use of the electricity that closely, he could use the premises undetected.

Since marijuana is the drug of choice for most youth because it is cheap, Boyd decided to start his own grow op in the old house. He purchased the male plants and the sodium lights as well as LED lights. Despite the fact that he wanted weed right away, he had to wait until late summer for the annuals to flower. Soil was not a problem for him as he found the remains of an old vegetable garden near the house. The soil was rich, perfect for plant growth. Since early May, his men had been bringing in the equipment, setting it up in the basement of the house. He was anxious to see how the plants were doing.

Finally, Boyd pulled alongside the oak dock that jutted out into the dark green water of the harbor. After cutting the engine, Boyd climbed up on the forecastle, prepared to cast the mooring line to one of the young falcons standing on the dock. "Here she comes, Peter. How is everything on the island?" Boyd threw the line to the teen, who deftly caught it, and fastened the brown rope to the thick spruce post at the far end of the pier. Boyd moved to stand near the side of the boat.

"Fine, boss. The plants are thriving. We lucked out with a constant supply of power as well as water from a local well. You picked out an ideal spot for the grow op." Peter moved toward the boat and prepared to grab the second line.

As he positioned himself, the craft brushed against the rubber bumpers along the dock. The tires made a slight squeaking sound as they made contact with the wooden hull of the *Bay Boy*. She swung out slightly from the pier before the line on her bow stopped her movement. In a matter of minutes, the small boat was secure. Boyd jumped up on the dock, and the two of them made their way to the clapboard house in the distance. The moon illuminated the pillar of the lighthouse then the house suddenly appeared through the thick stand of trees. A brilliant beam of light from the lighthouse bathed the house in a white glare for a second, blinding them both, then the beam swung out toward the ocean. The two men disappeared into the depths of the house.

When Boyd stepped down into the musty basement of the place, his eyes adjusted to the dim light of the room. He smiled at the sight before him. It was the self-satisfied smile of a man who felt he had the world at his feet.

One of his men was watering the plants that grew in rows along the walls. The tables ran the length of the building, with an open area in the center. All the young marijuana plants were doing well. They were not yet at the stage where the male plants had to be removed. The large blue lights gave an eerie cast over everything in the room.

"Everything on schedule?" He approached a young man as he watered the small plants.

"Everything's good, boss. We sure lucked out with the well and the pump. It makes watering these plants a lot easier."

"Very well. Did the crystal meth come in yet?"

"It's upstairs in the pantry, ready to be converted for street use. It's high grade, Boyd. Should get a good price on the street."

"Okay. Let's get this stuff ready for our users."

Back at Frank Peterson's house, final preparations were under way for getting Janice out of town. At exactly eight forty-five, Betty, dressed as her sister, left the house and got into her sister's small sedan. As she backed out of the asphalt drive and then turned toward the Micmac Mall, a black Town Car pulled away from the curb a short distance up the street.

The hunters had just become the hunted.

Frank watched the large luxury Town Car move down the street, keeping a respectable distance from their prey. Betty drove over to the mall parking lot, exited the car, and then made her way to one of the large department stores. Zellers had multiple levels, so it made a perfect place to shake her pursuers. She moved through the bedding section, doubled back toward the food aisle, and then to be certain they were not on her tail, she hid for a few minutes in the pharmacy section. While she was there, she got a good look at them as they passed by the drug aisles. After waiting for a few minutes, she took the escalator to the second floor. After hiding in the women's washroom for a few minutes, she moved out into the mall. After she had lost the two hoods who shadowed her, she doubled back to the car. With a sly smile, Betty headed back to her own house to meet up with the rest of the family.

After Frank was satisfied they were in the clear, he, with Janice and the children, headed out to the small compact parked at the curb. He unlocked the blue-colored Mazda and climbed behind the steering wheel. With squeals of excitement, the kids followed. This was all a big adventure for them. Ben was too young to understand the seriousness of the situation.

"Wow, this is cool. We get to stay up late tonight." Ben was excited about being able to stay up later than usual.

"Aunt Janice?"

"Yes, Amy. What's on your mind, sweetie?"

She smiled, turning toward her aunt. "You really do look like mom. You have to go away for a while, don't you?"

"Just for a week or so. Until I'm safe from Uncle Boyd. He does bad things." Janice sighed, resigned to the fact that she was going to be a prisoner in her eccentric aunt's house.

"Mom told me that drugs make you sick. She said that I should stay away from those type of people. I saw a man with drugs a while ago at recess." She looked at her aunt, and Janice's heart went out to her. It wasn't easy living in the world today, even for an eight-year-old. Janice gave her niece a quick hug.

"Everyone buckled in?" Frank Peterson turned to face the kids in the backseat. He gave a thumbs up when he saw that the two of them had succeeded in fastening the black restraining devices. As he pulled away from the curb, Janice tried to keep them occupied by playing a game of identify the car. Traffic was light, so they quickly made their way to Betty's house in Westphal.

"Is Aunt Audrey okay with us showing up late at her house, Dad? She won't turn the gun on us will she?" Janice was apprehensive about staying with this aunt. She hadn't seen her since she was a little girl. "I need to let Roger know what is going on. He'll be worried." She gazed out the window, her thoughts on a certain handsome police constable.

Frank turned slightly, glancing at her. He knew she missed seeing her sweetheart, so he said softly," You can call him when we get to Betty's place. As he's a police officer, do you think that might put Roger in a compromising position, Janice?"

"He can keep it quiet, Father. He knows if he reports it, my life will be in danger." Janice smiled and realized Roger would do all in his power to protect her. She watched the streets slip by until they turned into a dead-end lane near the Shoppers Drug Mart. The car came to a stop in front of a brick duplex. "We're here. I have the key, so we can wait for Betty inside." Frank looked over into the backseat. Ben was slumped against his sister, fast asleep. Amy was struggling to stay awake as well. She gave a big yawn and smiled sleepily at her grandfather. "Guess a couple of kids need to get to bed." Frank pulled up the cuff of his white shirt, noting the time showing on his silver Rolex. The luminescent hands said 9:00 p.m. It was going to be quite late when they reached Aunt Audrey's place outside Windsor. He hoped he could remember the way there.

Janice opened the back door, released the seatbelts that held the kids prisoner, and then tried to rouse them. Amy turned toward her aunt. "Are we home, Aunt Janice?" She yawned several times as her aunt gently lifted her sleeping brother from the car. The five-year-old hardly noticed he was being carried into the house.

"I'll take him to the bedroom. Amy, honey, can you help me with your brother?" Janice walked carefully down the narrow hallway, turning at the first bedroom on the left.

"I'll get the bed ready for him. Sometimes I help Mom put him to bed." She moved just ahead of her aunt, quickly turning on the Bud Lightyear table light beside the narrow bed. In the soft light, Janice could see that Ben had a thing for *Toy Story* characters. She smiled tenderly at her nephew, taking in pale green walls, a *Toy Story* theme curtain at the window, as well as Woody/Bud Lightyear motifs through the bedding and the stuffed toys in the toy box. There was also a pirate theme evident in the shams on the dressers. He was a typical five-year-old. Janice placed Ben gently in the bed, pulled the blue covers up, and then bent over to plant a soft kiss on the child's forehead.

He didn't even stir.

"Okay, sweetie. You're next." Janice drew her niece against her, and together they moved into her room. The pink-colored bedroom was just across the hall. When she flipped the light switch, her breath caught. The room was the perfect place for a young girl. A white dresser with a mirror stood along the left wall, next to a closet. The bed was pink with flowers throughout and had matching sham and pillow covers. The bed also had a frilly canopy over it. Amy showed her aunt her collection of Barbie dolls. They sat in a glass-fronted case near the window. A computer desk sat on the other side of the window.

"Your bedroom's very pretty, Amy."

"I think so too. Mommy let me pick out the colors." She yawned again then stretched. While she got ready for bed, she heard her grandfather just outside the door.

"Is everyone decent in there?" He tapped lightly on the pine door.

"Yep. I'm ready for a good night kiss, Grandpa." Amy slid under the thin summer bedding. She smiled broadly when the door opened, admitting her Grandfather Peterson.

He got a quick kiss from his granddaughter then she turned on her side. "Your mom should be home any minute now." He had no sooner mentioned it, when they heard Betty's voice in the hall, just outside the door.

"Hello, I'm home. Is everyone settled in for the night?" She opened the pine door and stepped into her daughter's room. "Looks like the kids are asleep."

Betty made her way over to Janice, giving her a tight hug. Both of them gazed down at Amy's sleeping form.

"Amy was asleep before her head hit the pillow, sis. It's been pretty exciting for them." Janice ran her hand over her niece's forehead. The girl barely stirred. "Speaking of exciting, thanks for the little decoy job at the mall. Did you lose the guys that have been watching me?" She brushed a strand of hair behind her ear.

"No problem. They're probably still looking for me." She gave her watch a quick glance. "It's after nine in the evening. We need to get you on the way to Aunt Audrey's place. Dad, do you have the directions with you?"

Frank retrieved a piece of paper from his pocket. "She lives just outside Falmouth. It'll probably take us a little over a half hour to reach her place. Janice, you need to contact your boss then we need to get on the road. Do you have a GPS device in your car?"

"It's in the glove compartment." She moved to give her sister a big hug, suddenly aware of the burning in her eyes. By the time the two of them pulled apart, she had tears in her eyes. "I'm nervous about staying with someone I haven't seen in years."

"It's going to be all right. I'll say a prayer for you." Betty removed her costume, while Janice did the same. In minutes, they were back to normal again. Janice excused herself to phone her employer. She just hoped the woman didn't give her a hard time, or fire her. She was worrying for nothing, because Dr. Anderson said she understood. She had quite a few sick days accumulated, so it wouldn't be a problem.

"I have two weeks sick leave I can use. Let's go before I lose my nerve." Janice headed for the living room where her father was waiting.

He handed her the car keys. "You want to drive, honey?" He gave her a look of concern when he noticed the tears still standing in her violet-colored eyes.

"No. The way my nerves are, I don't think that's a very good idea, Daddy." She passed the remote and the keys back to her father. After a quick embrace and goodbye, the two of them headed out to Janice's small car. It was slightly after nine in the evening. It was a beautiful evening, with a full moon and the sound of birds chirping in the nearby trees.

Once in her car, her father started the engine, pulling out into the street. Traffic was light, so in only minutes, they were on the main highway toward Windsor. Janice placed the GPS on the holder on the top of the dash, adjusting the coordinates for their trip. The map for Route

101 came up on the small screen then the familiar female voice told them which way to go.

"Great device, the GPS. Can't get lost even if you tried." Frank observed with a wry smile at his daughter.

"How long has it been since you saw her, Dad?

"At least ten years. I was talking to her son, who told me she lives in the same house. It's on the outskirts of Falmouth. Apparently, there's a small brook nearby and a wooden bridge. If I remember correctly, she has some farm animals, a barn, and an old stone fireplace. You'll love it." He looked at his daughter, trying to reassure her she would be safe at this aunt's house.

"Dad, what are we going to do about Boyd? She turned to look at him as he adjusted his speed. Her face showed a deep frown.

"As long as he doesn't do anything illegal, we can't do anything. I want you here, so his men don't know where to find you. Once my brother gets his money, he'll back off." Frank tried to sound positive, but Janice heard the hint of uncertainty in his voice. The issue of caring for Boyd's friends also worried him.

They drove in silence for the remainder of the trip. Janice motioned to him about the directions they were to follow once they were off the main highway. Her father slowed down then took a left turn under the overpass. It was darker here because of the lack of street lights. Janice could make out a couple of houses far off the road. Their lights blinked at her through the trees.

As they approached the end of the paved section of road, Frank slowed down to absorb the slight bump where the pavement ended. Janice noticed the change in the sound as the tires made a crunching sound as they proceeded over the gravel. A turn up ahead indicated that they were almost at her Aunt Audrey's place. Sure enough, as they started around the bend in the road, she spied a narrow dirt road off to the left. She could also make out the faint outline of a small wooden bridge.

"We're here, Dad. Her house is way back in the woods." She sounded nervous even though she knew she was being unreasonable. Her father was right; this was her only option for now.

Frank took the narrow heavily rutted road toward the small house in the distance. The lights from the old house seemed to beckon them, urging them forward. As the sedan moved over the wooden bridge, Janice heard the hollow sound of the tires against the wooden planks. There was a slight drop as they exited the bridge then the house seemed to appear from between three large oak trees.

Before they even reached the house, she saw the front door open and a tiny woman appeared on the front porch. She waved to them as Frank pulled up nearby. He shut the engine off then the two of them climbed from the car. Aunt Audrey stepped down off the porch.

"Well, for land sakes, child, look at you. The last time I saw you, you were just a little sprite. You have grown into a real beauty. The image of your mom. I'm sure sorry to hear of her passing, dear." She moved forward to give her niece a big hug. She was surprisingly strong for a tiny woman, and Janice felt the breath knocked out of her.

"Hello, Aunt Audrey. How are you? I hope we're not putting you out any." She managed to answer, once her aunt loosened her grip on her. Her arms were very strong. Maybe she exercised to stay in shape. She couldn't have been any more than five feet tall, she had soft fuzzy white hair, and her face was wrinkled by age. That face was glowing with love for her. When she looked into her aunt's hazel eyes, she saw that love. It drew her in, comforting her.

"No trouble at all, child. Your father told me about your problems with that no good brother of his." At this point, she gave a loud humph. "As far as I can remember, Boyd always was bad news. Well, you'll be safe here. I have ears that can pick out something amiss a mile away." Her aunt gave a slight chuckle, turned to Janice, and then grinned. "My hearing isn't as good as it used to be, though. I have a rifle that will make up for my hearing problems."

"Sorry we had to be so late. Hope we didn't keep you up, Aunt Audrey." Janice offered by way of apology. Maybe this would work out okay after all.

"You're not keeping me up, dear. I never go to bed before midnight. My mind's too active."

As they moved toward the steps, Janice took in details of the old homestead. A pole with a light made a bright circle of white at the end of the driveway. It was too far away to illuminate the house, but it made the bridge stand out in sharp lines. The house itself was painted an off-white. Green shutters edged the windows on the façade, and several trellises rested against the side of the old building. She could see the bushes clinging to the wooden lath. The narrow driveway at the side of the house revealed the dark outline of a clapboard barn. Off to the left of this structure, she could see the henhouse. Even though she couldn't see them, the sounds of hens cackling came to her ears on the clear night air.

Janice decided that she liked her aunt's farm. It would be a lot quieter than her place back in Dartmouth. "Dad, could I borrow your cell phone? I need to get in touch with Roger. He's probably wondering where I am." She was upset with herself that she hadn't called him before this. As she approached her father, he handed her a small black phone. She opened the device, quickly dialed a familiar number, and then waited for her boyfriend to pick up.

The call connected and she heard the answering machine kick in. She heard the sound of sirens then a deep voice." You'll never get away with it, so you might as well give us your name and information. We know where you live. We'll get back to you, if you have enough courage to leave your name and number. This tape will self-destruct in ten seconds. As Janice smiled at the original, if somewhat corny message, she heard the sound of laughter. After leaving her message, she handed the closed phone back to her father with a weary sigh.

"He's not home, Father. Probably off getting groceries at the mall. I'll try him later.

"Come on, you two. Enough jawing out here for everyone to see. We need to get Janice here settled for the night. She looks tired out, Frank." Audrey glanced at her niece with concern as she appeared to wilt beside her father.

As the three of them moved into the house, Roger was starting to get worried about Janice.

He had tried to call Janice at home, with no luck. Frowning, he headed for her sister's place. Betty had opened the door, and with an audible gasp, let him in. She quickly explained the situation that had developed during the evening. Moving to the desk, Betty jotted down the address and a map, so Roger could find Aunt Audrey's place.

"You just missed her by minutes, Roger. So much has happened, there was no time to call anyone. Our aunt agreed to keep her there for a couple of weeks. It's late, but from what I hear, Aunt Audrey keeps late hours. It should take you half an hour to get there, unless you speed. It wouldn't look too good if a member of the police force got a ticket for disobeying the law. However, she could sure use a friend right now." Betty touched his arm, giving him a gentle squeeze. She had a knowing smile on her face.

"Wild horses couldn't keep me away. I have a lot to tell her. And considering what you just told me, I'm worried about her." With squared shoulders, he pulled the doorknob, preparing to drive to Falmouth. His watch said 10:00 p.m.

"Good night, Roger. Give my love to Janice."

"I will. Wish me luck." With that, he closed the door, making his way to the red car waiting at the curb.

He put a rock CD in his CD player, and pulled out into traffic. Once on the highway, the GPS on his dash lit up, giving directions to Falmouth. It took about twenty minutes for him to reach the turn off that Betty had mentioned. Heading under the highway overpass, he moved along the old secondary road, heading toward the aunt's farm. Lights blinked at him from among trees on his right. He slowed his Chevy as he approached the end of the pavement. A slight bump indicated that he had entered the gravel part of the back road. The GPS indicated that he was getting near the turn to Aunt Audrey's farm. "Turn here." There was that monotonous female voice again.

As Roger slowed to make the turn into the narrow lane, he saw the outline of an old farmhouse just ahead of him. The road grew rougher, so he pulled over to the right side of the entrance. Finally, he came to rest a couple of yards from the white clapboard house. Here, he could see the shape of a small car in the driveway near the side of the farm. The place needed a coat of paint. He smiled at the quaintness of the structure, the shutters, the old barn, complete with a henhouse and a corral. A light shone from the side window, so he knew someone was still up. A quick adjustment and he shut the GPS off. He shut the engine off then released the seat belt. Roger climbed out of the car and headed for the porch steps. Despite the fact the A-frame house needed a coat of paint, a porch ran the complete length of it, giving it an inviting appearance. Unaware of the terrain, he stepped on some dry twigs. The snap sounded abnormally loud in the stillness of the night.

Before he reached the bottom of the steps, someone turned the outside light on. A bright white light illuminated the front porch, as well as several feet into the yard. Still in the shadows, he was invisible to the occupants of the place. The squeak of hinges indicated someone had just stepped outside.

A short elderly woman stood at the top of the stairs, looking out into the dark. Roger chose that moment to step into the arc of light.

"Hold it right there, mister. I don't know who you are, or why you're here. If you came to rob the place, you can turn around and go back where you came from." Audrey was angry, her voice revealing her protective attitude. She also had her feet spread apart, a sure sign she meant business.

"My name's Roger Abbott, ma'am. I'm a police officer in Avonvale. I'm here to see Janice Peterson." He hoped he could calm her down. She was a tiny woman, so how intimidating could she be? He mentally adjusted his opinion when he saw the glint of metal in the porch light. Looking down, he saw that she was holding a rifle and the barrel was aimed right at him. As a policeman, he had faced his share of antagonists with weapons. He knew better than to underestimate this pint-sized granny. With a weapon, she held the trump card.

"Never heard of you or this Avonvale place. If you're a cop, how come you don't have a uniform on? And what do you want with Janice? Are you the young man that she called earlier?" She wasn't convinced of his intentions. Considering the late hour, he couldn't blame her. Normal people didn't show up on stranger's doorsteps at such late hours.

"I haven't talked to her tonight. Since I'm off duty, I don't have my uniform on, ma'am. Let me show you my warrant card for proof." As he started to move forward, she brandished the rifle. Was she bluffing or was the thing loaded?

"Hold it. Any closer and I might let Bessie here do the talking for me." She gripped the gun even tighter. "Most people pay attention to her."

Roger detected a slight movement behind the elderly woman, the squeak of hinges meant someone else was moving up behind her.

Then he heard the most beautiful and beloved voice call out, "Roger, what are you doing here? How did you find me?" As she stepped down into the yard, her face broke into a brilliant smile. His heart seemed to stop as he absorbed the sight of her.

"Janice, do you know this man? Is he the friend you called earlier?"

"Yes, Aunt Audrey, he's a very close friend. He's here to make sure I'm safe." She gazed at him, her heart soaring at the sight of him.

She softened her voice as she addressed them both. "Well, why didn't you say so in the first place, girl? Let's go in before the whole country wants to know who he is. You may come in, young man." She gestured for him to follow.

"Could you lower the rifle, ma'am?" He was still a little leery of the gun then relaxed as she let it drop to her side.

"Sorry. I keep it to scare off predators that try and get at my chickens. Usually, it's coyotes or sometimes foxes." She pushed through the screen door then she laid the Winchester against the closet wall. Come in and have a glass of lemonade, Mr. Abbott. And please, you don't need to call me Ma'am. I haven't been called that in years." She gave a hearty laugh.

"Okay. May I call you Aunt Audrey?"

"That would be okay with me. May I introduce you to Frank Peterson. He drove Janice here." She moved aside so they could shake hands.

"We meet again, Roger. Sorry I had to steal her away from you, son. You probably know by now that my brother has made threats against her. Since you're here, I'll take my leave. Audrey, I really have to get back. Early day at the hospital tomorrow. It may be a holiday, but health problems don't take a day off. I have to let the hospital know that my car is still in the parking lot. It will be okay until I get it tomorrow. I'll leave your car in the drive at home." He gave his daughter a hug and a few words of encouragement then he grabbed his jacket. "Call me in the morning, honey."

"I will, Daddy, and thanks. It looks like I might have a good July 1, after all." Janice smiled at Roger, their hearts connecting across the room. No words were needed.

They failed to see the knowing smile on Aunt Audrey's weathered face.

The three of them made their way to the front door to wish Janice's father goodbye. Once on the porch, Roger enjoyed the cool evening breeze, the chirp of crickets in the bushes, and the warm glow from the moon just overhead. As they walked Frank to the car, he heard the flutter of wings off to his right. As he looked up, a large black bird swooped down nearby. The crow landed on the railing of the front porch. Once Frank left for the city, he looked back at the bird.

"What's that crow doing here?" Roger gestured toward the creature that had settled on the white railing. It looked in his direction, giving him a loud caw caw.

Aunt Audrey smiled, revealing that this was not a chance encounter. "That's Charlie, Mr. Abbott. He's a good friend."

Roger didn't know what to say to her after that comment. He had never heard of anyone having a pet crow. Unless they were eccentric.

"I bet you never heard of a crow for a pet. I rescued him a few years ago, after he hurt his wing. He often comes for a treat. Charlie's very tame, son. Often, he takes food right from my hand. And he's very gentle too." At this point, Janice's aunt put out her right arm. A second passed then Charlie spread his wings, moving to sit on her extended arm. With her left hand, she plucked a piece of apple from her pocket. The bird caught sight of the fruit and moved to pluck it from her hand.

"Janice, would you like to feed him? He won't bite you, I promise. Here, use this apple slice." She withdrew a thin apple slice from her pants pocket, passing the fruit to her niece.

Once Janice had the fruit and was holding it out to the bird, Charlie seemed to get the unspoken message. The large black bird jumped from one arm to the other. With her arm held stiff in front of her, Janice watched as the bird eyed the piece of fruit she held. Within seconds, the scrap of apple disappeared. She was very aware of the bird watching her, of sharp claws digging into the material of her blouse.

"Do you think I could pat him, Aunt Audrey?"

"Go ahead, girl. I think he likes you. Hold him up closer to your chest."

Janice moved her arm closer to her body, aware that the bird was watching her very closely. As she reached out to touch the tiny black head, the eyes looked right at her. The first contact surprised her, the black feathers were so soft and smooth. The bird seemed to relax as she continued to caress the small head.

"This is awesome. I think he likes me rubbing his head." She seemed enthralled by the whole experience.

"Amazing. If I hadn't seen it with my own eyes, I would never have believed it could happen." Roger was impressed. This woman had a way with animals which made her pretty special. The fact that he was willing to take to Janice was equally amazing.

"Okay, now. Charlie, you need to go so Janice here can get settled in for the night. It's late." With a couple of loud caws, Charlie disappeared into the night. The three of them made their way back inside.

CHAPTER NINE

They went into the house as darkness embraced the countryside. Crickets chirped, and they could hear the distant yip of coyotes calling to each other.

Once inside, Audrey showed Janice her bedroom, while Roger waited in the small parlor. The room was painted an off-beige color. Dark brown-colored furniture gave the whole area a fresh, earthy appearance. He liked this woman's color sense. A lot of the things in the parlor were remnants of an earlier age: an antique clock on the stone mantle, a spinning wheel in the far corner, as well as silver candlesticks on the end table. The ancient stone fireplace was well made and appeared to have been used. On the stone mantle, he could see an old gold-edged photo as well as a kerosene lantern.

He found some interesting reading on the coffee table that sat in front of the couch. As he thumbed through an old issue of *National Geographic* magazine, he heard footsteps in the hall outside.

"I see you found my *National Geographic* books, Mr. Abbott. Keeps me in touch with the world. You'd be surprised what you can learn. Last month's issue had a good article about the coyote. It's good to know, because they are outside, as you probably have heard." She saw him look up. "Don't look so worried, son. They're more afraid of us than we are of them." She gave Roger a sly wink as Janice came into the room behind her.

"The bedroom's charming, Aunt Audrey." She gave him a quick smile then went to him as he sat on the couch. It's so good to see you. I guess you know all the details now, eh?" Janice felt a calm settle over her, and she knew it had everything to do with the handsome man next to her. She looked at his firm square jaw, the hazel eyes, and the fine sandy-colored hair.

Roger was lost in the depths of those eyes. He almost forgot to breathe, and he couldn't remember what she said if his life depended on it.

"Humph. Hello, you two." Audrey gave them a bright smile and a lilt of laughter. It was very obvious to the older woman that these two were very much in love. "I guess three's company. Since you don't need me, I'll just slip into my room."

They hardly heard her as Roger leaned closer to Janice. She sighed when his lips gently brushed hers. Her lipstick tasted faintly of strawberry, and her hair was as soft as satin.

That first kiss came as a revelation for both of them.

By the time they broke the kiss, they were both aware that their relationship had just changed. They had passed the casual and entered the serious side where hearts became even more involved. After another tender kiss, Roger reluctantly drew away and looked into Janice's deep violet eyes. He almost caught his breath when he saw the love shining there.

With a soft tender whisper, Roger revealed his feelings for her. "Janice, I love you so much! I don't know exactly when it happened, but you slipped past my defenses."

"I love you too. I've been praying for this moment for a while now. It seems like I've known you a lot longer than a few months. Are you still having the dreams?" She leaned against him on the couch, content to be near him and hear his sweet voice.

"Not the nightmares about Anna. Due to help I got from the minister and my faith, I've been able to let her go. I know she is in a better place, as Amy told me not so long ago. That child is very wise for her age. I know now that she would want me to find someone so I can be happy again." He whispered so softly in her ear, she could just barely hear his declaration of his newfound love for her. "I want to see if we have a future together, Janice. I was so worried about you, I had to come see you." When her eyes met his again, they were full of tears. She smiled at him, feeling those tears slide down her cheeks.

When Roger moved his hand up to wipe away the tears with his thumb, she touched his outstretched arm. "Why the tears? Are you okay with this?"

"More than okay. They're just happy tears, Roger. It's going to be great having you all to myself for a whole day."

Outside the room, Aunt Audrey has decided to stay close by, just to be sure Roger had good intentions. She didn't want her niece upset any more than she already was. Audrey heard the tender admissions by the two of them, and despite herself, she felt hot tears fill her eyes. She brushed them away impatiently then whispered, "Bless their hearts." Satisfied with Roger's intent, she made her way to her room at the rear of the house. Then she remembered that Roger would probably need a place to stay for the night.

Roger and Janice made their plans for the next day then kissed again. This was something they could both get used to. As they pulled away, Roger looked down at his watch. "Good heavens, it's after eleven o'clock. I need to get going so you can get some sleep. I'll just find a place in Windsor for the night."

"You might have some trouble. I heard Aunt Audrey mention some sort of celebration in town. She said most of the places would be full by now."

"Then there's no other course. I'll have to go back to Dartmouth and come back tomorrow." He was disappointed, but there didn't seem to be any other answer.

"When do you move into your house in Avonvale?"

"In a couple of weeks. I've been there several times, moving the rest of my stuff, but I still have to connect the phone. Guess I'd better get moving." He rose from the couch, bringing Janice with him. As they hugged each other, Aunt Audrey appeared around the corner.

"I couldn't help hearing that you have to go back into the city. I only have the two bedrooms here. Sorry there's no room, son, but if you don't mind roughing it a bit, you could bunk out in the barn. If you have a mind to, I'll give you some blankets, a pillow and a light. You may have to share with some of the local critters, but they won't hurt you." Audrey gazed at him, waiting for him to accept or reject her suggestion.

Roger considered the offer then asked," What sort of critters are we talking about, Aunt Audrey?"

"Just mice, maybe an owl, or barn swallows. Believe me, hay makes a nice soft bed." She reached for a Coleman lantern that had rested on the end table near the door.

The part about a nice soft bed sounded great. "You've got yourself a deal. See you in the morning, Janice. Sweet dreams."

"Sweet dreams yourself. Don't let the critters keep you awake," she teased.

"I'm thinking of something or someone else who will definitely keep me awake." He winked at her and they gazed intently into each other's eyes. No words were needed.

"I'll show you where the blankets are. There's power in the barn, and the well is just at the back of the house. I had a pump installed recently, so both the house and the barn have running water." She led the way to a small closet in the hallway, withdrawing two blankets and a white pillow. A trip to the bedroom procured two keys, which she gave to Roger. "The larger key is for the double front doors, the smaller silver key will unlock the side door. I would prefer if you would use the side door. That way, I can keep unwanted critters from getting into the barn." She handed him the keys. "Welcome to my farm, Mr. Abbott. Hope you enjoy the place."

With a final kiss for Janice, he followed Audrey outside. The night was cool but not unpleasant. He could hear the faint cackle of hens, mixed with the neighing of a horse. She held the lantern high, illuminating the door and the rusty brass doorknob.

Roger inserted the key and the lock clicked. Pushing the door inward with a loud squeal of hinges, Audrey reached in and flipped the light switch.

As Roger took in the interior of the building, he saw a small blue Honda, of dubious vintage as well as a red tractor. Several farm implements hung on pegs along the far side of the wall, and a ladder lead to the loft overhead. The smell of hay lay heavy in the air of the barn. Both of them moved toward the ladder.

"Sleep well, Mr. Abbott. I'll wake you around 7:00 a.m., if that is okay with you." She handed him the blankets as well as the lantern.

"Thank you, and please, call me Roger."

"Roger it is. If you wish, the door locks from the inside." She quickly withdrew, leaving him alone in a completely foreign environment.

Being a resourceful person, he snagged an old rope by the post, uncoiled it, wrapping it around the blankets. He held the Coleman lantern, slipping the handle over his wrist as he climbed the wooden ladder. After securing the rope close enough that he could reach it, he continued up the rough-hewn ladder to the loft. Lush straw lay in thick piles all around him. By the smell and look of it, the stuff was fresh. Roger smiled slightly. "This just might work."

Setting the lamp on the floor, he reached over the edge of the loft and grabbed the rope. A hefty tug brought the blankets to him. A quick visual inspection told him the best place for his bed would be near the post, about two feet away. The light gave off a soft glow, lighting up the area he was in. The post nearby had several hooks on it, one of them containing a length of rope. Sweeping the hay to one side, he made a small hollow where he could spread the blankets. It took him about a minute to get the blankets ready. The hay was crisp and fresh and had a sweet smell. Dust motes were visible in the light from the lantern.

Wearily, Roger settled down into the soft cushion, aware only of the quietness in the place. Occasionally he heard the scurry of mice then the soft call of barn swallows at the far end of his makeshift bedroom. And despite his reservations about sharing the place with animals, Roger fell into a deep sleep. Tonight, he dreamed of Janice. Anyone watching him, would have seen a mixture of emotions cross his face. A faint shadow hung just out of sight in the background.

Janice too slept well, and, yes, her dreams were about him.

While the two of them slept, forces were at work back in Avonvale that would test Roger Abbott's courage and skill as a member of the police force. When he returned to work in about four days' time, his hours would be spent in the investigation of the local drug smugglers.

Earlier in the evening, as usual, Boyd sent out another shipment of drugs. This time it was heroin and crystal meth. He already had someone waiting in Truro for the stuff. The sale would bring in a lot of money.

The small transfer truck barely got outside the Avonvale town limits when a large black pickup truck pulled alongside, forcing the larger vehicle to the shoulder of the road. As the truck jerked to a stop, a couple of men in black jumped from the half ton and began spraying the Boyd truck with bullets. The driver was killed instantly, while the second man managed to get down from the trucks running board, giving himself some shelter. His protection was short-lived as one of the attackers rounded the side of the disabled truck. Both men began shooting at the same time. Boyd's man was shot and killed, but not before he was able to get a shot off at his enemy.

The one shot found its mark, the black-clothed man was shot low in the left shoulder. As he staggered back to the truck, they could hear the sound of sirens converging on the scene. The driver jumped in the truck and gunned the engine, taking off and leaving his badly wounded friend to fend for himself.

The Avonvale police pulled alongside, taking the wounded man into custody. While they waited for the ambulance, the man was read his rights and questioned about the aborted robbery. The two officers spread sheets over the bodies then they placed orange-numbered markers for the key sites of the shooting. Faced with the possibility of a long stay in prison, the man, whose name was David Hart, decided to cooperate with the law.

Pieces fell into place. A rival drug cartel had been ordered to hit the Boyd truck and procure drugs that were hidden among electronic equipment. When questioned about their knowledge of which truck held the drugs, he revealed they had a hidden spy within the circle of Boyd's men. However, he was firm in his refusal to identify the man. A police dog was brought in to sniff out the hidden contraband. Rex had the hidden drugs located in a matter of minutes. Using a crowbar, along with one of their truncheons, they pried up the wooden lid of the crate.

"Pay dirt. It looks like we finally got a break," Constable Peters said as he reached into the box, uncovering the bags of white powder. "Looks like crystal meth. Seems like we have a date to talk to this Boyd. The origin of the crate says China. It's possible the stuff could have come in from the orient, and Boyd might be unaware of it being there."

While the officers made arrangements to talk to the trucking company owner, the paramedics arrived, taking the wounded man to the hospital. He would be placed in protective custody.

Boyd Peterson answered the door a short time later, and when told of the attack on his truck, appeared genuinely shocked. He assured the police he knew nothing of the hidden drugs in the shipment. As it came from the Asian countries, he reasoned that the stuff had been shipped for the benefit of the rival drug gang. His business was completely legitimate.

Once the cops left, Boyd sprang into action. He had handpicked those whom he felt he could trust to hide the drugs. There were only a half dozen of them involved doing the work after the company closed. It couldn't be too hard to weed out the spy and deal with him. Picking up the cell phone, he called an emergency meeting for eight o'clock that evening at the shop. One way or the other, he would get to the bottom of this.

The guilty party would pay.

The next day was a holiday, July 1.

Around 10:00 a.m., one of Avonvale's police cruisers was patrolling the area near the town's water tower. As they approached, a young man in faded blue jeans, blue shirt, and baseball cap staggered out into the street. The car made a quick stop to avoid hitting the man. Based on his behavior, he appeared to be very intoxicated.

Officer Jacobs, a seasoned cop, walked up to him. As he drew closer, he could hear the fellow babbling something. He seemed to be confused. It was also evident that the man was having balance problems as well as breathing difficulties. It didn't take an expert to tell he was high on drugs. Before they could reach him, the youth staggered wildly to the left then dropped to the ground.

A quick check of his vitals revealed the man was dead.

"Any identification on him, Simms?" Officer Jacobs placed orange pylons around the body then blocked the street with yellow police tape.

As the other officer looked at him, Simms withdrew a black leather wallet. A quick flip through it revealed a large wad of twenty-dollar bills, credit cards, plus driver's license, and ID. The man's name was John Ballantyne, he lived in Avonvale, and he had no kin listed. Most of this information wasn't unusual, but under the heading of occupation, he had listed truck driver for Boyd's Transfer. Simms got an odd look on his face when he saw the information. It was so fleeting, it went unnoticed.

Both officers looked at one another. It certainly was a small world. It looked like another visit to this Boyd Peterson was in order. The first thing they had to do was call in the emergency, mark the area around the victim, and then take pictures of the body. As the EMTs pulled up, Constable Jacobs went to talk to the paramedics. After requesting an autopsy, the ambulance pulled away, heading for the city. The older officer was in the cruiser, booting up the small computer located on the consul of the vehicle. He was looking for a possible listing of John Ballantyne on a local rap sheet. He had a gut instinct that told him Boyd Peterson knew something about this young man's demise.

Unaware of the events unfolding back in his home town, Roger was just beginning to stir from a wonderful sleep. Dawn was sending the first yellow rays of sun into the barn, the thin shafts of light spreading through the cracks and across the loft. He heard the faint screech of something on the edge of his consciousness. It was loud and very annoying.

Roger rubbed the sleep from his eyes then sat up. Now that he was awake, he recognized the sound. There was no mistaking the loud, raucous call of a rooster.

Good heavens, the sound was enough to wake the dead!

His body felt refreshed, even though his ears were still ringing. A quick glance around his makeshift bedroom brought him face-to-face with a hoot owl. The brown bird was sitting on the rafter directly over him, studying him with its beady eyes.

A ringing bell brought him more fully awake as Aunt Audrey showed up in the space below him. "Rise and shine, Mr. Abbott. Roger. I guess you heard my alarm clock already. Always on time, that rooster. I trust you slept well," she called up from the base of the ladder.

"I slept like a log." Flipping his wrist to one side, he glanced at the hands of his wrist watch. It said 7:00 a.m.

"See you in the house. We're having fresh eggs and bacon, with buttermilk pancakes."

He heard her moving out of the barn as he approached the top of the ladder. The thought of that breakfast had his mouth watering. Throwing the blankets down ahead of him, Roger started down the ladder. The sun cast bright yellow rays across the dirt floor, illuminating the interior. For the first time, he noticed the stall to the back of the barn. It was occupied by a large brown horse.

Once at the bottom, he grabbed the blankets, and then made his way to the house. On the way, he saw the chicken coup, the corral, with a single cow, and the stone well nearby. Looked like a typical farm.

With an accompanying squeal of hinges, he entered the modest home. His nose was immediately aware of the enticing aroma of bacon and eggs. The sizzle of the skillet came to him as he made his way into the yellow kitchen.

"You're right on time, son. Everything's ready. You can sit next to Janice. She's a little easier on the eyes than this old bird." She laughed at that, and he was almost certain she was pushing the two of them together. Not that he was going to argue. He was in total agreement with her.

"Thank you. Good morning, Janice." He grinned as the two of them positioned their chairs at the old oak table. The checkered table cloth added a cheery atmosphere to the small room.

"Ahem. Before you dig in to your breakfast, we need to thank the Lord. Roger, would you do the honors, please?"

Roger was a bit apprehensive about praying out loud, but he closed his eyes then offered a short heartfelt prayer.

"Thank you. There's lots, so don't be shy about seconds."

For the next half hour or so, they praised Audrey's cooking. Both of the young people thoroughly enjoyed the meal.

As Aunt Audrey cleared away the dishes, she looked over her shoulder at them. "Don't fret yourselves about the dishes. Now, what have you got planned for the day? I've got a map of the area that might be of help to you. Or you could take a trip to the valley. Grand Pre is a lovely spot to visit." Audrey made her way into the den. A few seconds later, she reappeared with an old dog-eared map in her weathered hand.

"Janice and I would like to see Grand Pre, I think. I remember it was a very peaceful place to visit. Would you like to come too, Audrey?" Roger offered because he felt indebted to her for putting him up, but he secretly hoped she would decline. That way, he would have Janice all to himself. He would get his answer in the next breath.

"You don't need me with you. Even a blind man can see that you are both very much in love, so I think that three would definitely be a crowd. I always hoped that Janice would find someone special. I know that she has. Roger, you are always welcome in my home any time you are in this area," she added with a sly smile. "Next time, I promise not to come after you with a rifle."

He laughed at the scene that had greeted him. "That's okay. I would probably do the same thing. Sorry, I scared you. I was really worried about my sweetheart." It sounded right even though there was a shadow in the hazy background of his mind. He ignored the faint warning. Roger checked his watch, as he took the map. 8:45 a.m.

"Perfect day for a trip to the valley. We should take a picnic lunch." He suggested, thinking of how special that would be with Janice. He was going to make this day as special as possible for her.

"Why don't you both go for a walk while I prepare something for you to take." Audrey shooed them both out then went to work in the kitchen. They were out on the front porch in each other's arms, so didn't hear Aunt Audrey preparing a picnic lunch for two special guests. For the first time in ages, she had a new focus in life. Making these two outside happy. They also didn't hear her whistling as she went about her tasks.

Roger drew Janice to the barn. He wanted to see the horse.

As they entered the side door, light spilled over the threshold. A quick sprint brought them to the stall. The horse, which was a mahogany-colored mare, came up to the rail to meet them. She nudged Janice's extended hand.

"Hello, beautiful. I suppose you want a carrot?" She giggled as the horse licked her fingers with that huge tongue. "Be patient, Lucy." Withdrawing a carrot from her pocket, she offered the treat to the horse. The vegetable disappeared in a mini-second then the horse came sniffing Janice's hand for more treats.

"Don't be greedy now, girl." She laughed.

"How do you know her name? Looks like Lucy likes you, Janice. I'm a city boy, so haven't had much exposure to animals. I could get to like it, though." He had an almost wistful tone to his voice that she didn't fail to catch. He placed his hand on the animal's neck, enjoying the soft hair against his fingers. Lucy made a soft sound then turned, giving him a nudge with her nose.

"Aunt Audrey told me earlier. I think you're a hit. She's a pretty good judge of character." Janice gave the horse a hug then turned to him. "We better get started on our trip. Aunt Audrey will probably be wondering where we are."

Roger's voice held regret when he answered her. "You know, I'm going to miss this place. It's so peaceful here. A person could get in touch with the important things in life with no distractions. Bye, Lucy."

"I knew you'd enjoy it here. Maybe we can come back sometime."

He noticed that she said *we*. His heart seemed to expand at the thought of the two of them together.

Hand in hand, they walked across the barnyard and entered the side door. As they moved into the cheery kitchen, Aunt Audrey met them with a giant wicker basket in hand.

"There's lots of food here. The sandwiches are in a cooler bag inside. Enjoy your day. Drive safely and I'll see you around suppertime."

"Thanks for everything, Auntie. I love you. I'm glad that I get to spend time with you again." Janice felt tears in her eyes as she reached to give her aunt a big hug. She couldn't wait to spend a whole day with Roger.

CHAPTER TEN

"Same here, child. I guess you're not a child any longer, are you?" Audrey sniffed a few times then pulled away from her niece. "Enough tears now. Have fun." She even winked at him as they walked to the car.

Reluctantly, Janice released her aunt and went to join Roger who was putting the basket in the backseat. He straightened, waved to Janice's aunt, and then slid behind the wheel of his Chevy Malibu. Once she was in the car and buckled up, he backed out of the drive. Both of them gave her aunt a wave then he turned the car toward the road. Positioning the GPS on the dash, he adjusted the device for their trip to the valley. He made a face as that droning female voice once more announced their position.

"You don't think much of the voice on the GPS, do you?" Janice had that knowing look on her face when she noticed his scowl.

"It's that obvious, is it? She's boring enough to put someone to sleep." He sighed then reached out to turn down the volume of the device.

The drive to Grande Pre took about a half hour, giving them time to talk about their lives, and they found out that they had many similar interests. Both of them liked skating, both adored children, and both liked to read western novels, especially Zane Grey. They also had a passion for opera. Roger was impressed by her dedication to helping children learn to skate. He was comfortable with this conversation until it started heading toward more personal things, like religion and past loves. Despite his overcoming the guilt about his wife's death, with the accompanying nightmares, he still was very cautious about giving his heart to someone else. He still didn't know Janice that well. Best to go a bit slower. He decided on a diversionary tactic by putting in a CD of a recent young opera singer, Jackie Evancho.

A minute later, the sweet sounds of Jackie Evancho filled the interior of the car. Janice hummed along with one of the familiar tunes, much to Roger's delight. She had a beautiful voice. That voice stirred his weary heart.

The GPS announced that they were approaching the turn that would take them to Grand Pre Provincial Park. They moved along a rough back road, crossing a marshy area with its dykes and fields of tall grass. Off to their left, they caught sight of well-tended lawns, old willow trees, and then the visitor's center. He looked farther to his left, and on a slight rise, sighted the old church of St. Charles.

"It's so peaceful. I love the lawns and hedges. Thank you for suggesting it, Roger." She gave his arm a gentle squeeze as they turned into the gravel parking lot. He pulled into an open space near an antique car with New Brunswick plates. The small parking lot was almost full. After shutting off the engine, he jumped from the car, making his way to where Janice was just opening her door. With a curt bow, he extended his arm, drawing her up against him. He backed up a bit, as those scary feelings began to grow inside his breast. Maybe this wasn't such a good idea after all. Both of them could be hurt if this didn't work out. One major heartache was enough, thank you.

"It's a perfect place for a romantic picnic." She admired the lush lawns and the aura of quietness that seemed to permeate the site. She failed to see the faltering smile on Roger's handsome face. As the two of them paid at the visitors' center, he picked up a map of the area as well as two bottles of water. The weather was warm, with a slight breeze. The two of them made their way along the gravel path then Roger guided her off the path, making way for some tall oak trees near the church. Leaves rustled in the warm breeze, bees buzzed nearby, and he heard the sharp call of a blue jay calling to its mate. After reaching the perfect spot, he bent over, spreading the blanket he had brought on the lush grass. Janice lowered herself to the thick plaid blanket and smiled up at him. As happy as he was, he felt a faint warning stir in the back of his mind. They had both revealed some very personal things about each other, along with some of their ambitions. Janice, he knew, wanted to be a coach and teach children how to figure skate. He, on the other hand, wanted to get in print a book he was writing. He had been a closet writer for almost six years now. They both had similar philosophies. However, they were different in their ability to deal with the loss of a loved one. That difference was to prove a large stumbling block.

"This is a perfect spot, Roger. It's so quiet here." She seemed relaxed, ready to enjoy the day with him. She was unaware of the war he was having with his feelings.

He began to get cold feet. That uneasiness he had felt earlier pushed into his consciousness. As he looked down at her, he took a mental step backward. Suddenly he was face-to-face with his biggest enemy.

Fear.

What was he going to do?

Apparently, he carried some excess baggage after all. His dreams of his deceased wife had stopped, he had moved forward.

Or so he had thought.

What he hadn't come to terms with was the ability to let his heart open to new love. To Roger, it felt like standing at the edge of a cliff with no rope to help him across the chasm. It was a terrifying revelation.

He managed to whisper, "I always feel calmer when I'm here. Let's see what your aunt gave us for lunch." Food was a good way to take the conversation in a more comfortable direction. That made him relax somewhat. Janice looked at him oddly, and he wondered if she sensed his reluctance to open his heart to her. As he pulled back the checkered cloth, a virtual smorgasbord of goodies was exposed. "Aunt Audrey sure knows how to get up a picnic. There's cheese, fresh bread, fruit, and some ham in the cooler." He was impressed.

For the next half hour, they enjoyed the bounty in the picnic hamper. As they ate, he was very aware of the trees rustling, of birds calling to one another, and of the sounds of people talking in the distance. The specter of his growing fear was hovering in the background, ready to pounce on him.

Janice sensed the change in Roger's attitude as she gazed into his hazel eyes. His were shaded, hiding the emotions that she knew simmered just below the surface. His eyes held a hint of sadness in their depths. With a growing sense of dread, she touched his arm. The movement seemed to rouse him out of his stupor, for he looked into her eyes. Sorrow overwhelmed him when he saw the love shining in their violet depths. The intensity of the deep violet in her eyes scared him.

There was no avoiding it.

Both of them were going to be hurt!

"What is it? I can feel you withdrawing into your safe little world." She saw it as she looked intently into his eyes then added, "You're afraid, aren't you, Roger? I thought you loved me, and that your past was over and done with. It's not, is it? It's still there between us. Why are you so afraid of me?" She let out a strangled cry, pushing herself away from him. Pain pierced her like a stab through her heart as realization hit her.

Had she misread his feelings for her?

She pulled away from the blanket and ran for the shelter of the church a short distance away. As she ran, sobs racked her body. When she saw the clusters of visitors near the church, she veered in the direction of some weeping willow trees.

How appropriate! The trees suited her situation perfectly.

Roger stood, almost in shock, at her sudden flight. Quickly, he made his way to her. What would he say? If he loved her as he claimed, he had to climb over this hurdle first. He doubted in her present state she would even listen to him. Tentatively, he approached her. Even from this distance, he could see her body shaking. As he drew closer, he heard Janice sobbing. Those sobs were like a knife to the heart.

She apparently felt his presence behind her, for she turned, exposing him to the anguish that was very evident on her heart-shaped face. Fresh tears made their way down her cheeks. It was useless to try and stop the flow, for they refused to be stopped. She had been so stupid.

It looked like she was going to suffer for her wrong assumption.

"Please leave me alone, Roger! There's nothing you can say at this point that will make things better. I need time to think. Will you take me back to Aunt Audrey's? In our present situation, it would better if you just dropped me off. Aunt Audrey is very protective of me, and I know she will be out for blood when she finds out what happened. Please!"

Roger nodded, and with a heavy heart walked with her back to the picnic basket and blanket. The sight of them seemed to mock him. Leftovers.

Was that all he was going to have in his life?

Leftover memories?

As they made their way back to the car, she would not even look at him. When he made a token gesture of opening the door for her, she ignored him. He really couldn't blame her. Why was he letting his insecurities ruin the best thing to come into his life?

Because he was a fool!

The half hour drive back to her aunt's place was made in silence. It was one of the longest, most agonizing half hours in his life. Even with the radio blasting the latest rock music, it did nothing to lighten the mood. Janice wouldn't look at him, instead her gaze fastened on the passing landscape that whizzed by outside. Her tears had not subsided. They still hung on her long lashes, ready to drop. His eyes felt scratchy, his heart raw.

As they approached the turnoff for Falmouth, he turned and in a hushed voice said, "Please, Janice, don't write us off. I just need some time to—" Before he could finish, she interrupted him.

"I don't want to hear your excuses. I'll give you some time, if that's what you think will help. But I won't wait forever, Roger. I really thought we were growing closer." She dug into the interior of her purse, producing a slip of paper. After grabbing a pencil, she scribbled her number for him. "This is Aunt Audrey's number. I'll be there for the next couple of weeks. I'll tell her not to hang up on you, because after today, she will probably not welcome you with open arms."

"I'll remember that. Well, we're almost there," he sighed wearily as the car turned into the long lane leading to the farmhouse. As he brought the car to a stop, Janice jumped out, making a wild dash for the safety of the house. Almost with a sense of dread, he placed the picnic hamper on the top step of the porch, and then withdrew to the car.

Roger turned the key and the car came to life. Quickly, he gunned the engine, sending gravel spraying from beneath the front tires. Once he was on the road, he headed back to Dartmouth. He had some last-minute things to collect from his uncle's house then he could officially move into his new place in Avonvale. He thought about what Janice's father had told him. If he needed to talk, he would be willing to listen. That sounded like a good idea right about now. He could use a little advice. As he pulled out on the main highway, the past few hours began to replay themselves in his mind, much like watching a bad movie, even though you know it should be turned off. A glance at the clock on the dashboard told him the time was eleven in the morning. Sudden tears stung his eyes, then he felt their wetness on his cheeks.

Because of the tears, he was looking at things through a blurry windshield. He felt something brush the side of his Chevy then he heard the loud blast of a car horn. Automatically he pulled the wheel to the right. When his vision cleared some, he realized he had drifted over the center line.

"This is crazy. I can't drive when I'm like this." He acknowledged out loud.

Shaking, he realized he needed to stop to regain control of his emotions.

Roger gradually slowed the car down, moving into the right lane. Ahead, he saw a good place to stop in safety. Seeing the direction sign, he noted he had gotten only as far as the Windsor turnoff. The sedan finally came to a stop on the gravel triangle formed where the ramp met the main road. It was just big enough to give him a safe place to park. At this rate, it would be supper before he got home. He sat there for quite a while.

While Roger struggled to gain enough control so he could resume driving, Janice was in an emotional vacuum. She had burst through the front door, startling her aunt. Before Audrey could utter a word, her niece had run down the hall, slamming the door to her room. As Audrey approached the pine door, she could hear the muffled sounds of sobbing coming from inside. She realized something had happened with Roger. Something that had hurt Janice deeply. With a firm resolve, she made her way to the door to give him a piece of her mind. She remembered telling Roger that he better not break Janice's heart, and it appeared that he had done just that. She even considered taking the rifle just to prove her point.

However, she was to be cheated of the pep talk she would give him. Once on the porch, she saw his car start, saw the spray of gravel fly from beneath the tires. Several stones clattered as they hit the side of the house. Just before he pulled out, their eyes met. Hers were full of anger; his regret and something she couldn't tell from this distance.

"Hmm, good riddance. He's not good enough for her, and if he comes back, I'll fill his backside full of lead." With that declaration, she stomped back into the house to deal with a very unhappy niece.

It seemed to take a long time, but Janice finally emerged from the safety of her room. Her eyes were puffy and red. She sniffed several times. "Oh, Auntie. I've been such a fool. I really thought I could love Roger enough to help him overcome his fears. He's scared of me. Why? I would never do anything to hurt him."

Audrey tried to quell the anger she felt for Janice's sake. She thought about some of the things her niece had shared about her boyfriend. Now she was forced to change some of her initial feelings she had since the fiasco this morning. "Let's sit for a spell. I know you'd never hurt him. Roger is gun shy. He's been badly hurt by giving his heart then losing. Maybe he's not as strong as you have been. How much do you know about his past, child?"

Janice managed to compose herself enough to talk without crying. "I mentioned he lost his wife four years ago. But he assured me he was past that and that he's let her go. I know he was brought up by an uncle. His parents were killed when he was around six or seven."

Aunt Audrey didn't say anything for a while then took her niece's hand. "That's your answer. He's had a lot of tragedy in his life and was robbed of parents when he was very young. In his mind, if he gets too close to someone, they die and leave him alone. What you need to do is be his friend. Forget the romance part for a while. Just be there for him. If the rest is meant to be, it will happen on its own." She had tears in her eyes, and suddenly Janice broke down, throwing herself into her aunt's arms. For several minutes, both women hugged and gave in to the tears.

"There, there. Feel better now? They say tears are good for the soul. Guess we've had enough between us to last a lifetime, eh?"

"Thanks, Aunt Audrey. I love you. How did you get to be so wise?" She saw the wry smile spread across her aunt's weathered face.

"Trial and error, dear. I'm still dumb about some things, even now. I should have been quicker to spot the fear in your young man's eyes. He sure left here in a hurry. You would have thought the devil himself was after him."

"I hope he's all right. Surely, he'll pull off the road if he feels it's dangerous to drive." Janice couldn't help worrying about Roger, despite the heartbreaking hours she had just endured. She didn't even want to think of him in the ditch somewhere.

"I know everything will be all right. He'll be kept safe, so don't worry about him, Janice."

While hearts were at stake with Janice and Roger, back in Avonvale, two of Roger's colleagues in the police force were knocking on the door of 13 Shore Road. A brown-haired Sara Martin answered.

Surprised to see two officers at her door, she said, "Good morning, officers. May I help you? She moved back slightly so they could step into the entrance.

One of the constables, whose name badge said *Bennett*, addressed her. "We found a young man a couple of hours ago on the road a short distance from here." At her confused expression, he went on to explain further. He died of a drug overdose. His ID said he worked for Boyd's Transfer. Is Boyd Peterson at home, ma'am?"

Apparently Boyd heard them talking, for a minute later, he came up behind Sara. "Can I be of help to you two gentlemen?" He didn't like the cops snooping around.

"Possibly. Do you have a John Ballantyne working at your firm, sir? We found him on the road, where he unfortunately succumbed to a massive drug overdose."

"Let me check the company records." Boyd disappeared for a minute then reappeared and gave them a curt nod "Yes, he was a driver. No kin listed. Do you want me to come down to identify the body?" He glanced at the officer closest to him, saw his affirmation. "He did have some drug issues, we were trying to help him kick the habit. I thought he had made some progress." He wore a serious expression on his face, and Sara gave his arm a gentle squeeze. To anyone watching the exchange, it appeared he was genuinely upset about the latest developments. But Boyd Peterson was a master at masking his true feelings. This trait he had perfected early in life to protect him from a cold-hearted father. Ironically, he was becoming the very person he had tried to escape in his youth.

He gave Sara a quick kiss then left with the police to identify the remains of John Ballantyne. He knew that there would be an autopsy on the body. He supposed he would have to have some sort of funeral for the man, if no kin could be located.

In Dartmouth, Frank Peterson was just getting home from the hospital. He thankfully had an early day. There was only one small encounter with the young intern who had opposed him before. This time though, the man saw his mistake, actually making corrections. He threw his keys on the hall table then hung his suit jacket over the back of the wing chair in the living room.

Since it was past lunch, a quick meal done in the microwave was the best option. The house was so empty without his daughter. She was safe for now, but what would happen if his brother didn't get his money? He did not look forward to the meeting tomorrow at the bank. His call to the police in the HRM did get some results. They were driving by his house at regular intervals, so the dark sedan that had been parked up the street was no longer there. Betty had a pretty good description of the two men as well as a description of their car.

Recalling his discussion with his brother, he came to the conclusion that Boyd had always felt like an outsider. He was filled with sorrow at the path he knew he was going down. It could only lead him to heartache and a long period behind bars. His father had always favored him over Boyd. Why, he didn't know.

Why had his father not split the inheritance between them?

Frank was still thinking about the encounter with his brother when he heard the ping of the microwave. Pulling out a chicken alfredo entrée, he moved to the dining room table. Before he had taken a bite of the dinner, the doorbell's chimes echoed through the house.

"Who could that be at this hour?" Rising, he made his way to the front door. A peek through the side window by the doorway revealed a sandy-haired young man standing on the porch. "Roger, what are you doing here, son?"

As he unlocked the door and pulled it open, Roger stumbled over the door sill. His face was pale, and his eyes were red.

"Roger, what's wrong? You look like you've lost your best friend." Frank looked with compassion into his distraught face, the fear very evident for anyone to read.

"That's not far from the truth, Mr. Peterson. Janice and I are no longer together. She was deeply hurt because of my fear. I'm still caught in the aftermath of my wife's death. Why can't I trust my heart?" He let his countenance fall. Tears burned in his eyes.

Frank offered him a seat." Don't be so hard on yourself. You've had a big loss in your life. Sometimes it takes time to trust your heart to another again."

CHAPTER ELEVEN

"Be her friend. Don't try and force your heart. Life is a gamble no matter who you are. All we can do is hang on and enjoy the ride. Believe me, I've been there. The pain will go away and you will trust yourself to take that leap. Concentrate on being the best friend you can be for Janice. If it's meant to be, it will happen. And if you work things out, you have my blessing if you wish to marry Janice."

"Thank you, sir. She's really hurt, so I don't know if she will let me talk to her, or even let me ask her for forgiveness." Roger slumped in his chair, feelings of remorse assailing him. "All I can do is tell her how I really feel." With a new resolve, he rose from the wing chair.

"Good luck, Roger, I'll be praying for both of you."

When Roger left Janice's father's place, he was still at loose ends. After driving around for a couple of hours, he decided to visit his uncle's place one last time. It was now late afternoon, so he hoped he wasn't going to give his uncle George the impression he showed up for the food. If he did get to spend supper, that would be cool.

Traffic was starting to get heavy as he turned on to his uncle's street. He had just turned into the driveway when the front door opened. His uncle waved as he stopped near the hedge. Jumping from the car, he made his way to where his uncle waited on the steps.

"What brings you to this neck of the woods, son? How are things going with the renovations at your new house? Do I get a tour?" George was quick to pick up the strained expression on his nephew's face. It was also very obvious that Roger had suffered trauma of some sort. "What's wrong?"

"Janice and I had a major argument, Uncle." Roger went on to explain the past several hours with her in Grand Pre. His emotions were very raw and close to the surface.

"I'm real sorry to hear that. Give her some time, son. She'll come around. I'll be praying for you. Now, it's nice to see you again. Now that you're here, would you like to stay for supper?"

"That would be nice. I'd like to check out the rest of the loft then I have to head for home. Tomorrow I'm back to work, and I'm nervous about messing up. The chief has been watching me lately to see if I drop the ball. Ever since the fiasco four years ago, I feel like I always need to prove myself." He looked at his uncle for some support. He knew his uncle would do what he could to boost his feelings about himself. He sat at the small round table and enjoyed supper with his uncle. The advice he got from the older man was invaluable too.

"I remember that was a very rough time for you. Your mind was not settled on your work because you were mourning the loss of your wife. It was probably not the best idea for you to be working back then. I know you blame yourself for messing up the drug investigation, but if I recall, there were some other factors at play as well. It wasn't all your fault, so don't beat yourself up about it. I still think you're a good cop, have good instincts, so I know you'll prove that to the force in Avonvale."

"I appreciate your confidence in me. According to one of my colleagues, it's the biggest case we've had in the past two years. I can't prove it, but I have a gut feeling Janice's uncle Boyd is up to his bushy eyebrows in the drug business."

"Never ignore your gut feeling about something. Those promptings are often correct." Uncle George rose to give him a quick hug. "You'll do all right, son. Just don't give up."

"Thanks, Uncle. I'll check the loft once more before I head off. You've given me a lot to think about." He gave the older man quick handclasp then moved to the door. Tomorrow was going to be a big day.

As Roger backed out of his uncle's driveway, he waved at him as he stood on the porch. Quickly, he pulled out into traffic, heading for the Eastern Shore and home. The drive took a little over an hour and was made without incident, although he still felt the nagging feeling in the back of his brain about his day at work.

The loss of Janice's love also bit into his heart, much like broken glass into one's finger.

Within an hour, he was at the entrance to Avonvale. The blue sign with the gold letters proclaiming the name of the town appeared on his right near a red hydrangea bush. Roger drove along Shore Road, passed Boyd's Transfer then swung inland to Rose Street. Number 3 was his new home. After pulling into the gravel drive, he stopped the car near the new shed he had built for his yard tools.

His house was a simple two-bedroom bungalow with a porch along the length of the front. Painted a pale yellow with dark green shutters at the front windows, it had a cheery summery feel to it. Withdrawing the keys, he unlocked the side door and moved into the kitchen area. This room was painted a pale green, with white trim. The new cabinets were installed now but still needed to be painted then fitted with hardware. The appliances were sitting in the dining area for now, and dust covered everything. He moved into the hall, heading for the first bedroom on the left. It was a typical man's room, dark blue in color with pale wood trim along the edges. With a queen-sized bed, dressers, and a table, it looked pretty spartan, but it was his and he was proud of it. Once he had placed his keys on the top of the dresser, he made his way back to the kitchen to prepare a drink.

Back in Falmouth, Janice was lying on her bed. She had a heart-to-heart talk with her aunt and found her advice was just what she needed. Still, her heart was tender, and tears were not far from the surface. She heard a knock on her door and slowly went to answer it.

"How are you feeling, hon? How would you like a little visit to the barn to check on Lucy?" Audrey looked intently at her, waiting for her answer. She hoped to get her niece out of the house for some fresh air and interaction with the farm animals. If she could forget herself for a few minutes, maybe she could get a new perspective. Animals were good therapy.

"Yes, that sounds like a good idea. Animals are always good listeners."

"And they don't talk back, or break their promises." At this point Audrey raised her eyebrows as she glanced at her niece.

Roger was assigned twelve-hour shifts, with four days off after working for four days. He started at 6:00 a.m. The alarm blared its warning at 5:00 a.m. Wearily, he turned the clock off and scrambled out of bed. Once up, he made his way to the bathroom for a quick shower. That should be good to bring him awake.

Thankfully, the stove and fridge were connected, so he could prepare a meal. Ignoring the dust on the counters, he made a quick breakfast consisting of bacon and eggs then he grabbed his keys and locked up. Once in the car, he turned the radio to some old rock music then pulled out into the street. The trip to the police station was made in about ten minutes. He parked the car in his spot and made his way into the station. In the officer's changing room, he, along with several other men, changed into his dark blue uniform. Once dressed, he strapped on his belt. Adding the truncheon as well as his holster and revolver, he reached for the radio that clipped to his shirt.

Roger nodded to his colleagues and made his way into the large room where a cluster of officers of various ranks were gathered.

Once everyone was present and seated, Sergeant MacDonald stood to address his men. Behind him, seated on the small raised area, was the chief of police and his assistant.

"Good morning, men. While I pass out your assignments, I have an update on the drug ring in New Brunswick. The RCMP is investigating on their end. The man shot the other day during the hold up of Boyd's Transfer truck mentioned who he works for. The bad news is that he passed away this morning, so will not be able to help locate the drug ring in town. Your assignments are being passed out by Lieutenant Jacobs."

Roger accepted the printed list from his superior, glancing down at the list. Just as he suspected. He was put on the beat with Officer Wylde, an older man. They were to continue questioning those involved as well as checking with the HRM Port Authority about drugs being smuggled in on container ships.

It was a busy day, frustrating at times, with the end result that they were able to get the authorities in HRM to step up their checks of containers coming in. The sheer volume of containers made it hard to check every one of them. Something could slip through.

Roger was tired by the end of his shift and anxious to change into city clothes again. As he slipped into his jeans, he heard his name called.

"Abbott, you have a minute?" Staff Sergeant MacDonald approached him, an envelope in his hand.

"Yes, what do you need, sir?" He tried not to let the nervousness show.

"This is a record of the drugs stolen from the pharmacies. We think the same people are involved in the robberies as in the concealed drugs in the transport trucks. If I remember, you were involved several years ago in the city in a drug bust. Apparently, at that time, you missed some important clues and the guilty parties got away. You have another chance to make things right. Don't mess this up. These men need to be put behind bars before more innocent youth become victims. You up to it, Abbott?" His supervisor looked at him with the stern expression that he so often wore when he was worried about the performance of his officers.

"I won't let you down, sir. We're going to watch Boyd Peterson and his business." He sounded confident, but he wasn't because as yet, he had nothing concrete on Boyd. Suspicions wouldn't hold up in a court of law.

"Very well. Here's the file on the robberies from the drugstores. Go over it with Officer Wylde." The commanding officer passed the brown manila folder to him. "See you tomorrow at six." With that final comment, the sergeant turned on his heel and made his way back to the main part of the precinct.

Roger knew the man meant well, but his bedside manner needed work. He was well respected and ran a tight ship. It should be an interesting week. And it sounded like his performance would determine his future here.

During Roger's first day back to work, Frank Peterson and his brother met at the local bank where Frank had his rather sizable bank account. At 10:00 a.m., they met with the loans officer in a corner office. Frank noted the muted colors on the walls, designed to relax clients. It didn't seem to be having much effect on Boyd. He looked ill at ease, wishing the whole ordeal was over.

"This way, gentlemen. I believe, Frank, you wish to transfer a sizable sum of money to your brother's account. Let's check the accounts." The gray-suited man who sat opposite them appeared to be around thirty or so and was most efficient. Within the half hour, they had made the transfer and had the proper papers signed.

"I'm glad that's over. Now I can get on with my business, and you can rest assured my men will leave you and your daughter alone. A deal's a deal, Frank." Secretly he still planned on having his men watch Janice, just in case he needed a little insurance. His brother could still go to the cops. This would give him the leverage he needed.

Nothing else was said as both brothers made their way to their own vehicles then pulled out into traffic. Frank set out for work, while Boyd went toward Avonvale and his trucking company.

Later the next day, Roger headed out. The night was warm, a cool breeze was blowing in off the ocean. As he pulled out onto the main road, he glanced at the trucking company on his left. Trucks pulled in and out of the gravel lot. Before he knew it, he was at the entrance to his street. Once home, he pulled the car around back next to the stone well in his yard.

Once the door was unlocked, he moved into the kitchen. He threw the keys down on the counter and grabbed a frozen dinner out of the freezer. While he waited for the microwave to ping, he turned on the flat-screen TV in the small living room. Since nothing interesting seemed to be on, he flipped the set to off. Later, he would phone Janice. He hoped they could come to some sort of compromise. While he ate his meal, he grabbed the phone and dialed the number for Janice's aunt. In the next heartbeat he would know if he had another chance with her.

"Hello." Janice's aunt picked up.

"Hello, Aunt Audrey. Please don't hang up. May I speak to Janice, please?" He held his breath.

"I wondered when you would call, Roger. When I first heard about your little disagreement, I wanted to strangle you for hurting her. I was wrong to think that way. Life is full of pain. It's a part of living. She has been moping around here for the past couple of weeks. I know she loves you, and I know you love her. I hope you won't think I'm being too forward, but I'd like to help if I can. The two of you need to take some time to really get to know one another. When I was dating my husband, we went together for a couple of years before we decided to tie the knot. There's no hurry, son. You have to be sure because this decision will have an impact on both of your lives. I know you're scared. Janice is too. It's normal where hearts are involved. Trust the feelings in your heart." There was a moment's hesitation before she continued, "Enough of my rambling on. You can ignore me, or maybe something I said can help with you two. I'll get Janice for you." She pulled away from the phone and he could hear her calling Janice.

A couple of seconds ticked by, but they seemed more like minutes as he waited to speak to Janice.

"Roger, is that really you? I thought maybe you didn't want to talk to me after the scene at the park a couple of weeks ago." She sniffed, obviously her emotions were very close to the surface. "I'm sorry I jumped all over you about whether you really loved me, as well as accusing you of still being in love with the ghost of your wife. I guess I panicked. Will you forgive me?"

"It's okay. Actually, I was going to ask you if you would forgive me for leading you on then backing away. The truth is, I was terrified." Roger sensed the irony of the situation that both of them were asking for the same thing.

"Boy. I guess both of us are in the wrong. I'm willing, if you are. Aunt Audrey and I had a very revealing talk, and I think I want to try again. That's if you do. And, if you must know, Roger, I'm scared too." She hoped he felt as she did. It sounded like he'd also reconsidered their relationship.

Roger laughed then. He couldn't help it. "Funny you should mention your aunt giving you a pep talk. My uncle George and your father both helped me see things a little clearer. Your aunt just gave me some wise counsel too."

"Are things clearer now? Can you trust your heart enough to give it to someone else? I want us to have a chance to explore our relationship to see if we have a future." He could hear the passion in those words. That gave him the courage to take the next step.

"I want that too. How would you feel if we went out on a date when I have a day off?"

"That would be fine. When do you get another day off? I know you've been involved in the drug smuggling case."

"I work four days on, two off. How does Saturday at 2:00 p.m. sound? I could come out to pick you up then I'll take you to an afternoon movie."

"I'd like that. See you Saturday, Roger. I'm looking forward to it. I've really missed you."

"Same here. Give my love to your aunt." Reluctantly, Roger listened to her disconnect. For a couple of minutes, he hung on to the phone. When he realized he was listening to the buzz of the dial tone, he hung up.

He decided to take a quick run to the local grocery store for some special food for the weekend. With a new spirit of contentment after his call, he headed for Meyerhoff's Department Store. The brick structure sported a tan-colored awning as well as an assortment of garden tools off to one side. There was even a couple of ride-on lawnmowers near the front entrance.

As he entered through the aluminum doors, he met several of his new neighbors. Several nodded to him as he moved into the produce section. Grabbing a handful of the fresh produce, he moved to the other aisles. It took about a half hour to complete his shopping then he pushed the stainless steel cart toward the checkout. With just a couple of yards to go to join the line, Roger heard some teenage boys talking near the magazine racks. He picked up conversation about the usual things boys were involved in. A quick glance revealed three boys, about sixteen, discussing the latest video games, girls, and the basic dislike of having to do homework. Nothing interesting. That was until he picked up their remarks about someone being on Spooner's Island. From what he was able to understand, two men seemed to be using the island for something.

The grocery order was momentarily forgotten as he approached the young men. A few people glared at him as they maneuvered their carts around his. Pulling it off to one side, he cleared his throat. "Excuse me. I couldn't help overhearing you talking about someone on Spooner's Island." Reaching into his pocket, he produced his police ID card.

One of the three, who seemed to be the leader, spoke up, "We haven't done anything. officer. We're just hanging out." He lifted his head slightly, challenging Roger. Was that a look of guilt on his face? It was so fleeting, he wasn't sure it was real or not. He knew a lot of teens were nervous around law officers.

Roger noted that all three of them were wearing T-shirts with the emblems of well-known baseball teams across the front. One of the boys had his hair dyed a bright red. Like a lot of the youth he had seen, these boys had pierced ears. They also had on those baggy low-hung jeans with the huge pockets on the back. He marveled that gravity didn't cause the denim pants to drop to the floor. As it was, the top of their underwear was visible above the waistband.

Trying not to smile at the sight that produced, he mentioned his concerns. "Sorry, I was eavesdropping on you, but I overheard you mention that you had seen someone on Spooner's Island. The place is off limits, so whoever is using it may be breaking the law. Would you be able to describe the men you saw?" He hoped the boys were observant because he could sure use a break right now in the drug ring case.

The leader of the three described two men, around forty years old, who had taken a boat to the island earlier in the day. The image of one of the men matched Boyd Peterson's profile perfectly. Roger felt his pulse kick up a notch at the possibility they might have some leverage against the guy. "Thank you. You have been most helpful. I would really appreciate it if you didn't mention this to anyone because it could compromise an investigation. Are you cool with that?"

"Sure, that's cool with us. We're glad we didn't get arrested for something," one of the other boys added, with obvious relief evident in his tanned face.

Roger gave the boys a final nod and made his way to the checkout. He had wondered when someone would see Boyd Peterson. The fact that he went on the island in the daytime surprised him. It appeared the man was starting to get overconfident. What was he going to do with this new piece of information?

Something told him to take a quick run down to the gut by Boyd's Transfer company. Slipping behind the wheel of his car, he turned the car toward the coast.

A couple of minute later found him parked next to Boyd's business. As he made his way down the gut to the small beach, he could hear the sound of surf in the distance. He was almost at the bottom when he heard voices.

Men's voices.

Hiding among some brush along the edge of the beach, he peered at two men standing near a small aluminum boat. He didn't recognize the older man, but there was no doubt that the other was Boyd Peterson. They were transferring briefcases. Roger wondered just what was in those briefcases. Seeing the transaction was almost complete, he backed away and headed for his car. Just one more suspicious encounter with Janice's uncle. There seemed to be a lot of them lately. He filed this new information for later.

Tomorrow was Saturday, the day of his date with Janice. His future relationship with her was at stake, so he prayed he wouldn't do or say anything to blow it. It was just a movie and a dinner out, so it shouldn't be too complicated.

The rest of the day dragged for him. Even a favorite CD couldn't hold his interest. Finally he decided to call it a day. Thoughts of tomorrow's date hovered in his mind. He slept fitfully that night.

When morning came, he heard the alarm buzz in his ear. A quick check on the weather revealed a beautiful sunny day. Sunlight's rays cast their yellow glow across the hardwood floor. Shaking off the last of his sluggishness, he made his way to the bathroom for a quick shower.

Refreshed now, he went to prepare breakfast. In his plans for the day, he was going to take Janice on a tour of the town. Then maybe they would go see *Pirates of the Caribbean* at the local theatre.

He wanted to take Janice to see one of the local museums. It held many interesting old artifacts from the early days of the community. Spooner's Island played a very important part in the life of the town, so he was going to suggest a visit. Maybe that would settle his thoughts about the place. This visit was going to be a little different, it would be done after dark. Hopefully, she would be agreeable to the little adventure. He didn't stop to analyze his motives for checking out the island too closely.

It had something to do with the hope he could get evidence on Boyd Peterson and everything to do with his need to prove himself.

CHAPTER TWELVE

After lunch, Roger headed for Falmouth and his date with Janice. To say he was nervous was an understatement. As he made his way into highway 101, he turned his CD on. His favorite music filled the interior of the car, and in about two hours, he was turning off at the Falmouth off ramp. In another minute, he would be at her Aunt Audrey's farm. His palms were sweaty, and he could feel his heart palpitating. He wasn't this nervous when he took his entrance exam at the police academy.

As he pulled into the driveway, the screen door flew open, revealing Janice in blue jeans and blue flowered blouse. He was so struck by her beauty that he almost drove his car into the side of the house. He applied the brakes just in time to avoid a collision.

Boy, that was close.

The last thing he wanted was to damage her aunt's house. It showed just how distracted he got whenever Janice was around.

As he exited the car, Janice ran to meet him. Catching her by the waist, he lifted her off the ground then spun her around. Both of them ended up laughing. "Roger, put me down. You're crazy, you know." Her mouth split in a huge grin. Obviously, she was enjoying herself as much as he was.

"Sorry. Actually, I'm not sorry at all. I'm so glad to see you I just can't contain myself. I feel like a school boy on his first date, I'm that nervous. Ready for a little adventure?"

"What kind of adventure are we talking about?" She looked at him, daring him to reveal some of the secrets he was keeping from her. "It's not dangerous or illegal, is it? Is it something I'll like?"

Roger gave her one of his mischievous grins that hinted at secrets for later in the afternoon. Giving Aunt Audrey a time when they'd be back and a wave goodbye, he helped Janice into the car. Being a gentleman was good for impressing a girl, and the basic laws of courtesy always gained one some points.

Once seated, he turned to her, "Did you tell your aunt we'd be gone most of the evening? Does she trust me with you for that long, Janice?" This was a big day for both of them, a day that would tell if they could move forward in their relationship. It felt a little like walking a tightrope, always worrying about falling. The scary thing about this wire he was on, and Janice as well, was the lack of a safety net underneath them.

"Aunt Audrey trusts you, Roger. She knows you would not do anything to endanger my life, and she knows that you love me. And I know deep down, you love me too. What is this big secret? The suspense is driving me crazy." She turned toward him, her eyebrows raised in question.

"Okay, first, we're going to take a little tour of my hometown then a museum." He hesitated when he saw her eyebrows go up, questions in her deep violet eyes. "After that, I plan to spoil you at the fanciest restaurant in Sheet Harbour. Later, well, you'll just have to be patient." With that rather cryptic remark, Roger concentrated on driving. He decided to scratch the movie. With the highway busy with commuters, he needed to keep his eyes on the road. That proved to be a very difficult task.

While Roger and Janice were driving toward Avonvale, Boyd Peterson was getting ready to ship more drugs out of town. With the spy out of the way and the wounded man in the hospital gone, he had free rein to do whatever he wanted. It was a heady feeling for him. He had an impromptu meeting with some of his coworkers to plan the next step. He laughed at the term workers. The marijuana plants were thriving and would be ready for harvesting soon. There was a big demand in Avonvale for this drug. It was cheap and easy to get. He had his money from his brother, but he still might contact him again for medical help. After a severe rebuke for losing Janice at the mall, he had reassigned the two men somewhere else. It was a thorn in his side to have two women outsmart his men who were supposed to be undercover.

He learned a valuable lesson. Never underestimate the resourcefulness of women when faced with an obstacle.

Boyd was enjoying a little downtime with Sara at home. He knew she loved him, and in his misguided way, he supposed he loved her as well. While she prepared lunch, he went into the den to check on his files. Seated at the old oak desk, he turned the black laptop computer on. It beeped once then the blue screen appeared, followed by the desktop picture of a tropical beach scene. As he glanced at the photo, he imagined Sara and him on a beach something like that. With the money coming in from the drugs, he could be in Florida by Christmas. It never occurred to him that the money was procured at the expense of people's lives.

"Sara, tonight I need to go to the island. Do you want to come, or do you want to stay here? I don't know what you do with yourself all alone in this house, but if that's what you want, I'm good." Boyd looked at her, trying to gauge her feelings. He had no doubt she loved him and would be loyal to his cause, but he would have felt better if she would offer to help more. Still, her offering to help boosted his inventory with some much-needed drugs.

He brought up the inventory for their drugs and the cash value on the street. Also listed was the total of the assets they already had in the safe in the corner of the room. So far, the total balance was in excess of seventy-five thousand dollars. Added to that was the money from his brother Frank. With the other gang being investigated by the RCMP, he had a clear path to do as he wished. Boyd felt like shouting from the rooftops.

He planned on getting his hands on more of his share of his brother's fortune. It belonged to him, and he was not going to be cheated out of it. As for his drug smuggling operation, with the lack of officers and the slowness of the local police, he would have no worries about being found out.

He spent the rest of the afternoon at his trucking company, watching over the affairs of his other business.

A short distance away, Roger was preparing to enter the town limits. They passed the "Welcome to Avonvale" sign then turned down Main Street toward the museum. They stopped in front of a gray clapboard building proclaiming Sheet Harbour Heritage Museum on the large sign above the green door. Janice wasn't overly impressed with the musty reminders of past decades. Some of the old quilts interested her, as well as a beautiful old spinning wheel that sat in a far corner. About an hour later, they headed down Marine Drive toward the restaurant in West Sheet Harbour.

"Well, here we are. You'll love the food, Janice. It's all homemade." He pushed open the oak door, entering a well-decorated room with wine-colored drapes, matching table cloths as well as pale pink walls. Each table was set with a candle in the center as well as fine silver.

As he approached the desk, a maitre'd addressed him, "Mr. Abbott. Welcome to Holmans. Your table is ready sir. Follow me."

The dark-suited older man moved gracefully between the tables that were situated at various spots across the room. He finally stopped at a round table for two at the far corner near the window that overlooked the harbor.

"Here we are, sir. Here's your menu. Take your time. I'll get you water." He quickly backed away and turned toward the back area of the establishment.

"This place looks expensive, Roger. Although I really like the ambiance. The soft music is a nice touch too." She looked at him with an aura of serenity evident on her face. He knew he had made the right choice coming here.

"Don't worry about the expense. You deserve the best, so I'm not concerned with the cost." A wink had her blushing.

The waiter came and took their orders and left an appetizer. When he came back to deliver their food, Roger thanked the young man. For the next three quarters of an hour, they enjoyed some of the best food they had eaten in years. Afterward, he left the waiter a generous tip.

The rest of the afternoon was spent exploring West Sheet Harbour, the town of Avonvale, as well as visiting his new house. They found that they both enjoyed the outdoors, both of them liked to do things spontaneously as well. It was shaping up to be a very enlightening day for both of them.

It was 2:30 p.m., time to drop Janice off at her father's house. They would meet again at dusk, when he would propose their trip to Spooner's Island.

"It's been a wonderful day, Roger. What else do you have up your sleeve? Is this the secret you were hinting at earlier?" She gazed at him, curious to know what he might be thinking.

Roger looked intently into her eyes, hoping she would go for the last little adventure. This one could test their courage if they saw any of Boyd's men.

"I'll pick you up at dusk for the rest of our adventure. I promise this will not be dangerous, Janice. You'll just have to be patient a little longer." In his mind, however, was the hope that they wouldn't have any confrontations with Boyd's men.

After giving her a soft kiss, they drove to her father's place in Dartmouth. Reluctantly, he took his leave. Deciding against going back to Avonvale, he decided to visit some friends in the city. The time seemed to drag, but he finally stopped at a local A&W for a quick bite to eat. Then he made his way to visit Janice.

She answered the door on the first ring, rendering him speechless with her beauty.

"Come in, Roger. Have a seat while I finish my supper. Now can you tell me what this big secret is all about, or are you going to drive me crazy while I wait?"

"If you'll agree, I'd like to go exploring Spooner's Island after dark. The place has always intrigued me." He held his breath, wondering if he had gone too far. Her eyes widened as she finally answered. The minute seemed to stretch on forever.

"Do you really want to go on the island? I always heard the place was haunted. What do you expect to find, Roger?"

"If you're okay with it, I want to check into the possibility that your uncle Boyd is using the island as a cover for drug smuggling." He went on to explain about the conversation he had overheard at the grocery store.

"Do you think you can rely on the honesty of some teenage boys?" she sounded skeptical of the idea, but if he could convince her, she would go along on the trip with him.

"My instincts tell me they are telling the truth. I think we need to check it out. Since you and your uncle have a history, if you want to back out, I'll understand." Roger took her hands in his and waited for her response. This would tell him if she trusted him.

Janice thought for a moment then squeezed his hand, "Count me in. If we can get anything on that buzzard of an uncle, I support you all the way." The passion in those words surprised him. Her lips were set in a thin line, and there was a fire in her eyes that told him she was dead serious. It was a side of her he had never seen before.

They visited for the next hour or so then when her father came home, he told Mr. Peterson they were going into the city for the evening. Just a little lie, to protect Janice, and to avoid the possibility of opposition from her father.

At 8:30 p.m., they said goodbye to her father, heading for Avonvale.

Roger pulled out into the road and drove to his house so they could change clothes. He appeared a few minutes later dressed in black jeans, black shirt, and a black vest with pockets. He handed her a black shirt to wear over her light blouse.

"We'll need to be as invisible as possible, hence the dark clothes. Can you put your hair under a black cap?"

"This sounds like stuff out of a spy movie. You've been reading too many police novels. I trust you though, so let's go for it."

After getting some last-minute gear, they were off to the dock at the side of West Side Sheet Harbour Road about a mile away. There was a small parking lot next to the dock, so he found a space next to a battered Chevy pickup. After helping her from the car, he went around to the trunk. Flipping the lid up, he grabbed a couple of rolls of gray duct tape, two LED flashlights, and his belt and revolver. "All set. Let's see about renting a boat."

Janice felt her pulse increase at just the thought of being on the island with Roger. She wasn't worried about being in danger, not with him beside her. The two of them approached an older fisherman who was mending some nets. As she watched, Roger shook hands with the man, and then made his request. She could tell by the body language and smiles that he had made a satisfactory arrangement. When he returned, he was excited and waved a set of keys in front of her face. "We have the use of that silver boat next to the Cape Islander. I also asked the captain of the *Lady Louise* if he could give us some cover over and back. We'll need about an hour, so he's going to cover the sound of our boat so we can get on the island undetected."

"I'm impressed. You're good at this cloak-and-dagger stuff, you know. Where did you learn all this?" She was intrigued by the detail of their trip.

"From watching all those police shows, of course. *CSI, Flashpoint, Unforgettable, Charlie's Angels*, those types of shows. You can learn a lot from watching TV." His smirk gave him away. She swatted at his arm when she realized he was having some fun with her.

"I don't believe you. Those shows aren't real anyway. What's the duct tape for?" Janice moved closer to examine some of the equipment he had assembled for their trip to the island that sat just offshore.

"You never know when the stuff will come in handy. I like to be prepared for anything unexpected." He stuffed some of the gear in the pockets of his vest then the two of them approached a long silver speedboat. After moving down a sloping ramp to the smaller wharf, he helped Janice into the back part of the twenty-five-foot craft. He was pleased that the aluminum boat had a divider about midway where he noticed a small wooden steering wheel as well as a windshield. Jumping into the front part of the boat, Roger located the storage locker near the gunwales in the bow. The keys he had would unlock this box so he could obtain the safety life jackets they both needed to wear. The bright orange seemed to stand out in the darkness around them. Good for finding someone who fell overboard, but not the best thing to be wearing if you wanted to sneak on an island undetected. As soon as they were near the island, they would ditch them.

"Ready? I hope you don't get seasick. It looks like a bit of a swell out there tonight." He was reassured by her smile.

"It will take more than a little swell to make me sick, Roger. When I was younger, my sister and I would quite often go out on trips with father in his sailboat. So I have my sea legs, if that's what you're worried about."

"Good. It's just a little after ten fifteen, so we better get going."

Roger took his position in the stern by the large Evinrude motor. A quick pull on the black plastic handle of the rip cord started the engine. It roared to life, with an accompanying puff of blue exhaust smoke. The slight acrid smell of gas wafted over them as the smoke drifted by. Once they had her started, Janice cast off the line and they steered the craft out into the channel. Off to their left, they heard the louder, steadier sound of the larger fishing vessel that would escort them as far as the island.

It didn't take long for them to feel the movement of water beneath them, causing the light boat to pitch. Water sprayed over the bow occasionally, the coolness wetting their faces. It took about ten minutes to reach the long dock that jutted out on the lee side of Spooner's Island. He killed the motor, allowing them to drift toward the pylons of the wharf. In the distance, both of them heard the splash of the waves as they crashed on the rocks of the shoreline. Every thirty seconds, a bright flash of light passed over the area, indicating that the light from the lighthouse was at work. The light was something they would have to avoid, if possible.

"Duck. We're going to coast in underneath the wharf and hide the boat out of sight." Nodding to her, both of them leaned forward as the small boat slipped out of sight under the decking. A slight jolt told Roger the bow had just touched the shore, so he stepped out into the shallow water, pulling the boat up out of the water. With Janice helping on the other side, it took them only a minute to secure her. The coolness of the water soaked through his jeans, making him shiver slightly. He watched as Janice made quick work of tying the rope around one of the pylons. She seemed to be as excited as he was, and he could tell she was very efficient with handling that rope. That pleased him. The area around them was pitch black, and the smell of seaweed and salt air very evident. Both of them crawled out from under the dock, taking stock of their surroundings. As they knelt side by side, Roger saw a narrow walkway ahead of them. It was gravel, and it cut through the thick stand of trees that covered part of the island. He withdrew the small LED flashlight and aimed it low to the ground in front of them. The beam revealed a thin patch of grass along the edge of the path. This was where they would walk, so the sound of their footfalls would be muffled.

"Ready, Janice? Keep low and walk along the grass at the edge of the path. When we get to the clearing, we'll have to stop and plan our next move. I'm concerned about getting caught in the beam from the lighthouse. We'll have to move around the edge of the clearing so we won't be as visible." He moved alongside her, the two of them creeping along the grass edging. It was slow going, and a couple of times, Janice almost stumbled on some roots that stuck out of the ground.

"You okay? The ground is a little rough here. Let me shine the light on the ground for you." As he swung the small light beam to the earth, he saw several roots stretched across their path. He took her hand and helped her over the roughest spots.

"I'm fine. Thank goodness I wore hiking boots. It looks like we're almost at the clearing, Roger. What's the plan?" She gazed intently at him, waiting for directions. She wasn't afraid, but all her senses were on full alert.

"We have to time the light beam. Here it comes." Taking his watch out, he looked at the luminescent hands. When the beam swung around again, he checked the minute hand: *thirty seconds*. No time to run across this clearing. From here, it looks like it's a little over a hundred feet across. Hopefully it won't be too much of a problem. We'll have to go along the edge of the clearing." He was just preparing for their dash around the edge of the lawn, when he heard Janice gasp.

Turning, he saw her hand over her mouth, and she pointed to her feet. When he directed the flashlight downward, he saw a small garter snake slither off into the dark.

"It's nothing but a garter snake, Janice. Are you okay? It won't hurt you. You probably scared it. We'll need to be really quiet from this point on." Roger saw the startled look on her face. Her tentative smile told him that she would be fine.

"Sorry. I don't do snakes very well. I could feel it against my foot. They terrify me. I know it's silly."

She apologized for being such a wimp.

"It's okay, really. Everyone has a phobia about something. I guess it keeps us from getting too comfortable. With me, it's heights." He took her hands in his, offering her his support.

Off to their left, they heard the sound of someone approaching. Both of them flattened themselves against the ground, making their bodies harder to see in the dark. This was where the dark clothes would prove critical. The grass was cool, the breeze blew warm against their faces as they waited for the person to come nearer. The young man was dressed in dark gray clothes and wore a black baseball cap, and to Roger's dismay, carried an automatic rifle.

This would be their first real obstacle to overcome.

They had to put the guard out of commission before proceeding.

"How do you want to handle the guard, Roger?" she whispered in his ear so they wouldn't be heard. To her, it seemed like a very large obstacle.

He was pleased at her calm attitude, despite the seriousness of their situation. He turned to her, his voice just barely above a whisper. "How's your throwing arm?" When she nodded in the affirmative, he continued, "Find a small round rock, take a good swing, and then throw it somewhere in front of him. When he looks away from us, I'm going to sneak up behind him and knock him out."

Janice found a small round rock just right for their purposes. "How's this?" She held it up for his inspection.

"Perfect. This will do for something to knock the fellow out."

When he held up a branch, her eyes widened. It was quite straight, about three feet long, so it would make a perfect weapon. She was impressed by his resourcefulness.

"That should give him a nasty headache, Roger."

"That's the general idea." He gave her a thumbs up.

On their prearranged signal, Janice drew her arm back, letting the rock fly. She had a pretty good arm, for the thing bounced off some rocks near the lawn, just in front of their antagonist. As suspected, he turned in the direction of the noise. Roger waited for the light to pass over the area then as soon as darkness fell again, he sprang into action.

As Janice watched from her hiding place, she saw him move quickly up behind the man. Just as he raised the branch, the guard started to turn. Roger swung the wood with all the strength he could muster and caught the man in the side of the head.

Crack!

Just at that moment, the light swung by him. The sound of the branch seemed to echo through the night air, and there was no doubt in her mind that the branch had hurt. She saw the young man slump to the grass, unconscious. As planned, Roger dragged his inert body back to where they were hiding. The lighthouse's beam chose that moment to swing around again, catching him in its brilliant glare. Luckily, no one was around to see them. He also managed to snag the rifle, but he really hoped it didn't come to gun play. He didn't want to take the chance that Janice might get hurt.

"Next step, we tie the guy up." He pulled a roll of gray duct tape from the front pocket of his vest. "Janice, hold his feet together while I tie the tape around his ankles." When she grabbed the man by the feet, he smiled in approval. "Good job. You're awesome."

With Janice holding his feet, Roger quickly wrapped duct tape around the fellow's ankles, effectively tying him up. Next, he moved to their victim's arms. After straightening out his arms, he said in a low voice, "Okay, so far so good. Hold his hands so I can tie his wrists together."

As she held his hands, she looked up into his face, noting the determined line of her sweetheart's lips, the frown on his face. He pulled more tape from the roll, twisting it around the cuffs of the dark work shirt. She had never seen him so focused about something.

"He's not going anywhere. What's next?" She released the arms, glad to be free of the job. The warm breeze continued to blow around the trees, making the leaves rustle. The only other sound audible was the roar of the surf as it crashed against the far cliff behind the lighthouse.

Roger quickly put a length of tape across the guy's mouth as well as two pieces of tissue over his eyes. Seeing Janice's eyebrows raise in question, he pulled more tape out and tore off a strip. The noise seemed loud enough to alert someone, but nobody came. This piece was used to cover the man's eyes, making him sightless. As a final precaution, he grabbed a piece of stick about two feet in length, fastening it to the bound feet and wrists. Satisfied with the result, he whispered in her ear, "Ready? This is where we need to be as quick as possible. I just checked my watch. We have a half hour before our cover swings back by the island. You've been great. Up to plan B?"

"Yes. Why the branch between his feet and arms? He looks like a bound heifer."

"Just a precaution. If he comes to, and I suspect he will, he won't be able to reach up and pull the tape off his mouth. The eye covering means we won't need to worry about anybody identifying us. As long as he's quiet, we won't need to be concerned about him alerting the others. Surprise is the best weapon we have, Janice. Believe me, if Boyd is up to something illegal, he's going to get the biggest surprise of his life."

"I'm amazed at your cunning. If we can get anything on my uncle, it will be worth it." She gave his arm a gentle squeeze, making him very aware of her as a woman. The woman he was in love with, and suddenly wanted to be free to give his heart to. He suddenly realized that he wanted more than anything to be free of his fear and silently prayed that he could move forward. This cloak-and-dagger stuff, as she called it, was proving that they could work well together as a team.

Speaking of moving forward, they watched as the light turned, lighting up the area for a couple of seconds. Within the next second, the beam moved off toward the ocean. It was time to move into plan B. Grabbing Janice's hand, they ran along the edge of the opening, keeping a low profile as they approached the house. At this point, the woods grew near the house, making the approach easier.

They had barely reached the shelter of some trees when the light flashed by them. Perfect timing. A quick sprint brought them to the edge of the buildings.

As Janice caught her breath, he took stock of their surroundings. The house was old, with a stone, concrete foundation and sat about twenty-five feet from the nearby cliff. From here, the sound of the surf at the base of the cliff was very evident. The air around them was also damp and smelled of the sea. He noticed a small shed at the back of the property that probably held the fog horn equipment. A dilapidated white picket fence ran the length of the cliff, offering only a token barrier against the danger on the other side. The massive tower of the lighthouse was to his right, about thirty feet from their hiding place. Behind it, he could see the dark outline of the gully that lead to the small beach. From this angle, they would be under the beam when it came around again.

"How are you holding up? I really appreciate your support. We have to see if we can take a look inside. Without a search warrant, we can't step inside the house, but if we see something from the outside, it can be used as evidence." Roger motioned with his hand toward the back of the house. For a few precious moments, they gazed into each other's eyes then the special bond was broken as he looked away. Once they were at the corner of the old place, Roger peered around the foundation.

The wind was definitely blowing harder on the side closest to the Atlantic. His eyes could pick out a large cargo vessel several miles off shore, moving down the coast. A fishing trawler made its way into the channel, with an accompanying putt putt sound from the small engine.

Looking down, he noticed that this part of the foundation had two windows, one at each end of the building. A bright orange glow lit up the windows, so he knew someone would be in the basement of the house. Perhaps this would be the most dangerous part of their excursion, getting information, and then getting out of here as quickly as possible.

Any delays would mean they would not have the cover of the Cape Islander that they needed.

Motioning to Janice to follow, he inched along the wall, pressing himself close to the cold damp stone. It may have been July, but out here, it felt colder. The rough stone scraped against his fingers and moisture dampened his hands. Although his jeans had pretty well dried, they were still a bit damp from his dip in the water when they landed. He knew Janice had damp jeans as well. It would get a bit uncomfortable, but if they got something on Boyd, it would be worth all the little inconveniences. They would know in the next minute if the trip was a waste of time or not.

"I'm going to check out the basement. You stay here and watch for any other activity. I just hope no one comes out of the lighthouse." He moved to the small casement window and peered in. His breath caught.

CHAPTER THIRTEEN

He wasn't sure what he expected to see, but it wasn't this. Below him was a long brightly lit room. Blue lights were strung along the length of it, while overhead lighting cast a white glare over everything. He knew exactly what he was looking at.

Marijuana plants. Lots of them. The containers ran the whole length of the room, on each side. By the looks of them, they were almost ready to harvest.

Withdrawing his iPhone from the pocket of his vest, he rested the camera/ phone on the casement. Taking careful aim, he snapped several photos. The flash concerned him, but the room was empty. Moving farther along, he snapped pictures of the equipment as well as more plants. Crawling on his hands and knees, he came to the first window again. This time when he looked in, he saw two men enter the room through a side door. The first man he didn't recognize, but there was no doubt about the identity of the second man.

It was Boyd Peterson.

He threw a piece of stick toward Janice, drawing her attention. "Boyd's here," he whispered, the excitement evident in his voice.

"No kidding. That's good news," she mouthed.

Somehow, he had to get a picture of Boyd, placing him here with the drugs. The flash could alert the men, so he would need a cover. Just then the light flashed over him on its way out to sea. That was the answer. He'd let the light beam cover the flash from his camera.

This time when the lighthouse's beam came around, he snapped the final photo of Boyd Peterson. He was turned slightly away, so the flash would have gone unnoticed. A quick check of the photo showed him very clearly.

Mission accomplished. It was time to leave.

His luminescent watch hands showed they had about fifteen minutes to make it back to their boat. Joining Janice, he indicated that they should move out. As both of them slid along the stone wall, the beam swung by.

At the corner, they stopped, checking for possible dangers. The large clearing was deserted. Once the light had made its swing past them, they moved quickly, silently across the opening toward the safety of the trees. From there, they moved along the grass edging the path and passed the still-unconscious guard toward the dock. He had to grab Janice when she almost lost her balance among some wet rocks.

"Careful. The rocks are quite slippery here. Okay?"

She nodded, giving him a faint smile and gratefully accepted his outstretched hand. Once they were under the pier once again, they donned lifejackets, waiting for the fishing boat to appear. While Roger jumped into the craft, she untied the rope holding them to the pylon then joined him. Off to their left, he heard the welcome putt putt sound as the larger vessel came around the shoreline. As he pulled the cord and the engine came to life, the *Lady Louise* pulled abreast of them. Leaning over the gunwale of the aluminum craft, they pulled out from their darkened hiding place, making for the channel. In another ten minutes, they would be back at the pier, the whole ordeal behind them.

Both of them had worked well together tonight. Roger was so proud of Janice, she had come through in a big way.

As a precaution and to avoid being seen from the island, he turned the wheel to the left, putting them behind the other boat. With the wind behind them, they made better time and didn't have spray flying over the bow this time. The little problem they did have would be the rough spot left by the wake of the fishing boat.

"Hold on, Janice! The wake might be a bit rough." He grabbed the wooden steering wheel tighter as they crossed through the wake.

As he suspected, the swell caused by the other craft caused the light aluminum boat to pitch violently for a few minutes. Both of them felt the coolness of seawater against their faces as spray splashed against the windscreen in front of them. It gave them some protection. It took all his strength to hold the craft on course, but he managed it. It was hard to make conversation with the noise from the motors as well as the wind swirling around them. Finally, they were free of the drag from the other vessel and made for the wharves about ten yards away. The docks, with their bright lights, were certainly a welcome sight to them. He wanted to get away from here as quickly as possible, for he knew as soon as Boyd found out somebody had breached his security, he would be out for blood.

Guiding his craft up to the lower dock, Roger cut the engine. He glanced up at the larger concrete platform nearby. A ship was docked there, loading lumber for some distant port. The bright spotlights momentarily blinded him. Silence dropped upon them. They docked then they jumped dockside to secure their rental to the pier. Taking off their orange lifejackets, they stored them in the locker at the bow of the boat.

"I'll go pay the men then I'll get you back to your aunt's place." He glanced at his watch, "Just past 11:30 p.m. Hope your aunt isn't worried about you. I'll be right back." With that, Roger walked across the wharf toward two men who were standing by the Cape Islander that had shadowed them back. A quick handshake followed, then he passed some money into their hands. Turning, he made his way back to where Janice was standing.

"Let's get out of here. Believe me, once your uncle finds out he's had unwanted visitors, he'll hit the roof. I get the impression from what I know about him, he will be very dangerous, if crossed. The last thing I want is for him to find out that you've been with me." He gave her a hug then opened the car door for her. Once she was settled, he made his way to his side of the vehicle. To help dry their damp clothes, he turned the heater on for a few minutes.

It took them about ten minutes to get out on the main highway then they made their way toward Falmouth. Turning the radio down, he turned slightly toward her, "I know it's going to be hard not to tell your aunt and father about your little adventure, but you have to promise not to tell anyone yet. Okay?" His face was solemn, his eyes changed to that deep brown that meant he was concerned about something. Right now, it was important not to let the "cat out of the bag," as his grandfather used to say.

Janice looked tired, her head resting against the black headrest. "I won't say a word. It's such a departure from what we normally do, they probably won't believe us anyway. It was something that I'll remember for a while, Roger. I think you were wonderful. If you don't mind me asking, why was it so important for you to get something on my uncle?"

She looked at him intently, noting the firm Roman nose, the square jaw, and the deep concentration as he drove toward Windsor.

Without breaking eye contact with the road, he answered in a quiet voice, "I have always felt like I needed to prove myself, that I was of worth. I guess that started after my parents were killed. It came to a head the year my wife died. I was involved in a drug investigation involving your uncle, and because I was distracted, he got away. This is personal."

"This time, Boyd Peterson will not get away!"

Janice heard the determination in his voice as well as his fear that he would fail at this investigation. She had no doubt that he would succeed, he was focused and as tenacious as a bulldog. With great emotion, she said, "I am confident in your abilities, in your dedication to your job. I know you'll be successful. I don't judge people by their past, and from what I know about you, you're passionate and caring. I enjoyed my day with you, even the excursion to Spooner's Island. Before today, I wouldn't have thought about the place. And just for the record, I never believed the island was haunted." She hesitated then added, with concern, "This might be good news for the community and for the police, but I know it's going to be really hard on my dad. No matter what he says about my uncle Boyd, I know he loves his brother. It's weighed on him that he chose to work outside the law, Roger." Her countenance grew pensive as she thought of the implications for all of them when this became public. He thought he detected the sheen of unshed tears in her eyes.

And there was no doubt it would get messy, especially when the media got wind of it.

In a deliberate attempt to lighten the mood, she added, with hope in her voice, "Are you planning on attending church with us tomorrow? This is one time when a little prayer would sure help. And I know someone else who would like to see you at church tomorrow."

"I'm sorry about what this will mean to you and your family. I wish I could spare you all the heartache. I'll do all in my power to keep the media away from you, but it could get rough. These trials can stretch for months sometimes. But no matter what, Janice, I'll be there for you. I'd like to go to church with you. And yes, I think I know who else wants to see me." Here, he smiled at the thought of her niece, Amy. The girl had a big crush on him. "Shall I drive up to get you, or is your father getting you?"

He slowed as the off ramp to Falmouth appeared just to their right.

"Dad's getting me, and guess what?" Janice didn't give him a chance to answer before she continued, "As of Sunday, I'm no longer at Aunt Audrey's place. The danger is over, so I'm back home. I'll meet you at church. The service starts at 9:00 a.m."

"That's great. Well, it looks like we're here. Hope you can unwind enough to get some sleep. With all the excitement, it will be a while before I get to sleep, I know that." Roger pulled up in front of the farmhouse, all the windows seemed to be ablaze with lights. Aunt Audrey stood on the porch, waiting for her niece.

Bending over to give her a kiss, he reluctantly let her exit the car. For now, a quick kiss would have to be enough. With a final wave to her and her aunt, he pulled out onto the road, and then headed back to Avonvale. It would be after 3:00 a.m. by the time he got back.

It had been a long but very rewarding day. He would go slow with Janice and not rush things this time.

Back on Spooner's Island, Boyd had heard that one of his men was missing. It came to light when Jason Cox, his second in command, had made a check on the guard outside. Finding the young man missing, he had gone looking for him, finding his bound body in the ditch.

By now he was conscious and struggling in vain to get the tape off his mouth. Jason pulled him up, ripping at the duct tape. "What happened, Peter?" Jason didn't relish telling his boss, he knew Boyd had a violent temper. "How long have you been like this?"

"Ouch, that hurt. I've been here for at least an hour, maybe longer. All I remember, someone, or something made a noise in the trees. When I went to investigate, I got whacked on the side of the head. It felt like I was hit with a sledge hammer. My head feels like it's about to split open." The man rubbed a rather large lump on the right side of his head. "I was supposed to be watching the island. Boyd's going to have my hide for this." Knowing Boyd's temper, he was nervous about what would happen to him when the mishap came to light.

For the next ten minutes, they worked at removing the stick, and tape from his body. Peter stood, still a bit shaky from his ordeal. He managed to take a few steps before his legs gave out.

"Easy. I'll help you to the house. I think you need to lay down for a while, maybe we need to let a doctor look at that bump." Jason moved his colleague's hair to one side, revealing a very nasty bulge. It was a dull purple color, and a couple of places were red. "You're going to have one monster headache for a few days, mate."

The two men made their way back to the house where several others were searching the grounds. Boyd was looking off toward the ocean but turned when he heard them approach. His expression changed to one of annoyance when he noticed the guard limping.

"What happened to him?" Boyd swung toward Jason, who was still supporting his friend.

"He was in the ditch by the dock. Someone tied him up with duct tape and left him unconscious. I haven't had a chance to check out the dock for evidence of any visitors." Jason waited for the explosion that he knew would come.

"You're supposed to be watching the island, Peter. If someone has been on the island, you better pray they didn't see anything. I will not tolerate failure. Jason, take him inside where I don't have to look at him. Tomorrow, he goes back to the mainland. Both of you, get out of my sight!"

Once they were out of sight, he aimed the flashlight on the ground, looking for any sign of their intruders. At the edge of the house, in the scrub grass, the beam of the flashlight revealed some of the blades here was pressed down. Following along the side of the house, he could see the area where someone had pressed close to the building. Boyd wondered if they had looked in the basement windows. When he rounded the corner, he had his answer. It was obvious someone had been here. Now, the question was did they see anything in the basement, or were the main lights off? He began to feel an uncomfortable flutter in the pit of his stomach.

And as he thought about the implications of discovery, Boyd felt something else.

For the first time, he felt fear. Fear that this whole thing would blow up in his face.

It was Sunday morning. Roger rolled over and hit the off button, silencing the loud buzz of the alarm. Boy, the thing was loud enough to wake the dead. The red numbers said the time was 6:45 am. He had about a half hour to get ready. After a shower, he felt more awake and ready for the day. By the time he finished his breakfast, it was time to leave. Taking one final look in the floor-length mirror, he nodded in satisfaction at his reflection. Dressed in a dark gray suit with white shirt and red tie, he was ready for church and seeing Janice again. The fact that she was going to be there probably had a lot to do with the extra time he had spent on looking his best. Suits were not his favorite way to dress, but it was for a good cause.

Roger locked up, making his way to the car in the driveway. Quickly, he backed out into the street then headed for Dartmouth. He made good time and pulled into the church parking lot at exactly 8:50 a.m. It was a beautiful day, warm, with the sounds of birds calling to each other from the nearby trees.

Near the main doors of the old edifice, he spotted Janice, her father, Betty, and her children.

"Hi, Roger. Nice to see you. I can probably guess who you came to see."

Betty gave him one of those knowing looks that said she was well aware of the growing relationship between her sister and him. The smile told him that she approved. As he joined them, Amy tugged his sleeve.

"I had a birthday yesterday, Mr. Abbott. I'm nine. We had a big cake with pink frosting." She was as animated as ever, and he felt himself responding to her. "Is it okay if I sit next to you in church?"

"If your mom says it's okay, then sure, I'd love to have you sit with me." He couldn't help but notice the way her eyes lit up. From what Janice had told him, she missed her father desperately and apparently wanted him to be her friend while her dad was in Afghanistan. He didn't mind, actually he was flattered that she liked him. Kids seemed to be as foreign to him as someone from Mars. Being an only child, he had no experience with siblings.

At this point, her mother leaned down and said, "You can sit next to Mr. Abbott if you promise not to talk during church, honey." She gave her daughter a hug, then they made their way into the interior of the building.

"I'm cool with that, Mom. I can show him my new watch. Oh, there's Becky Summers. Can I go talk to her, please?" Amy waved to her friend then raced off toward the front of the entrance. A minute later, they heard the giggles of two very excited children sharing the week's news.

Betty gave her daughter a tilt of her head then spoke to Janice and Roger, "That child has more energy than three adults. She's still coming down from all the sugar she had for her birthday, sis. She was so excited when she heard you telling me that Roger would be here. Ben is just now coming out of his shell, and he wants to see him too." She gave her sister a quick knowing look then added, "I think I can guess someone else is happy to see Roger here, right?"

"I'm sure glad to see him. That adventure the other night brought us closer together." Her sigh was loud enough to catch the attention of some of the parishioners closest to them. Janice felt her skin heat, and she was sure she was blushing.

"It sounds like you had quite a day yesterday. How are things between you two? I know it was pretty rough there for a while. He's a nice guy, so I'll be praying that things will work out okay." She took a quick glance toward her daughter then they headed for the inside of the church. The massive oak doors were open, revealing the long interior.

Roger moved up beside Janice, whispering in her ear, "You look wonderful in that blue dress. No regrets about last night?" His direct gaze told her that he was remembering their trip to the island.

"None. I enjoyed having a whole day with you. Both of us are back to work tomorrow, so we'll have to see when we can get together again. Right now, I think we need to get inside before the service starts. Don't let Amy talk your ear off, okay?"

Janice felt that now familiar flutter in her stomach, something that always happened when he was around. She now knew in her heart that he was the man she wanted to spend the rest of her life with. The big obstacle now was to convince Roger that it was okay to open his heart again.

After moving into the main area of the Gothic cathedral, they made their way to some pews about halfway up toward the raised area where the choir sat. Roger admired the dark oak rows of pews, the ornate brass fittings on the pulpit, and especially the rows of stained glass windows that cast a kaleidoscope of colors into the room. Since he was paying more attention to the décor than the people around him, it wasn't surprising that he ran into Betty's back.

"Sorry. I was so caught up in admiring the décor that I didn't realize you were so close." He grinned rather sheepishly as he followed them into the pew about four from the front.

"No problem. Is it the décor of the church that has you enthralled, or is it my sister?" She looked over at her sister. Her smile said that she was very aware of the dynamics of her sister's relationship, and she was happy.

"I guess I can't slip much passed you, can I? I'm still trying to overcome this fear about being hurt. This is one place where I hope to get the inspiration I need."

Betty called to her daughter, who was still talking to her friend. When she did join them, she slid in next to Roger. There was Amy, Roger, Betty, Ben, Janice, and her father. Looking up at him, she gave a thumbs up and whispered, "You look really handsome, Mr. Abbott. I think you look really cool in a gray suit. I like the red tie. Mr. Abbott, do you think I look good in pink?" Here, she fluffed the lace overlay of her pink dress. Her white shoes and white ribbon in her hair gave her the appearance of a princess.

"You look very nice, Amy. I think the service is going to start, so we'll need to be really quiet so we can hear the minister. What do you think?" He looked over her head, catching her mother's eye. A slight nod indicated that she was okay with his counsel. At this point, Amy moved closer to his side.

The organ began to play, filling the room with the strains of a well-known hymn. Once the song was over, the white-frocked minister made his way to the raised pulpit that was situated to their right. As he stepped up, the light from the closest window seemed to illuminate him. Roger noted that he appeared to be in his thirties, had dark brown hair, and dark glasses that seemed to balance on the end of his nose.

"Good morning, everyone. Thank you for coming today. I pray that you will leave here today happier than you were when you came in. Let us pray."

A short heartfelt prayer followed that touched Roger. As the preacher began his sermon, Amy leaned over, whispering in his ear. "You really like my Aunt Janice, don't you, Mr. Abbott?" She was looking intently at him, completely ignoring the words of the preacher.

"Yes, I do like your Aunt Janice, a lot. We've been dating for a while now."

"Do you love my aunt, Mr. Abbott? I can see that you like to look into her eyes a lot. Are you guys going to get married? That would be awesome."

Amy had raised her voice to the extent that the woman in front of them turned around and looked at them. Roger felt his face heat then Amy's mother leaned over and spoke to her, "Shh. You have to be really quiet, honey. Sorry, Mrs. Anderson," she offered an apology to the elderly woman in the pew ahead of them.

"That's okay, Betty. Having had children, I know how inquisitive they can be. No harm done, dear."

The woman eyed Amy, giving her a slight smile. She indicated that she was not upset, that she understood. Then she pinned Roger with a shrewd gaze. Raising her gray eyebrows slightly, she turned back to her worship.

Amy was watching Roger, noticed the shadow cross his face, and then whispered, "You look afraid, Mr. Abbott. Why are you afraid? I know we don't need to be afraid if we have friends around. I'm your friend."

"I would like that very much. How did you get to be so wise? You sure you're not really older than nine, Amy?" He was impressed by the child's insight. The preacher was forgotten for the time being as he talked softly to her.

Off to his right, he caught some movement, and saw Ben slip from the pew, making his way to where he sat. The five-year-old wedged himself between Roger and Amy. Looking down, he saw the boy attempt to climb on his lap. Unprepared for this show of affection, Roger felt his cheeks grow red. He regained his composure quickly and placed his right arm around Ben. A glance up toward Janice, and he saw her staring at him, her eyes bright with unshed tears. It was a tender moment that was broken when Betty spoke, "Ben, you can sit next to Mr. Abbott, but don't crawl on his lap, okay? You guys need to be quiet so everyone can hear the preacher." At this point she gave Roger and Amy a pointed stare that said she meant business.

Roger grinned rather sheepishly, and tried to concentrate on the rest of the sermon. Amy's words kept going through his mind. The sermon didn't interest him until the minister started talking about love. Most of it he forgot, but the sentence about perfect love casting out all fear struck a chord. With sudden comprehension, Roger realized that his love could cast out all fear if he let his heart free of the shackles that held it bound. He also knew that if he gave in to this fear, he would lose Janice.

That thought caused almost physical pain.

Leaning over to whisper to Amy, he cautioned, "Guess we better behave ourselves, Amy." Just to soften the words, he hugged her. Not to be outdone, Ben gave his arm a squeeze too.

The service was almost over, the final hymn started, and he gave Janice a knowing look. No words were spoken, but a lot was said in that glance. They thought that no one else was aware of the intense stare, but they were wrong. Amy was very astute in her observations and gave him a big grin, along with a high-five. It appeared she was determined to get them together.

As they began to gather their belongings and head toward the aisle, Betty spoke to him, "What was all the whispering about?" Kneeling down on her daughter's level, she waited for her response.

"Sorry, Mom. Mr. Abbott looked so sad, I thought maybe I could make him feel better. I didn't mean to upset anyone, honest." She let her gaze drop to the floor, prepared for her mother's lecture.

The lecture never came.

Betty was so overcome by her daughter's compassion for Roger that all words failed her. "You really like Mr. Abbott, don't you, honey?"

Amy nodded.

"Your daughter is very wise for her age, Betty. She gave me some valuable advice that I really appreciate, so don't be too hard on her."

"She is a very special child. I still can't believe in a few short years she'll be a teenager. Thank you for being her friend. Right now, she needs a friend, someone to be there for her until her dad comes home." She had a bit of a catch in her voice that Roger picked up on.

"If I can help in any way, let me know."

Mrs. Anderson moved up next to them, "I couldn't help overhearing your daughter, Betty." She leaned down, giving Amy a gentle smile.

"Sorry we disturbed you, Mrs. Anderson. I've already told her that she should be quiet in church," Betty apologized.

"No harm done, dear. Who is the nice young man with her?"

"Roger Abbott, he's Janice's boyfriend. Amy has apparently taken to him." Betty gave her daughter a hug.

"Well, children know who they can trust. They're pretty good judges of character, Betty. It looks like the two of them have bonded. He obviously adores her. It's hard to miss the looks between them."

The adults made their way toward the doors where the minister was waiting to shake hands with his parishioners. As Amy ran ahead to talk to one of her friends, Janice nudged Roger, "She hasn't stopped talking about you since she found out you would be at church today. Guess what she told me earlier?"

"I can only imagine. She's a very special little girl. I like her a lot, Janice."

"The feeling is mutual, believe me. She told me that she loves you, Roger. I was so touched I almost started crying."

Roger didn't say anything for a minute, as he couldn't form the words. The fact that Amy loved him blew his mind. Not a whole lot of people would say that. The fact that it had come from a child humbled him.

Finally finding his voice, he said in a hushed voice, "I'm okay. I just never expected her to grow so attached to me, that's all. If you want the truth, I love her too. She's a very compassionate child." He looked thoughtful as he stared at Amy's retreating back.

Janice studied him for a second, the soft expression on his face obvious for all to see. The love he had for her niece shone from his eyes. She actually felt a little bit jealous, she wanted some of that love shown to her.

Roger picked up the subtle change in her expression and gently whispered in her ear, "You don't need to feel jealous, Janice, I have lots of love to go around." Somebody bumped Roger from behind, making him aware they were blocking the aisle. "I think we need to move so these people can get by."

Both of them moved into the space between the pews and nodded to friends who passed them. A few of them gave Roger a quick once over. The fact that they were seeing each other was apparently very evident to some of the Peterson's closest friends. Some smiled, while a few looked at him and frowned.

"Hope I passed inspection. Some of your friends looked at me like I was some sort of bug under a microscope." He raised his bushy eyebrows at this point then gave her a grin. He enveloped her in a firm hug, leaving little doubt about his feelings for her.

Janice leaned against him, enjoying the feel of his arms around her. He was so gentle, yet she could feel the passion in him. When they broke away, her face flamed red. To make things even more interesting, Amy picked that moment to join them. She didn't have to wait long for her answer.

"I saw you hugging Mr. Abbott, Aunt Janice. I know you love him. How come your face is all red?"

She was saved from trying to answer her niece when Amy's mother spoke up, "Amy, why don't you let your aunt have some time alone with Mr. Abbott, honey? Come along, the minister wants to introduce you to his granddaughter, Jessie. Then you need to get to your Sunday school class."

She gently guided her daughter along the aisle to where the minister was shaking hands by the open door. She looked back at them over her shoulder, giving them both a sly wink.

"Whew, that was close. I honestly didn't know how to answer her, Roger. She knows we like each other, love I'm not sure of. Maybe it's time we had a heart-to-heart talk with her, and let her know where we stand. I know she'll be pleased if we were in love. Which we are." Here, Janice hesitated, not sure if she could actually believe he was willing to give his heart to her.

CHAPTER FOURTEEN

"That is an excellent idea. I know I don't want to play games anymore. The past couple of hours I have thought about us, the fact that I need to let my fears go and to trust in my heart. You never did answer Amy as to why your face was red. Remember, you have to keep our trip to the island to yourself for now. Say a little prayer for me. Tomorrow, I tell the captain about my discovery on the island. I am worried he will not be pleased that I did it on my own. There's no regrets, though. I had to prove that I'm efficient and can use my head."

"I'm not concerned, Roger. I have every confidence you will come through." Her smile went right to his heart. His day seemed brighter because of that simple smile. "To answer your other question, my face turned red because I was embarrassed, especially when my niece caught us."

"You don't need to be embarrassed. Anyway, I think you look cute when your face turns red."

"You do, don't you?" They probably looked like some love-struck teenagers.

Reluctantly, they moved to the doors, where they shook hands with the minister, then moved into the hall for classes.

Finally, it was time to go home. Biding Janice, her sister, and children a goodbye, he made his way to his car.

Once on the road, Roger replayed the last couple of hours in his mind. His heart had changed, expanded. The band around his middle seemed to have disappeared, and for the first time, he felt free. Besides the talk from the minister, Amy Richards, with her childlike wisdom, had a lot to do with his change of heart.

Free to love, free to give his heart to Janice Peterson.

The alarm sounded its warning at 5:00 a.m. the next morning. With the sun just coming up, Roger groaned, pulled the covers off, and then crawled out of bed. With sleep still dragging at his feet, he made it into the bathroom to take a quick shower. Nothing like a shower to wake one up. He wasn't looking forward to telling his captain about his trip to Spooner's Island. The whole thing could get him in trouble. Breakfast was taken care of in minutes then he grabbed his keys and headed out to his car. It was starting to get light as he drove to the police station.

It was 5:35 when Roger entered the locker rooms to dress. Once he had his uniform and belt on, he made his way to the main squad room for the morning briefing. Taking a seat next to Officer Butler, he studied the board on the front wall. There were a dozen photos of men who had been implicated in the drug ring in the town. Among those pictures, he noticed a black-and-white shot of Boyd Peterson.

Public enemy number one.

"Good morning, gentlemen." Among the good-hearted laughter at the sergeant's use of the word *gentlemen*, he continued, "I will give you our latest update on the drug gang. First, the drugstore robberies have stopped. Officer Watson and Officer Jacobs found the abandoned car the other day at the bottom of a ravine outside Avonvale. The registration said it belonged to John Ballantyne. We think he was involved in the drugstore break-ins. Mr. Ballantyne unfortunately succumbed to a drug overdose. It has been ruled a probable homicide. The death of the wounded member of the rival gang was also a homicide. Apparently, someone disguised as a nurse slipped past the guard at the door. There is no clue to the identity of the man, but we suspect he may work in the hospital. Someone obviously knew what they were looking for.

The RCMP in New Brunswick have broken the ring up there with connections to this operation. So far, we have nothing concrete to go on, hence no arrests. Mr. Peterson insists he knows nothing of the contraband in his shipments, so until we have concrete proof, we can't do anything. Keep your eyes and ears open, if you suspect anything, let me or the super know."

At this point, he moved to pass out some white papers.

"Here are your assignments." Sergeant MacDonald passed out the printouts to the senior officers.

Roger was assigned to work with Officer Butler again, which he was okay with as the two of them got along like brothers. Before they left for their rounds, he stepped up to where his commanding officer was discussing some police business with one of his supervisors.

While Roger was preparing to discuss his trip to the island, the object of his investigation was getting ready to cover the evidence. First, Boyd moved all the stolen drugs from the back room of the house, concealing them in an alcove in the old tunnel. He thanked the old rumrunners for giving him such a great hiding place. Next on the list was dismantling the grow op on the island. The plants were almost ready, so he should be able to use most of them. As it was, the operation would take them several days. The paper trail had been destroyed, so the cops couldn't use that against them. He put all his files on a memory stick, deleting the incriminating information on the hard drive of his laptop.

Several of his men, including Jason Cox, thought he was being paranoid, but he wasn't taking any chances. The fact that someone had been on the island, and the fact they might have seen the marijuana plants, made him very nervous.

Roger stepped up to talk to his superior, and with a hushed voice, he said, "Excuse me, sir, but could I have a couple of minutes?" He grew nervous as the older man turned to study him.

"What is it, Abbott? Can it wait until later? As you can see, I have a busy morning." Sergeant MacDonald appeared impatient by the delay, so Roger decided to lay it on the line so his commander would understand.

"It has to do with the drug smuggling case, sir. I think I might have broken the case." Roger noticed his facial expression change slightly.

Definitely interested.

"Let's go into my office where we'll have some privacy."

Once they were seated in the small white-walled room, he continued, "What do you have, Constable Abbott?"

As Roger related his visit to Spooner's Island, he saw his boss sit a bit straighter, indicating that he was listening. His gray eyebrows rose slightly. He was hoping that he wouldn't get shot down because he had done the sleuthing on his own time.

"What's so intriguing about Spooner's Island, Abbott? No one's been on the island in years. And you did this on your own?"

"Yes, sir. I went at night so I wouldn't be seen. The island is being used to grow marijuana, sir. I have the pictures to back up my claim." Roger reached inside his shirt pocket, producing the color photos he got with the iPhone. As he slid them onto the oak desk, Bill MacDonald leaned forward, his eyes widening when he saw the evidence.

"Where did you take these? You didn't go inside the house, I hope. Without a search warrant, we can't use anything taken from inside. Did you have someone with you?"

Roger debated whether or not to mention Janice then decided against it. No sense in getting her involved in a police investigation. He had to protect her. "As you can see, sir, the pictures were taken from outside through the basement windows."

"It looks like you stumbled onto a marijuana grow op, but that still doesn't place Boyd Peterson there." He still wasn't convinced the photos would be of any use.

"Check out the last photo, sir, I think you'll find it the most revealing."

As his commanding officer flipped through the last photos, his eyebrows lifted, and a slight smile caused his mouth to twitch.

"Okay, it appears we have something to go on after all. Well done. How did you manage to get on and off the island undetected? You took a big risk."

Roger went over the details of his adventure, leaving Janice out of it, and saw his commander's approval.

"Smart thinking. You just might make a good detective after all. We need to get to work. Go with your partner, check out the transfer company. I have to go into the city and obtain some search warrants from the magistrate. It appears we might just be able to nail Boyd. I've been wanting to catch this guy for months."

"I know, sergeant. Glad I could help." Roger's heart felt lighter as he made his way back to the squad room and his partner.

Janice had a half day at work. Most of her day went smoothly, except for the incident with a six-year-old boy who didn't want his tooth filled. She tried to quiet him down, but in the end, the dentist had to cancel the appointment until later. She had felt sorry for the kid, but there was nothing she could do about it.

Once she left the office, she decided to do some shopping at the Micmac Mall. Pulling out into traffic on Main Street, she failed to notice the black Lincoln Town Car that pulled out behind her. The vehicle followed at a discreet distance so it didn't alert her. As she pulled into the parking lot of the mall, the larger car moved to a row several yards away, pulling in next to a red Volkswagen.

Janice went inside and headed for the Zellers store. With all the other shoppers around in the mall, she didn't notice the men following her. She had no reason to believe her uncle would still be watching her.

About a half hour later, she was leaving the Zellers store when she happened to see two dark-suited men off to one side. They seemed to be looking at her, but she couldn't place where she had seen them before. However, the sight of them gave her a feeling of unease, so she picked up her pace as she exited the building. Once in her car, she breathed easier.

The other car pulled out of the lot, intent on other pursuits.

That evening, Roger called Janice to set up a date with her for the following weekend, which was the middle of the month. His heart did a somersault in his chest when he heard her sweet voice on the other end of the line. His heart felt light the rest of the evening, and he couldn't wait to see her.

When Roger went to bed that night, he fell into a restless sleep. As his sleep grew heavier, he began to dream. These visions were becoming less frequent, and they weren't about Anna anymore. He saw a long bridge over a gorge ahead of him. Approaching the rope bridge, he could hear the roar of the water a long way below him. A fine mist floated up to him and dampened his clothes. Grabbing the rough hemp rope in each hand and with a lump of fear lodging in his throat, he inched across the narrow passage.

This time, he saw Janice standing at the far end of the foot bridge, waiting for him. Her smile seemed to erase all fear as he was drawn to her beautiful face. Within minutes, he was beside her and the ordeal was forgotten as they embraced.

As Roger embraced her, he woke up. Unlike earlier dreams, this time he was not upset but felt a strange sense of calm in his heart. He felt this was a sign that it was safe to trust his heart again. Specifically, it was safe to trust Janice. It was the final confirmation that he could move on with his life.

The week seemed to drag as he performed his duties as an officer of the law in Avonvale. Most days, he, along with his partner, cruised the streets of the town. Other than stopping a drunk driver, it was quiet. The drugstore robberies were still waiting to be solved as well as the two suspicious deaths. Roger heard the captain confirm the police search of Boyd Peterson's place was scheduled for Thursday at 8:00 a.m. The magistrate had taken longer to issue the search warrant than Sergeant MacDonald would have liked. However, he was pleased his superior had taken his claim seriously. He finally felt a sense of closure at the thought of nailing Boyd's hide.

Roger was to be cheated of the satisfaction of catching Boyd Peterson by surprise. Someone was working within the police department and was tipping Boyd off as to police activities. Even as he waited for Thursday, things were starting to unfold on Spooner's Island.

Later that evening, he decided to go for a walk. As his place was close to Shore Road, he found himself walking along the sidewalk opposite Boyd's Transfer. It was a warm late July night, birds chirped in the nearby trees, and the traffic was light. He felt a cool breeze blowing in off the ocean, bringing with it the smell of salt air.

As Roger approached the gully that led to the small beach, he happened to look out at the lighthouse. It was so faint that he thought he had imagined it, but he was almost sure that he heard the faint putt putt of a small boat out by the island. Because of the fog bank that hovered near the place, any boats were invisible from here. However, he seemed to be drawn to the place.

As the fog cleared some and gave him a clear view of the lighthouse and the out buildings, he could see a flash of orange through the trees. He stopped, curious as to the source of the orange tinge. Within five minutes, the faint tinge burst above the treetops. Flames licked hungrily at the old wood of the house.

As the fire began to rage on Spooner's Island, Roger quickly pulled his cell phone from his pocket and dialed 911. He waited for the fire trucks to arrive, wondering exactly how they would get out to the windswept rock.

By now the flames were leaping unchecked above the trees, and he could smell the strong, almost choking smell of burning wood. It stung his nostrils. He felt helpless to do anything more than watch the place burn. Sirens could be heard in the distance as the fire department converged on Shore Road.

Two trucks pulled up next to him. As the yellow-uniformed men jumped from the first truck, he went to talk to them.

"Did you call in the fire? Where is it?" An older man, dressed in heavy yellow fire equipment addressed him.

"My name is Roger Abbott. I'm a member of the police force here in Avonvale. I saw the fire start. It's going to be hard to get to." At this point, he pointed to the island where the fire lit the sky, turning it into a dull orange. He was sure he could feel the heat from here. Heavy smoke lay like a dark cloud over the town.

The fire marshal took one look, his face grim. "Looks like the house is already involved. That old place would probably go up like a tinder box. The only way to get to the island would be to take a boat out and use a portable pump. The best we can do is to keep the flames from spreading to the trees. Thank goodness the wind isn't very strong. Okay, let's do it." The chief, a stout man of about fifty, grabbed his mike and issued some orders to the waiting fire engines that sat nearby. As Roger watched, they pulled away, heading downhill toward the wharf. They quickly secured a fishing boat.

He glanced at his watch. It was 8:30 p.m. He pulled his black cell phone from his pocket and quickly dialed the station. They would need a couple of police cruisers to set up a roadblock near the firemen. People were already gathering to watch the old house on Spooner's Island as it burned. It seemed that fires drew people, almost like a magnet. He estimated there were close to twenty individuals milling about.

Two police cars came roaring up Shore Road, sirens wailing and lights flashing. The officers quickly got things under control. As Roger watched the fire burn a short distance away, he realized with sudden clarity that the fire would effectively erase the evidence he had photographed a few weeks ago. He felt his stomach knot in dread at facing his boss. He had been so close to having some concrete evidence on Boyd Peterson.

Now what would he do?

Roger walked back to his house, wondering what would happen to the search on Thursday. Some of the pushers and dealers were under arrest, but they refused to reveal who their source was. No doubt, they feared for their lives if they squealed. He had the sudden thought about going under cover to flush the big guys out. Later that evening, he talked to Janice. Just listening to the lilt of her voice lifted his weary heart. Since both of them had the weekend off, they made plans to visit the quaint fishing village in Eastern Passage. With regret, he finally let her go.

While Roger was worrying about the fallout from the fire, things were unfolding a short distance away at Boyd's house. He had moved his base of operation underground. Jason Cox, who was his second in command, and a few others he could trust, moved the drugs from his house to the tunnel that was hidden behind the living room wall. While they packed, Boyd deleted any remaining incriminating evidence from his computer. He began to relax as he stood watching his men haul the boxes into the dimly lit tunnel. The last thing to go was the heavy safe that held his drug money.

Boyd was a bit premature in his gloating. Something that lay unnoticed on the plush red carpet would come back to haunt him later.

That night, a shadowy figure slid into the secured area in the basement of the Avonvale Police station to an area that held evidence for use in pending investigations. Gloved hands grabbed several photos and slid back down the long corridor. He was in and out so quickly that no one saw him. Those photos were the last link to the burning house, just offshore.

The next morning, Roger entered the station with a feeling of gloom, wondering how he was going to salvage this situation. Even as he entered the briefing room and took a seat next to his partner, he was entertaining the idea of going under cover as a drug addict to flush the dealers out. His boss would probably give him flack for even suggesting it in the first place, but he was going to try it anyway. He owed the citizens of Avonvale his best, and he needed to prove to himself he could do the job.

Okay, so maybe ego entered the picture a little.

Sergeant MacDonald stood, motioning to the men to come to order. "Good morning. While your assignments are being distributed, I'll give you an update on the drug smuggling ring in town. Several of the street contacts have been arrested, but all refuse to talk. Most have been released on bail, pending their trials. Officer Abbott"—here he nodded to Roger—"had information on a marijuana grow op on Spooner's Island, but unfortunately the evidence burned last night. Our preliminary investigation into the fire suggests it was deliberately set. The remains of several gas cans were found near the scene of the blaze. We are canceling the search of Boyd Peterson's property until we get more information. So far, there's nothing to connect him to any of the drug trafficking. Keep your eyes and ears open, gentlemen."

CHAPTER FIFTEEN

There was a loud scrapping of chairs as those present rose, moving to the entrance and their cruisers. Roger was teamed up with his long-time partner and friend, Peter Butler.

Roger felt anger burn in his stomach as he thought about Boyd free on the streets of his town. He was even more determined than before to get something concrete on his adversary. Before he left the station, he decided to check on the evidence he had placed in the holding room. A quick check told him that someone had disposed of the final proof of the illegal drug grow op. He was back to square one.

He approached his supervisor.

"Sir, could I speak with you about the drug cartel? Someone stole the photos from the holding room. It seems we have a member of the force working for Boyd Peterson. That would explain why we can't seem to get ahead of them. I might have an idea that could flush them out." Roger was nervous, the suggestion he was about to make hanging over him like a fog.

"What is it, Abbott? I have a busy morning. Come into my office if you wish to discuss it in private." He sounded impatient, as always, which didn't do a whole lot to settle Roger's nerves.

"Sir, I realize we have no proof to go after Boyd Peterson, but I have an idea that could make them play their hand. Could I go undercover? I could pose as an addict wanting to buy cocaine. We could use the dealers we have in custody to link us up with a contact. We also need someone to watch the holding room. What do you think?"

"I'll have one of the men stay behind and watch the place. We could set up a remote camera as well. The man inside would explain a lot. Now, about your other idea. Have you ever done undercover work before,

Abbott?" He gave Roger a searching look, his bushy eyebrows raised slightly as he waited for the young officer to answer.

"No, sir, but I know that it could work if you'd give me a chance. I could use my partner as backup. It's important to me that I catch Boyd Peterson."

"Going under cover is risky. I can't guarantee your safety if the deal goes sour. You still interested?"

"Yes. This is personal, sir. He has threatened my girlfriend Janice Peterson. I want him off the street." He waited, with baited breath, while his superior either gave him the okay, or said no way.

"Would this Janice be related to Boyd Peterson by any chance?"

"Yes, sir, Boyd's her uncle. I worry she may be in danger."

"That does put you in a rather awkward position, don't you think, Abbott?"

"No, sir. I know I have to be professional and keep my personal feelings separate. I can do it, if you give me the chance. A friend of mine in Halifax works for a costume shop in the makeup department. He has agreed to supply myself and Officer Butler with disguises." He knew he sounded like he was begging, but a lot was riding on his being able to do this.

Part of it was for Janice, another part was to prove he could do it.

Finally, MacDonald made a decision. With a curt nod, he agreed to let Roger proceed as long as he promised not to take any unnecessary chances. His partner was to carry a cell phone and recorder so they would have some concrete evidence. He also agreed to initiate the first contact and set up the drop. For the next twenty minutes, they went over the details, the drug involved, the amount of money needed, and the time for the meeting. The drug would be cocaine, enough to cost about one thousand dollars, and all the bills would be marked. The time they settled on was Friday evening July 20, at 7:00 p.m. The drop would take place on Best Street where an alley joined Best to Arthur Street. It would be sheltered and private.

Roger thanked his superior then went to join Peter Butler in the briefing room. His excitement was pretty evident because several officers made a comment about his being unusually cheerful.

"Peter, the drop will be on Friday night at 7:00 p.m. The Sergeant finally agreed to let me do it. I'm determined to catch Boyd Peterson if it's the last thing I do."

Peter could hear the firmness in Roger's voice, and knew his friend would see this through to the end. For both their sakes, he hoped all went well.

"Okay, what do we have to do to prepare? You said something about having a friend at a costume shop. What disguises are we using? What drug are you dealing in? How do you want to play this out, Roger?"

"Cocaine, about one thousand dollars' worth. He quickly went over the details with his partner then they went out to the waiting police cruiser in the parking lot. The day was for the most part uneventful. They had a lunch at the local Wendy's then swung by the trucking company on Shore Road. Around the turn on Amber Crescent, they ran into a cluster of people milling about in the center of the road.

An older woman approached their car as they pulled up at the curb. Peter and Roger both pictured some sort of domestic dispute, which they both hated to get involved in.

"Trouble ma'am? Is anyone in danger, or does anyone have a gun with them? Has there been a robbery?" Roger asked, giving the elderly woman his full attention.

"No, no, it's nothing like that. My sister's cat is caught up a tree again. Could you gentlemen help us get the creature down? If you have a minute after, I can give you each a piece of fresh apple pie. Still warm from the oven."

Both of them smiled at the thought of fresh pie.

"We'll take you up on your offer after we get the cat back for you."

After they had cleared the area of spectators, they managed to secure a length of rope, a ladder, and a large hamper. Peter threw the rope over a hanging branch, then Roger began the climb the ladder up the tree trunk. With the rope around his waist, he looked up above him. Just over two feet away, he could see the small black cat, crouching on a branch. Its plaintive meows spurred him on.

He donned the heavy work gloves he would need in case the cat became frightened and scratched him. With soft whispers to the animal, he produced a small piece of catnip. When the cat sniffed his hand, he grabbed the animal, quickly placing the shaking feline in the wicker hamper. Once he had the lid closed and latched, he lowered the basket to the waiting people on the ground. His breathing began to slow down as the crisis ended.

A loud round of applause broke out among the twenty or so people clustered under the large oak tree. As he lowered himself to the ground, a few men pounded him on the back, while Mrs. Hanson, the elderly lady, went to get the promised apple pie. Within minutes they were both enjoying hot apple pie with a glass of cold milk. Reluctantly, they finished their treat then bade everyone farewell. Roger could get used to this kind of pampering, but knew it was the exception, not the rule.

The rest of the day went by rather slowly for the two.

After work, Roger decided to drive into the city to pick out a ring for his sweetheart. By the time he pulled into the parking lot of the Micmac Mall in Dartmouth, it was 8:00 p.m. Quickly he made his way to one of the many jewelry stores. The sheer variety of rings boggled the mind. Meandering among the rows of display cases, he tried to pick out something.

He must have looked totally confused because a clerk asked if she could be of help. They went over several styles, and he finally settled on a diamond solitaire with a gold band. As she packed it inside a blue velvet-lined box, he withdrew his credit card. A short time later, he left the mall with a broad smile on his face, his step lighter. He was home again by 10:00 p.m.

A half hour later, Roger curled up on the couch, grabbed the black cell phone, and called Janice. This calling each other in the evenings was starting to wear thin. Long-distance romances were not his idea of fun. However, as always, it was really nice to hear her soft voice. It boosted his weary heart considerably.

"Hi, it's so nice to hear your voice again. I miss seeing your beautiful face. All I ever see is a bunch of guys in dark blue uniforms, and not one of them has a sense of humor. Some of them are downright obnoxious." Roger felt that familiar flutter in the regions of his heart as he talked to Janice. For a few precious minutes, the miles seemed to dissolve. "All ready for a fun afternoon at Fisherman's Cove on Saturday?"

"I'm looking forward to it. I hear they have the best fish and chips in the city. Maybe we can go clam digging later."

"Maybe. Anyway, be prepared for a surprise. I hope you like it." He smiled at the thought of Janice trying to figure out what the secret was.

"Another surprise? Does it involve sneaking around? You're not staking out a restaurant, are you?" She liked to tease him sometimes about his cloak-and-dagger stuff. She could picture him in one of those spy movies as the hero of the story.

"Not exactly. But it does have something to do with a restaurant and the use of ice. Speaking of ice, how is your figure skating practice doing?" He knew this restaurant thing would definitely get her interested. It would probably drive her crazy waiting for two days.

"The local church hall has allowed me to teach the kids there. I'm enjoying helping the kids learn how to skate. You're really having fun with this, aren't you?"

"Definitely. Just be patient. Believe me, it's worth the wait, Janice."

"I'll try." For the next twenty minutes, they talked over their plans for the weekend. Reluctantly, they ended the call. "I love you, Roger Abbott."

He could almost hear her sigh as she whispered the words he loved to hear. "And I love you too. It feels so good that I can say that and really mean it. It's so good to be free of the demons that have kept me from feeling. You'll just have to wait until Saturday when I will show you just how much you mean to me." Roger smiled into the receiver as he revealed the feelings in his heart. A sense of freedom and coming home enveloped him, much like the warmth of a thick blanket. It took a minute for him to realize she had hung up and he was listening to the buzz of the dial tone. She always had a way of upsetting his equilibrium. For the rest of the evening, he was anticipating his date with Janice.

The next day was Friday, the day he went undercover to flush out the drug dealers. During the day, he and his partner made plans for that evening. He was to pose as a college student who had become addicted to cocaine. Peter Butler would pose as a street person. A quick inspection of the site revealed a long narrow alleyway with a drugstore on one side and a clothing store on the other. They made arrangements with the owner of the drugstore to use some crates near the place for doing business. Peter had permission to lay in the small alcove by the front door. For security purposes, Roger suggested the store close at 6:00 p.m. that evening. He was nervous; this was a very big risk, but he had to see it through. A lot was riding on the success of the ruse.

At 2:00 p.m., the two of them made the two-hour drive into Halifax to meet his friend at the costume shop. They met David Summer, the makeup artist who pulled out two disguises. Roger would be wearing dark slacks, a dress shirt, college sweater, with thick black glasses. He would have a beard, and black hair. Peter was shown his disguise. Worn jeans, a dirty shirt, jacket, with a scruffy beard. The man even produced a large bottle of scotch for a prop.

"Looks like you got the best of this deal, Roger. I definitely won't be fighting off the girls with this outfit, that's for sure. I'll smell like a brewery." Peter gave the outfit a slight grimace.

"Well, it's for a good cause. Believe me, with that outfit, you'll fit right in with the décor. I promise, you can have the first choice next time we go undercover. Okay, let's get changed."

"You've got yourself a deal. I guess I can live with this for an hour or so." For the next half hour, they had their makeup put on. The transformation was incredible. Roger didn't recognize himself or Peter when he looked at their reflections in the floor-length mirror. Peter was the perfect street person, right down to the gaunt appearance. He, on the other hand, could have stepped out of an issue of Vanity Fair.

For another thirty minutes, they went over the details of their disguises then paid their host. A glance at the clock on the beige wall told them it was already 4:45 p.m. They would have a slow trip back to Avonvale. Roger suggested they stop at a local Subway for a bite to eat, and when he mentioned he was paying, Peter quickly agreed.

As soon as they were on the road again, Roger looked over at his friend. "We'll separate on the street above the drop site. You can go first, stagger a bit and make your way down to the drugstore. I'll wait until almost seven then walk down for the drop. The guy's name is Jason. He has dark curly hair and will be wearing jeans, a light T-shirt, and jacket. I hope my act is convincing."

"You'll do fine. This is personal isn't it? Would your girlfriend Janice be related to this Boyd Peterson, by any chance?"

"Yeah, she's his niece. He's a real scumbag, has threatened her, and her father. If he fell into a dark hole, it wouldn't be far enough away to satisfy me, Peter." He realized he had revealed his extreme dislike of the man, but when it came to Janice, he seemed to be seized by very deep emotions.

The promise he had made to his commander entered his thoughts, and he knew he would have to keep a tight rein on his innermost feelings. It was important that he remain objective if he was to be convincing to this Jason.

They parked on the street above the alley, where Peter left to make his way to the drugstore. On the way down, he discreetly hid a small tape recorder behind some crates that rested against the stone wall of the drugstore building. To the right of the boxes, Peter noticed the loading door as well as a small light overhead. The area was basically a gravel walkway, edged with scrub grass along the edge of the buildings.

It was a warm evening, birds chirped in nearby trees, and a gentle breeze blew through the alley. There was still about two hours before sundown. Roger would have liked to have spent the time with Janice at a nearby beach, however, this was important, so he would have to grin and bear it.

As his partner disappeared around the front of the drugstore, Roger took a quick peek at his watch. It was 6:56. His contact should make his appearance any minute.

At exactly 7:00 p.m., a silver Mercedes pulled up to the curb in front of the alleyway.

Showtime.

As this Jason slid out from behind the steering wheel of the luxury sedan, he stood a little taller, trying to appear more confident than he was. It soon became obvious the man was not alone. A tall black man in dark clothing exited the other side of the vehicle. As he joined his contact, Roger assessed his age to be somewhere between twenty and twenty-five. Apparently, the guy worked out, for he had the physique of a football player. If he was nervous before, this made him even more unsure of himself.

"You must be Peter. I'm Jason, your contact. So you came for some cocaine?" He was in his late thirties, had dark, curly hair, and dark cold eyes.

At this point, he gave a slight nod to the man standing silently at his right. "You'll excuse me for being careful. Jake here is going to check you out to see if you're packing a weapon." His eyes narrowed as he gave Roger a quick assessment.

The bodyguard quickly frisked Roger, running his hands along his legs, patting the sweater he wore. It was a strange sensation. Usually, he was the one to do the checking. The check was done in about ten seconds, and he relaxed a bit. "No problem. I don't have a gun, and have never used one."

"Fine. Now that we have the formalities out of the way, let's get down to business. You want drugs, I want some money. Jake will keep an eye out while we conduct the exchange." Jake gave the street person slouched in the drugstore doorway a quick glance then ignored him.

Jason's eyes had a hard glint in them, and Roger got the impression this man was used to being in control. If he was Boyd's right-hand man, he probably was capable of disposing of opposition by the use of force, if necessary.

CHAPTER SIXTEEN

They moved to the crates that sat next to the building. Jason sat his black attaché case on the top and flipped open the locks. Once the lid was pulled back, a large number of bags were revealed. There were several eightball-sized bags as well as smaller bags of drugs. Roger saw some prescription drugs among the other bags.

Jason withdrew a small knife from his pocket, slicing part of the top of the closest bag. "Have a taste, my friend. You'll find it very high grade. You can snort it, or do whatever gives you the best high. There's enough cocaine here to last you for quite a while. Okay, let's see if you have the money."

It was Roger's cue to pay up. As he reached into his pocket for his wallet, the bodyguard gave him a quick once over.

Roger wet his index finger then reached in to take a small sample of the drug. This was going to be the most difficult part, convincing his adversary that he was a real drug addict. When he brought the stuff to his mouth, it had a sharp penetrating taste to it. Somehow, he managed not to show the grimace or feeling of dislike as the cocaine hit his senses. He must have been convincing because Jason closed the lid and moved to examine the bills passed to him. He straightened with a slight nod. "Good, small bills, just as I had requested. It's all there, so we have a deal. If you need any other drugs, just contact one of the pushers. It's been a pleasure doing business with you. This meeting never happened, if anyone asks you." Jason grabbed the money, while Roger picked up the cache of drugs.

Both men moved to the waiting Mercedes that sat idling at the curb. The whole transaction had taken them about ten minutes. Once they were in the car, and pulled out into the street, Peter appeared from his hiding place, joining Roger on the old cracked sidewalk. "I just called for our backup. They should block the ends of the street off." Moving to the crates, Roger reached behind the boxes, grabbing the small recorder. Snapping it off, he rewound the tape then played it back. As the familiar voices of Jason and himself came from the machine, he actually managed to smile. This just might be the big break they needed.

Both of them moved out to stand behind a parked car. At the end of the street, Roger saw a police cruiser pull across the road, effectively blocking any exit. He could see the red and blue lights flashing, casting their reflections against the closest buildings. The Mercedes stopped abruptly, then began to move backward away from the cruiser. In a matter of minutes they would be abreast of the two of them.

"Here, my friend. I think you will need these." Peter reached inside his soiled jacket and produced Roger's shield and service revolver. Crouching next to his partner, Roger waited for the sedan to approach them. He saw it back into a driveway then pull out, accelerating as it attempted escape. Both men checked their weapons and watched as the sedan approached them. It was now only about twelve feet away. As they waited another cruiser pulled across the road next to them. The red and blue lights cast their glow against the darkened buildings.

"Let's do it," Peter whispered. The tension in the air was palpable. He raised his gun.

"Believe me, I've been waiting for this moment for a while now." Roger also rose from his hiding place. The sedan came to an abrupt stop.

As they rose from their hiding places, Jason and his friend flung open their doors. Both of them had guns. Before they could even formulate a plan, the first police cruiser pulled up next to the disabled vehicle.

"Both of you, raise your hands and drop your weapons." Roger moved closer to Jason and kicked the driver's door shut with his left foot.

The drug dealer looked at him with unconcealed contempt. "Who the heck are you? Who's the bum you have for a backup?"

Peter Butler bristled at the insulting remark. His dislike of the fellow was growing stronger every second. He moved to the bodyguard.

Roger used crisp, firm tones. "We're undercover cops."

"Yeah, if you're undercover cops, I'm president of the United States!" Sarcasm oozed from his voice. So far, the black man remained silent, but he did smile at his boss's smart remark. "Look, I'm shaking in my shoes."

Roger and Peter both produced their badges, holding them out so there could be no mistake. As Jason looked at the ID's illuminated by the headlights, his face paled then a myriad of emotions passed across his features. He reminded Roger of a deer caught in the headlights of a car. It was almost laughable.

Almost.

"Now, I repeat. Drop your weapons!"

His command was reinforced by the uniformed officers who stood directly behind his dark-haired adversary. "I'd obey the man, if I were you."

Reluctantly, and almost in slow motion, both of them let their weapons drop to the asphalt street. The guns made a loud clatter as they hit the ground.

The uniformed backup quickly snatched up the discarded guns and continued to offer support to the still-disguised men.

While his partner checked out the guard, Roger said in a curt voice, "That's better. Now, please face the car, and spread your legs. I'm sure you know the routine." He felt just a tinge of sarcasm lace his own voice. He was starting to feel hot in his costume, but it was a small price to pay if they could get these guys out of business.

As Jason turned to face the Mercedes, he frisked him. Nothing hidden under his jacket, or hips. His right leg was clean. At the bottom of his left leg, he felt a hard lump, just above the man's ankle. Pulling up the material, he found a small holster strapped to the ankle. Withdrawing a small gun, he passed it off to the waiting officer behind him. "How does it feel to be the one enduring the checking out? You can turn around. Peter, how's it going on your end?"

Jason offered a smart comeback, trying to hide his nervousness.

"No big deal. You guys think you're pretty smart, don't you?" It was offered as an obvious challenge to both of them.

Peter yelled over, "Everything's fine here. This fellow had several weapons as well as brass knuckles. Real nice guy." At this point, Roger saw him turn the thug over to one of the waiting cops, who handcuffed him then led him to the closest police cruiser.

"To answer your challenge, no, we don't think we're smart. Just lucky." Enough small talk. He watched as Peter reached into the car and produced a small white card. "Registration card?" Roger gave it a quick glance.

"Yes. It says the car is registered to a Jason Cox." He gave a nod toward the man in front of him.

"Are you Jason Cox?" Roger almost bit out the words.

"What if I am?" Jason was still belligerent, still not willing to cooperate.

"Jason Cox, you're under arrest for drug trafficking, for resisting arrest, and for carrying a concealed weapon. That's just for starters. I'm sure we can think of something else. You have the right to remain silent." Roger read the last of the declaration to Jason as he pulled handcuffs from his pocket. He was thankful Peter had hidden all their equipment under his tattered jacket. It had been the perfect cover. The dealers had paid no attention to him.

"I want to talk to my lawyer. I'm not saying anything else until I see him."

"You can phone him from the station. Officer Simms, you can have him. We'll see you back at the office."

Once the patrol car had pulled away, Peter phoned a tow truck. Both of them were relieved the ordeal was over. Now they had to convince Jason Cox to confess. However, he seemed to be an unmovable as a stone wall. As they waited, they collected the evidence from the last half hour. Roger had snagged the attaché case from the Mercedes, adding it to the drugs he had procured. It was going to be hard to refute this and the tape recording of the transaction.

"I'm glad that's over. Once I make up my report, I'm off. I can't wait for Saturday." He got that faraway look anytime he thought about Janice. Lately, that was almost every waking moment when he wasn't doing police work.

"What's so special about Saturday? Just another day as far as I'm concerned." Peter didn't sound excited about the weekend, but he probably didn't have someone special in his life. He gave his friend a perceptive look then he smiled. "That's right. You mentioned that you had a girlfriend and that you were going to pop the question tomorrow. Good luck. I hope it works out for you two. You deserve a good woman." Their conversation was interrupted when a noisy yellow tow truck rumbled around the corner. While it sat idling with its orange lights flashing, a middle-aged man in blue coveralls jumped from the vehicle. He wore a yellow shirt with the company logo, *Jim's Towing*, stenciled across the front.

"You the two that called in for the tow truck? I thought a cop phoned us." The driver didn't seem impressed by them. However, once Roger flashed his badge, the man's demeanor changed. He saw the look of respect in the man's hazel eyes.

"We're with the Avonvale Police. This car is part of a drug investigation, so it needs to be taken to the compound at the station. Here are the keys. We'll meet you there. My name is Roger Abbott." He handed the keys to the man.

"Jake Owens. I'll meet you there, and we'll make out the paper work. His eyebrows rose just a bit as he waited for their reply.

"Yeah. Thanks." For the first time, Roger was able to relax a bit.

"No problem. Must be good money in crime to have an expensive set of wheels like this."

"There is, but unfortunately, it's blood money." Roger tried not to sound too cynical as he answered the man.

The man had the car hooked up in record time, then he hopped in the cab, and the truck pulled away. The flashing orange lights cast eerie shadows as they crept across the sides of the buildings. It was starting to get dark, and he could feel a cool breeze against his face. He picked up the spent shell casings from their guns.

As Roger and Peter made their way back to the car on the street above, he looked at the luminescent hands on his watch. It was 8:15 p.m. It would be late by the time he left the station for home. In a matter of minutes, they were pulling into the parking lot. The tow truck was just unloading Jason's car at the compound as they went inside the brick building. Passing the desks, they were subject to a couple of cat calls from the other officers. "Hey, where did you get the help Abbott? He could use a wardrobe makeover."

"Very funny. We just got back from an undercover sting. What do you think of the car we recovered? My dream car." Peter also gave them a faint grin. It was all in fun, the men liked to joke around a bit with one another.

"Congratulations. I somehow doubt on your salary you can afford a high-class car like that, Abbott. They just brought this Jason and his shadow in and put them in the slammer. Believe me, he didn't look too happy." Officer Bennett came over and slapped them on the back.

"Thanks. We still have to get something on Boyd Peterson. I have to get these reports done, so I'll talk later." Roger moved to his own desk, seating himself behind the scarred oak surface. Opening his laptop, he started to draw up the report for his super. As he typed, a feeling of elation swept through him. Finally, some movement on the drug dealer's case.

It was after nine when he finally shut off the computer then grabbed his street clothes. He and Peter would change into regular clothes then head home. He would return the costumes on Monday. Once he was in his clothes, he pushed open the aluminum door and headed for his car. As he pulled into his driveway, he gave a sigh of relief. For the first time, he felt his pulse rate drop to normal levels.

After arriving home and throwing his keys on the table, he got himself a cup of herbal tea. He retrieved the engagement ring from his bureau and took it to the kitchen. After placing the ring in some water in an ice cube tray, he set the tray in the fridge freezer. It was getting late, so he headed for the bedroom. Leaving the hall light on, he sat on the edge of the bed to remove his shoes. He was so tired he simply fell backward onto the patchwork quilt. As he relaxed against the old blanket that had been a present from his aunt, he fell into a deep sleep.

Roger again slipped into the hazy world of dreams. In this one, he began to replay his date with Janice. He saw the ring he was going to give her, saw the startled expression cross her face. The question of whether or not she said yes was not revealed to him. He continued to dream through the deepening hours of the night.

Brilliant rays of sunlight cast their yellow rays across his bed. He roused somewhat from his slumber, rubbing his eyes as he sat up. As he became more awake, he noted that it was a beautiful late summer day. A sense of freedom settled upon him as he thought about the special day ahead. He had a lot to do before his date with Janice. He was a bit nervous for he was going to go out on a long limb, trust his heart, and bare his feelings for her. The past several months, with their many dates, had only more firmly cemented their growing attraction for one another.

Once the breakfast meal was over, Roger changed into a pair of tan slacks and a white striped shirt. He spent the next hour listening to music then he locked up. Joining the other traffic, he made his way along the Eastern Shore toward the cities.

Now for part two of his plan.

It was around eleven, so he quickly drove to Eastern Passage. Once in the Seahorse Restaurant, he approached the manager and made his request. The man gave him a broad smile then indicated that he would take care of all the details. Roger left the ring with the kind middle-aged man. He had about an hour and a half before he had to pick up Janice and make it back to the Seahorse for their 1:20 p.m. dinner reservation.

For the next while, he enjoyed strolling along the boardwalk at the nearby Mac Cormack's Beach. The scent of the sea and the ever present screech of seagulls was invigorating. As he was nearing the end of the wooden walkway, he saw two men in dark clothes standing on the beach by the dunes. Normally, he wouldn't have given them a second thought. But this was anything but normal. He made believe he was bending over to tie his shoe.

They were talking then one of the men passed a briefcase to the other. The man who received the satchel turned a bit toward him. Roger stood still, stunned as he looked at one of the officers from the Avonvale police force.

The man was Fred Simms.

Interesting. What was he doing here on a nearly deserted beach?

As he made his way back to the shops, he tried to forget about the odd incident. No doubt there was a good reason for it.

Back in Dartmouth, Janice was putting on the last of her makeup, and arranging her hair in soft curls about her face. With a pair of peach-colored slacks, a flowered blouse, and brown shoes, she looked at her reflection in the bedroom's floor-length mirror. Perfect.

This should get Roger's attention.

Her father was still at work, so she locked the house and decided to wait outside on the front lawn. It was a warm afternoon, birds sang happily in the nearby trees, and the children played a spirited game of street hockey a few houses up from her. She was nervous, her palms sweaty as she waited for Roger to pick her up. For the past couple of days, she had replayed his cryptic comment about the use of ice.

What in the world did he have up his sleeve?

She would get her answer soon.

A flash of red caught her eye, and she turned to see Roger pull up to the curb in front of the driveway. She waved then opened the passenger's door.

"Wow, you look wonderful. If I didn't know better, I'd think I had just seen some sort of mythical princess or a forest nymph." He actually sat there with his mouth open, his eyes glued to her. It was obvious she had made a big impression on him. The sight of her made all the events of earlier in the day flee his mind.

Janice still felt a bit nervous, but his comment made her spirits soar and her heart flutter. Something deep within her told her that today was going to take their relationship in a whole new direction. The past couple of months had gone by in a blur. Each time they were together, she felt that they were drawing closer. He had been very supportive of her as she revealed her anxieties about her uncle Boyd. They both felt the chemistry that sparked between them. It drew them, almost like a large magnet.

"Thank you. You sure know how to charm a girl. Speaking of beautiful, you look wonderful. Like you stepped out of one of those old romantic movies. Where are you taking me?" She reached down to fasten her seat belt, her face growing warm as she stared at him. "How was your day yesterday? I heard you were planning on going undercover. I see you dyed your hair black. It makes you look more like Clark Gable."

"I did go undercover. The hair coloring was part of the disguise I wore yesterday. Clark Gable I don't know about. We caught one of the top guys in the drug gang. That's not important today. This is a day just for us. No one else matters. We're going to one of my favorite spots to relax in Eastern Passage. You ever been there Janice?"

"A while ago. I went with Betty and the kids. I don't remember everything about the place, but I do remember eating way too much ice cream. Do you have reservations made at a restaurant, Roger?"

As Roger pulled out into traffic and headed down the highway toward Eastern Passage, he gave her a mysterious smile. "As a matter of fact, I do." It sort of reminded her of the look that the cat had after swallowing the canary. She enjoyed the feel of the breeze from the open window against her face. Soft music came from the stereo, adding to the romantic atmosphere in the car.

As they came over the crest of the hill, she admired the fantastic view of Halifax Harbour with George's Island and the skyline of the city in the background. A large white cruise ship was docked at the sea wall behind the island.

"I forgot how fantastic the view is from here."

Roger was trying to concentrate on his driving, but with Janice next to him, it was proving to be a bit difficult. "It is a great view, but the view next to me is much better." He gave her a quick grin. By now they were at the base of the hill, approaching the traffic lights. He flipped his left signal light on then pulled over into the turning lane. The signal made a faint ticking sound in the background. When the light changed, he pulled into the line of cars heading toward Eastern Passage. He drove under the railway bridge then along the road opposite Shearwater Base.

Janice was quiet, relaxing against the black cloth seat. His tender comment sent her pulse tripping. The sound of the breeze, the soft strains of romantic piano music, all gave her a feeling of peace. Before she knew it, they were turning into the road that lead to the many shops in Fisherman's Cove. She sat up and admired the quaint brightly colored buildings with their wooden boardwalk in front. "This is really nice, Roger. What's this about the use of ice?" She gave him a questioning look.

"Just be patient. All will be revealed soon." He parked the car, moving to get the door for her. "We better go inside for our dinner date. The door, ma'am." With a slight flourish, he swung open the door and gently pulled her to her feet. For a split second they gazed into each other's eyes, then the spell was broken. With his hand at her elbow, they moved toward the front door of the restaurant. Both of them noticed the nautical theme at the front of the pale yellow building. A huge Seahorse Restaurant sign sat over the entrance, with the head of a very large shark holding it in place.

Roger pulled the white steel door open, and they moved into the interior of the restaurant. The place had an intimate feel, with dark rough boards on the ceiling and on the walls. Several glass cases displayed models of schooners, while nautical items like rope, bells, and fake fish covered the walls.

While they waited to be seated, Janice admired the décor, the delicious smells of seafood that lingered in the air. A young woman in black came up to them, asking them if they had reservations. With Roger's affirmation, she led them to a green-topped table by the windows. He pulled out her chair for her then took his seat across from her. The window let them see the outside patio area as well as the beach just beyond the railing.

"This is really romantic. I love the nautical theme." She gazed intently into his hazel eyes, getting lost in their depths. His expression softened, and he reached for her hands. His hands enveloped hers, giving her a feeling of belonging and safety.

The waitress approached and placed two medium-sized glasses of ice water on the table. The moment was broken and they pulled their hands apart. Two menus were placed in front of them, and the waitress left them to make their choice. Janice felt slightly flushed, so she reached for her water glass. She had just taken a sip of the ice cold liquid when her eyes noticed a strange reflection in the water. The overhead lights caught and reflected off something bright in the ice. Different colors shimmered and cast their reflections against the glass tumbler. As Janice held the glass closer, her breath caught. Her violet eyes widened in surprise.

She knew what she was looking at.

It was her engagement ring, and it was embedded in an ice cube!

CHAPTER SEVENTEEN

As she brought her hand to her mouth, tears filled her eyes.

"I can't believe you did this. How did you get it inside an ice cube?" As she looked closer and saw the details of the ring, fresh tears coursed down her cheeks. "Does this mean what I think it means?"

"I froze it last night. I thought it was a cool way to surprise you. And yes, it means I plan to propose." While he reached for a spoon, as if on cue, the waitress appeared again with a large pot with hot water. "I'll just dip it in the water, and it will be ready to wear. Thank you." He looked up at the young woman near their table. "Give us another ten minutes and we'll be ready to order."

"No problem. Take your time. I'll be just over there if you want me. Good luck."

Roger dipped the ice in the pot. When he withdrew it a couple of seconds later, the silver spoon held a beautiful diamond ring. A large stone sat in the center, surrounded by a gold band. Janice could only stare at it. Grabbing the ring, he made his way to her side of the table then he knelt on one knee on the floor beside her. She looked down at him, her heart in her throat. Words were out of the question. She couldn't have spoken if her life depended on it.

Unaware of the curious stares from the other nearby patrons, Roger held the ring in the palm of his hand, and in a very soft voice, opened his heart, "I never thought I'd find love again after Anna died. I was wrong. This time my love is so much sweeter, more complete." He hesitated then took the plunge. "Janice Peterson, will you consent to be my wife? I promise to protect, cherish, and love you for the rest of my life. Will you accept this ring as a token of that love?" As he stood and prepared to place the ring on her finger, she suddenly jumped to her feet, throwing herself into his arms.

"Yes, yes, yes! I'll marry you. I've dreamed of this moment. I love you so much, Roger."

Roger took her left hand, and as she watched, placed the engagement ring on her third finger. It fit perfectly. He embraced her again, and it seemed the world stood still. She smelled of strawberry-scented perfume. On Janice, it smelled of some exotic place, far away. He brushed his lips over hers.

Both of them became aware of others around them as a chorus of cheers and clapping reverberated through the restaurant. Several people came up to them and congratulated them. Both of them broke apart, suddenly embarrassed by all the attention. Roger had forgotten that they had others nearby, but he grinned, accepting the handshakes from the well-wishers.

"Excuse me. Are you two ready to order now?" Their waitress appeared out of nowhere, and they realized they hadn't decided on a meal yet. She gave them a knowing smile, before adding, "I take it the ring was accepted?"

"Yes. Thank you for helping me with my surprise for my fiancé. And if you could give us a couple of minutes, I think we can order something. Although I'm so excited, I don't know if I can eat a thing." He was still staring into Janice's eyes. She had managed to stop crying, but her eyes were still misty.

When she had left them, he reached up and very gently wiped the tears from her heart-shaped face. She gave him a brilliant smile. That smile went right to his heart.

"You are so beautiful. Even when you cry." Roger wiped the teardrops from her cheeks, his expression tender.

"I feel like I'm flying among the clouds. Sorry I started bawling like a baby again. It's just that I'm so happy I can't contain it. I hope we can come down to earth long enough to order."

"Yeah, I feel like I'm in another world myself. However, we do have to eat. I want the haddock platter, with lemon pie. See anything interesting?"

"I guess I'll have the scallop platter with a piece of coconut cream pie."

She handed the large plastic-coated menu folders to him as the waitress reappeared. "Ready to order, Mr. Abbott?"

Quickly, he gave the orders to her and watched as she wrote in her order pad. Then they were left to themselves for a while. Janice admired the décor of the place and realized that she was hungry. She gazed at Roger, the love shining in her eyes. That love was reflected back to her when he gazed intently at her. Time seemed to be suspended as they drank in the sight of each other.

The waitress made her appearance, interrupting their special moment, and Roger watched as she placed two large platters of food in front of them. She disappeared in minute later and they picked up their forks.

"This looks amazing." Janice reached for a piece of scallop. She closed her eyes and enjoyed the taste of the seafood against her tongue.

For the next half hour or so they ate. As they were nearing the completion of the dinner, their waitress brought their desserts. By the time they were finished, they were both stuffed.

"That was one of the best seafood dishes I've had in a long time." Roger sighed in contentment.

"This has been so special. What other surprise have you got up your sleeve?" She pushed away from the table and looked intently at him. Roger left a generous tip for their waitress then he moved to the other side of the table to pull the chair back for her.

"How does a stroll along the boardwalk sound?"

"That would be nice."

Once the bill was settled at the front desk, they moved outside. It was a hot afternoon and perfect for a walk along the beach's boardwalk. As Roger and Janice walked along the wood boardwalk, they were very aware of the screech of seagulls as they soared overhead. The salty smell of the sea and seaweed, the cooking odors from the restaurant, all added to the allure of being so close to the ocean. He took her hand as they continued along the winding walkway. The only other sound was the clomp, clomp of their shoes on the rough boards. To their right, the smooth crescent stretch of MacCormack's Beach snuggled in against the dunes and tall grass.

Roger pointed to a small fishing boat that moved slowly through the narrow channel between the mainland and Lawlor's Island. They could hear the putt putt of the small engine. The island offshore was so close they felt they could almost walk across the narrow stretch of water. Behind the smaller island was the dark green shadow of McNabs Island. Janice followed his gaze as they admired the beauty of the area. In the distance, they could see where the narrow channel merged with Halifax Harbour. The skyline of the city could be seen in the distance.

Several families were ahead of them, the children running toward the beach at the end of the wooden walk. "What would you say if I suggested that we join the kids for some time on the beach? Up to some sand and surf?" Roger swung her arm back and forth as they drew nearer to the end of the point.

"That sounds like fun. It's been ages since I had a chance to just let my hair down and relax on a beach. I haven't felt this relaxed for a long time."

Together, they stepped down into the grass near the sand. The small crescent of beach beckoned them. Once on the sand, they removed their shoes and socks. The brown surface was hard and cool beneath their bare feet. Some of the softer sand actually squeezed between their toes, much to Janice's delight. Feeling almost like children, they ran down toward the parking lot. Several people smiled at them as they raced by. At the end of the sandy strip, they stopped, panting for breath.

Both of them ended up in each other's arms. It felt like they had come home as they clung to each other. Roger was aware of the silky feel of her blonde hair, the faint hint of her strawberry perfume. They seemed to be the only ones on the beach as they looked into each other's eyes. He gently brushed his lips against hers, enjoying the strawberry-flavored lipstick. Passion flared between them. Roger's breath seemed to catch as he looked at her face. She was glowing.

"Roger, I love you so much. I still can't believe I'm actually engaged. I've prayed about this day for months." She gazed directly into his hazel eyes, into his soul. The love there drew her in with its intensity. An invisible current seemed to flow between them, holding them to one another.

"I know how you feel. It's what I've prayed for too. I feel like yelling it from the treetops, I'm so happy." His smile caused her heart to skip a beat.

While Roger and Janice were drawing closer, and opening their hearts to each other, back in Avonvale things were anything but calm. Jason's bodyguard broke down and confessed after a two-hour interrogation by members of the force. He readily admitted that Jason was Boyd Peterson's right hand man. He also confessed that Jason carried out execution-style murders.

The other development involved Jason Cox. Despite his arrogant, belligerent attitude, he had an Achilles heel. This weakness was going to crack open his hard, unyielding attitude.

Jason had claustrophobia.

It became clear something was wrong on Friday night when he was put in the small holding cell. By ten o'clock, he was beginning to sweat then he began to pace back and forth in his prison. Panic settled upon him like a fog until he couldn't breathe. It took a couple of officers to settle him down then he was given a shot to help him relax.

Downstairs in the evidence room, someone was looking for an attaché case. Unaware he was being watched, the officer grabbed the black case, turning to slide along the hall to the outside door. Before he was able to clear the doorway, Officer Bentley stepped out of his hiding place in the alcove.

"Can I help you with something, Simms?"

He watched as Simms went pale, a sure sign he was trying to hide something. The man tried to hide the attaché case behind his back.

"What are you doing here?"

"I could ask you the same thing. No one is supposed to be in that room, unless they have a good reason. What's your excuse, Simms?"

For the first time, Simms noticed the revolver his fellow officer held in his right hand. It dawned on him that the only recourse now was to confess. "I needed the money. This place doesn't pay enough to support my habit." His voice held an edge of bitterness that was hard to miss.

"What habit are you talking about? Are you on drugs?" Bentley looked closely at him, trying to detect evidence of recent drug use.

"No. My habit is a bit more expensive than that. I owe some one forty-five thousand dollars. If I don't pay, I'm a dead man!"

Bentley gave a low whistle. That much could mean only one thing.

Simms was a gambling addict. Big time.

"Come on. We have to have a little talk with the staff sergeant then the chief. You can explain everything to him."

When the two men approached MacDonald's office, he appeared, motioning them inside. Once the door was pulled closed, he told them to sit.

The next half hour proved to be very revealing. Apparently, Simms was in debt so deep that he decided to work for the drug cartel. The extra money he earned would help pay off his debt. What he didn't stop to think about was the debt he incurred while working for Boyd Peterson.

With a firm, no-nonsense voice the staff sergeant said, "Turn in your badge and service revolver, Simms. You will be contacted as the internal investigation begins. We'll see about the legal implications from accepting drug money. You could be charged with breach of trust. As of today, your assets will be frozen, pending further investigation. You will be able to apply for bail."

"Yes, sir," Simms answered with a flat, unemotional tone in his voice.

On Saturday, as Roger and Janice enjoyed their day, Jason Cox was being interrogated by Staff Sergeant MacDonald, and one of his detectives. It was obvious to the two men that Jason was ready to talk. He slumped in the high-backed chair, his eyes were bloodshot, and he glanced anxiously around the room. The prospect of being locked up scared him. To add insult to injury, his lawyer was out of town. And he had no recourse now but cooperate with the law.

"You ready to cooperate, Cox? Simms and your bodyguard have both implicated you in several murders. You are looking at some serious jail time, so you might as well come clean. Your choice, of course. It will go a lot easier on you if you cooperate."

"Of course." It was stated in a flat, defeated tone. Jason had the haunted look that often overtook men when they were caught and there was no way out.

An hour later, Jason was given some medication then locked up once again. A signed confession sat on the supervisor's oak desk, while the wheels were put in motion that would let them search Boyd Peterson's property. Jason had admitted that he had carried out the execution of Ballantyne. He had disguised himself as a male nurse to carry out the elimination of the wounded man in the hospital, using a massive drug overdose. Boyd had issued the order as well as setting up the fire on Spooner's Island to cover up evidence. Simms was the eyes and ears who tipped them off to what the police were planning.

With Jason's confession, the net was starting to close in around Boyd.

MacDonald felt that things were finally starting to move forward. Within the hour, he was on his way to the city to procure the necessary legal warrants needed to search the Peterson property. He thought about Roger Abbott, and a slight smile crossed his weathered face. Abbott should be in on the bust as he had given them the leverage they needed.

He had to admit, he was impressed by the young officer's tenacity as well as his street savvy.

Unaware of the dramatic turn of events back in Avonvale, Roger and Janice headed for Dartmouth. It had been a wonderful afternoon for both of them, but now he had to officially ask her father for her hand in marriage. He was very nervous, even though he knew Frank Peterson would not stand in their way. As he drove into the city, he felt his palms get clammy, his heart pound. Even the sound of one of his favorite songs by Abba didn't settle his bad case of nerves. Looking over at her, he was relieved somewhat when she gave him one of those brilliant smiles.

"Relax, Roger. Father already gave his permission, so there's no need to worry. I know Dad, and he won't bite. I love you, and I'll be there for you." She gave his arm a gentle squeeze. He got so distracted he almost lost control of the car.

"Better not do that till we get to your father's place, or I'll end up in the ditch. You sure know how to distract a guy." Roger gave her a quick glance, his smile lifting her heart. Reluctantly, he concentrated on his driving.

They drove into the city and took the highway that led to the Micmac Mall. As they turned off at the approach to the mall, he took her hand and gave it a reassuring clasp. They moved into the subdivision where Janice lived.

"Well, we're here. Looks like Betty is here too. She's going to be so excited to see this ring. If I know Amy, she'll be ecstatic. My niece has been pushing us together for months now. Not that we needed a whole lot of pushing."

"No we didn't."

He pulled into the driveway, just behind the small blue Mazda. Before they could get out of the car, the front door swung open. Betty and her children stood in the opening. As they moved toward the house, Amy ran to meet them.

"Guess what, Mr. Abbott? My dad is home from Afghanistan. I told him all about you, and he wants to meet you. And guess what else happened last week? I have a boyfriend. He's ten, and his name is Peter." She looked to her aunt, her eyes bright when she saw the shiny diamond ring on her left hand. "Wow. That's a pretty ring, Aunt Janice. Did Mr. Abbott propose to you?"

"As a matter of fact, he did, honey. Let's get inside and we'll tell you all about our day. And you're going to have to tell me more about this boyfriend of yours. I guess that means you're starting to grow up, eh?" She moved toward the door with Roger and her sister behind her.

"I'm not grown-up yet, Aunt Janice. I can't go out on dates, but he can come here if there's an adult in the house. It's nice to have someone special to share things with."

Roger leaned over, giving Amy his undivided attention, "I knew sooner or later you would find a nice boy, Amy. As you probably know by now, they're not all gross."

"No they're not. He's kind and likes some of the same things that I like. And he's fun to be with."

"That's great. Maybe we should get inside so I can talk to your grandfather. I have something really important to tell him."

"You've proposed to my aunt, and have to ask grandpa's permission, don't you?"

"Not much gets past you, eh?"

"Anybody knows that." She had a triumphant smile on her face as she said it.

Once they were inside, Roger was introduced to Betty's husband, Roy. He decided right away that he liked the man. At over six feet, he had an air of authority as well as kindness about him. With blonde hair, blue eyes, and a kind smile, it was not hard to see why Amy adored her father.

"Mr. Abbott, I've heard a lot about you from my daughter." He looked down at her, love very visible in his dark eyes. "Apparently, you two have become good friends. And she was right, you are quite good looking. Nice to finally meet you." As Roy extended his hand, Roger accepted the handshake. He had a firm handclasp.

"Nice to meet you too. And please, call me Roger. Amy has been a sweetheart and has helped me see things a little clearer when I was not sure what to do. She is very observant and very wise." He looked down at the nine-year-old, giving her a tender smile. This was a little secret just between them.

"Okay, Roger it is. Please, come into the living room."

Janice smiled at Amy then she showed off her engagement ring. As she held it up, the light from overhead caught and reflected off the diamond. It was quite dazzling.

Betty caught her breath as the light sent reflections from the ring against the walls. "Janice, your ring is absolutely beautiful. I can see that you are very much in love. Your face is glowing." She gave her sister a quick hug then turned to Roger. "Dad's in the den waiting for you."

While Betty and Roy took the kids off to play in the living room, Roger and Janice headed for the den. Despite the reassurances by everyone, he was still very nervous. It wasn't every day one asked a woman's father for her hand in marriage.

"Will you relax. Father knows why you're here and is very pleased. So you can stop sweating." She gave his arm a gentle squeeze to reassure him. The contact had a very strong effect on both of them.

"I'm just being paranoid, I know. Thanks for the pep talk. The squeeze was a nice touch too." He managed to settle down some as he approached the den, but now another emotion surged through his veins.

Desire.

It was very evident that Janice was feeling the same emotion. Her face looked strangely flushed, as if she had just run a couple of blocks. Both of them needed to get a grip on their feelings.

"You're welcome, although I don't think the squeeze was such a good idea. My stomach feels like it's full of a bunch of very active butterflies." She placed her hand across her stomach to emphasize her point.

"I know exactly how you feel. Looks like we're going to get to state our intent sooner rather than later. Here comes your dad." He pulled slightly apart from Janice then extended his hand as Dr. Peterson motioned for them to come inside.

As usual, Frank Peterson had a firm, yet reassuring grip.

"Welcome, Roger. Come in and have a seat on the couch. I take it this trip has something to do with Janice and you? Please, relax. I promise that I won't give you a hard time." As Frank took a seat on a deep burgundy wing chair, Roger moved to sit on the floral print love seat.

Taking a glance around the small room, he decided he like the intimate décor. Hardwood floors, covered with a dark oriental carpet, medium brown paneling on the walls, with white molding along the top. With dark furniture, shelves, and soft lighting, it had a very relaxing effect on his nerves.

"Sir, as you are probably aware, I am very much in love with your daughter. We have just come from a romantic dinner in Eastern Passage. I gave her a ring and proposed." At this point, Janice held up her hand, revealing the sparkling diamond ring. "She has accepted."

"It's wonderful that you two finally found each other. Both of you have been through some tough times. I am pleased with Janice's choice of a companion and will do whatever I can to help you both. Whatever you need, just let me know." Frank smiled fondly at his daughter then came to examine her ring. As he took her hand, she suddenly found tears standing in her eyes.

"Sorry, Daddy, I'm being a crybaby. I'm just so happy I can't keep the tears out of my eyes." She gave a couple of sniffs then her father pressed a handkerchief into her hand.

"Honey, it's normal to get emotional about something like this. This is one of the most important decisions you will ever make. You know, your mom was the same way. Tears came easily to her, whenever she was touched by something. You don't need to feel embarrassed by tears, they mean you have a tender heart."

Roger was watching the exchange between the two of them, and he felt his own eyes grow suspiciously moist. He realized he was one very lucky man. Janice was a very special, spiritual woman. He also realized that his nervousness had disappeared.

CHAPTER EIGHTEEN

For the next couple of hours, they discussed the details of the pending wedding. It was agreed that they would be married on the 15 of September. That would give them all enough time to organize everything. Frank would pay for the wedding. Betty agreed to take care of the caterers, invitations, as well as helping with the wedding attire. Roger's uncle would be notified to see if he wanted to contribute to the preparations as well.

Frank and Roger decided to go out on the patio for a few minutes for a man-to-man talk. His nerves had settled, replaced by a calm assurance that their plans would go well.

"You look more relaxed. How long can you get off for the honeymoon, son?"

"Probably about a week. I'm still involved with the drug smuggling case. Speaking of it, your brother is involved, sir. It will be difficult for Janice and for you. I'm going to hire someone to keep the media away from both of you. It's Janice I'm really worried about." He looked rather pensive as he looked into Frank's hazel eyes.

"Don't worry about me. I've suspected for months now that he has been dealing in drugs. It hurts me a lot, but I don't plan on it ruining my life. Janice, on the other hand, has a tender heart. I guess you know this already, don't you? A bit of security for her might be a good idea. I can pay for a security guard if you'd like."

"That's very generous of you, but I think I've got it covered. Let's talk about something a bit more cheerful, like my pending marriage to your daughter." Roger gazed into Frank's eyes. They smiled at each other, and Roger thought about how much he was going to like having Frank as a member of his family.

While they were discussing the details of the coming wedding, Janice, her sister, and the children were in the living room. It was a productive evening with preparations under way for the coming wedding. It was hard to say who was more excited. Janice and Roger. Or Janice's niece, Amy.

"So he finally asked you to marry him, sis." Betty took her sister's hand and admired the engagement ring.

"I knew he would, sooner or later. He's not hard to read. I hope I can sleep tonight, my stomach is so full of butterflies." Janice took her sister's hands in hers.

"That's normal, believe me. When I was engaged to Roy, I couldn't relax the week before the wedding, but once I saw him at the altar waiting for me, my nerves suddenly disappeared. It'll be like that for you too, honey." Both of them were rather teary eyed by now.

On Sunday, Roger went to church with the Petersons, although he found it hard to concentrate on the sermon. Janice sat next to him, jamming his thoughts. He felt that his life was going to be a lot richer, more meaningful, now that he had Janice to love and to cherish. Even the thought of going back to work didn't get him as uptight as before.

Monday morning dawned clear and warm. Sunlight's rays streamed through Roger's bedroom window. His alarm sent out its loud blare, rousing him from a sound sleep. His dream about Janice brought a contented smile to his face as he sat up in bed. He groaned when he saw the readout on the bedside clock. 6:00 a.m. Swinging his legs to the floor, he made his way into the bathroom to prepare for his day. Something inside told him that today was going to anything but normal.

An hour later, he pulled into the parking lot of the police station. Once inside, he made his way to the locker room to change. Several officers smiled at him, a few even gave him a slap on the back. Once he had his uniform on, he made his way to the briefing room. As he entered the small blue-walled room, a group of his colleagues began to applaud.

What was going on? Why was he getting all this attention?

He took his seat next to his partner, Peter Butler. The staff sergeant moved up to the small podium set up in front of a large blackboard. The board was covered with pictures of suspects and other information concerned with the pursuit of those wanted by the police in Nova Scotia.

"Gentlemen." Again there was a loud burst of laughter at the term he used. "As of today, I am happy to report that the drug ring operating in Avonvale is about to be broken up." He waited as there was a spattering of applause. "We have a couple of the key players in custody. And we have a signed confession by Jason Cox. Jason was Boyd Peterson's right hand man and has named him in the confession as the kingpin." He turned and received several high-fives from the men gathered in the room.

He came back down to earth when Peter added, tongue-in-cheek, "Don't give him too much praise, men. If his head gets much bigger, he won't fit through the door." He looked at Roger with raised eyebrows. That brought a round of laughter from the officers present.

"As of now I can still get my hat on, but thanks for the warning, partner. I'm just grateful we are on the winning team. You guys are the best." His high-five with Peter made a loud smacking sound in the small confines of the room. A couple of the others hooted in laughter.

"Okay, enough fun. I have just obtained a search warrant for Peterson's property. At 9:00 a.m., we are going to be knocking on his door. Now as to other business, we need to watch for speeders along Shore Road. There have been several complaints from local residents of young people out joyriding. Keep your eyes open, and have a good day. Dismissed." The staff sergeant came over to Roger as he prepared to leave for his beat.

"You have a minute, Abbott?"

"Yes, sir. What can I do for you?"

"First, I'd like to thank you for a job well done. And I'd like you to head up the search of Boyd Peterson's place today. If he is involved, and I'd bet my badge that he is, I'd like to see him behind bars. I have been blessed with a good group of men, and you are one of the best, Officer Abbott. That's all for now. Good luck."

The two of them headed out into the bright late July morning. The sun reflected off the light bar on the roof of their cruiser. Within minutes, they were on the road, checking the community for anything that needed attention.

"What was the little pep talk with MacDonald about? Did he chew you out for taking that risk with Cox the other night?" Personally, Peter felt Roger had come through in a big way, proving to everyone he had good instincts.

"He wasn't upset, on the contrary, he was very pleased by the latest turn of events. And"—here he raised his eyebrows to emphasize his point—"he wanted me to head up the search of Boyd Peterson's house."

"That's cool. You deserve it. Like I said before, I'm here to protect you from yourself, just in case you get a swelled head."

"I appreciate that. Now we need to have a plan of attack as we go to Boyd's place. We need at least five men, three for the trucking company, two for his home. Would you come with me to his house, Peter?"

"Let's go for it. If I remember, didn't you have a run-in with him about four years ago?" Peter looked over at him as he drove along Shore Road.

"It was a time that I'd rather forget. Boyd was implicated in the drug trade in Halifax, and at the same time, my wife, Anna, was killed in a car accident. There was no hard evidence, so he walked. He's not going to walk this time."

Peter looked at his friend, seeing the determination in his eyes as well as a firm resolve to see this through to the end.

"I know he won't slip through our fingers this time. Not with the confessions of his top men." Peter, too, was just as determined to nail Boyd Peterson. His own son had been approached by some of the drug dealers. He was grateful that his twelve-year-old son David had not been influenced by the lure of drugs.

They made their routine checks of the neighborhoods of the town. As it got closer to the time to search Boyd Peterson's place, Roger called the station, asking for backup for the operation. He fingered the dog-eared search warrant in his shirt pocket. They approached Shore Road, close to Boyd's Transfer. Peter glanced at the fluorescent hands of his wrist watch.

With a nod to his partner, he added, "Let's go, it's eight fifty."

Roger pulled the police cruiser over to the side of the road near the transfer company. Several more cruisers pulled into the parking lot. A couple of officers made their way to his car.

"What's the plan, Abbott?" Two constables stood near him as he shut the car door. "You said you needed to search the transfer company. What are we looking for?"

"Anything unusual. Did you bring the dog?" At their quick nod, he continued, "If they have hidden drugs, old Rex will sniff them out. See you in about an hour. Good luck."

While the three men made their way to the shipping company, Roger and Peter walked down the gravel path toward the house. It was hidden from the road by several tall trees, making it an ideal place to carry out illegal activity. Once they were among the trees, Roger saw a large Cape Cod-style house with a bright red door. He watched as Peter moved ahead of him into the wooden steps.

Peter pulled the door knocker. The sound sounded hollow against the weathered wood. Both of them waited, wondering if Boyd was home.

The door swung open, revealing Boyd's girlfriend, Sara.

"Can I help you officers? Is everything okay?" She looked from Roger to Peter for an explanation. As Roger held up the search warrant, her expression changed. She definitely looked wary.

"We have a warrant to search this house. We have reason to believe that Boyd Peterson is dealing in drugs. Several of the men we have in custody have fingered him. Is Boyd home, ma'am?"

"He's in the den, Officer Abbott. You and your companion, Officer Butler, may come in." With a search warrant, she didn't really have a choice.

Reluctantly, she moved to the side so they could enter the large living room. Roger saw in just a glance that Boyd had money. Throughout the room, he noticed expensive mahogany furniture, paintings on the walls, as well as a beautiful oriental rug on the pale hardwood floor.

"You look vaguely familiar, Officer Abbott. Have we met before?" She peered a little closer, trying to see if he was someone she knew.

"I don't believe so. Maybe you've seen me around town. We really need to search your place."

Before the two of them could check out the living room, Boyd stepped into the room. He had entered so silently Roger had not heard his footfalls on the carpet. That was a bit unnerving.

"May I help you?" As he came closer to Roger, his eyebrows rose in question. "I know you from somewhere." He brought his hand up to his chin. "Abbott." He thought for a minute then his face took on a hard edge as he recognized the young officer. "Abbott, yes, I know you now. You're that upstart rookie cop who I had the misfortune of running into four years ago. And I saw you a couple of months ago at my brother's place. You're seeing his daughter Janice, aren't you? I've been trying to remember where I saw you before. What are you doing, coming back for a second try at me? You're wasting your time, there's no drugs here."

Roger saw the hard eyes, the defiant look. It was the same one he had seen on Jason Cox's face a few nights ago. "I have reason to believe that you have drugs on the premises. And no, I am not doing this to soothe my ego. And I don't feel that we are wasting our time. If you have nothing to hide, you won't mind if we take a look."

"Go ahead. If you want to waste your time, I won't stop you. I really need to attend to some business at my trucking company." He made a move toward the door.

Peter stopped him as he grabbed his briefcase from the small table near the entrance. "We are checking your company as well. Until we finish the search, you'll have to remain here. Sorry."

Both of them noticed Boyd's face redden as he tried to get control of his temper. "This is an outrage. Sara and I have nothing to hide. I'm not under arrest, am I?" He was determined to give them a hard time.

"I'm sorry you feel that way. However, it's the law. And no, you're not under arrest." Roger turned toward the den, whispering under his breath, "Yet."

Boyd Peterson stood off to one side as they went into the small den. With beige walls, green furniture, and flowered curtains at the single window, it had an earthy, welcoming appearance. Peter went to the large oak desk. Looking under the green blotter, he moved on to the small laptop computer. Pushing the *on* button, he waited as the unit booted up. Once the desktop picture appeared, he called Boyd in.

"We need to check your files. Could you please open any files you have on your computer?"

"Very well. As I said before, you're wasting your time." With a quick tap on the keyboard, he opened the personal files. As he had said, there was nothing out of the ordinary. Peter felt a shaft of disappointment. This was going to be a bit harder than he had thought.

Roger had made his way into the large dining room. It ran the length of the house. With light birch walls, red carpet, and deep cheery wood tables, it had an intimate feel to it. The wall facing him was partially taken up by floor to ceiling book cases. In the middle of the wall there was a large stone fireplace which had had a wide oak mantle running across the top of it. To the left of the bookcase was an open area with a red wing chair in the corner.

As Roger approached the bookcase, admiring the eclectic collection of books, he gaze fell to the bottom row. At the far end were several hard-covered books about law. *Principles of Law, Crime in Canada*, just to name a few. He had to cover a smile when he thought of Boyd Peterson reading law books.

The Petersons were talking in low tones in the other room, so he continued his perusal of the large bookcase. Just before he turned away from the unit, he glanced at the deep red carpet. Roger felt a flash of excitement as his sharp eyes caught a smudge of something on the dark fabric. It looked suspiciously like dirt.

Once he was on his knees and he had closer look, he knew exactly what he had seen.

It was a large footprint.

And to make things even more interesting, part of that footprint disappeared under the bottom of the shelving unit.

When he finally got to his feet, he heard someone behind him. Turning, he came face-to-face with Boyd's girlfriend, Sara.

"You won't find anything in here, Officer Abbott. This room is not used very often, so what you see is basically what you get."

"That may be. However, I did find a dirty footprint on the carpet." When he pointed to the spot, he noticed Sara's face go pale. If nothing was amiss, why did she look worried?

"Peter, come in here. I think you might find what I discovered quite interesting," Roger yelled over his shoulder.

While he waited for his partner, Roger thought about the strange smudge on the floor. Then he thought about the possibility that someone had moved that book shelf. His eyebrows rose as realization hit him. He had heard about some of these old houses having passages down to the beach. Apparently, they had been used years ago by rumrunners.

Of course. It had to be the answer.

When Peter joined him, he was excited, "I have a feeling there's something hidden behind this shelf unit. Take a look at this footprint." He pointed to the smudge of dirt. Sara had left the room, so they were by themselves.

"Now that's interesting. Are you thinking the same thing I am? A secret passageway?"

"Exactly." Roger moved to the edge of the row of shelves then ran his fingers along the wall by the wooden storage unit. As he dropped his hand lower toward the bottom, he felt a small button like device. A gentle press on the thing caused the shelf to move. There was a loud clunk then the shelves began to slide to their left. Once the wall was exposed, they had their answer. A small door was set into the floor, leading to someplace beyond the house.

"What do you think you're doing? You have no right moving my furniture around!" Boyd stood there, hands on his hips. Anger creased his face. When he saw the door exposed, his expression changed very dramatically.

His face showed surprise, and something else.

Was it fear?

Peter thought it rather amusing that he had the nerve to tell them they couldn't do their job. The hint of fear that they had seen was gone. It was replaced by his trademark arrogant attitude. Peter had to admit, he was good. Never show weakness to your adversary.

Were they considered his adversaries?

Probably.

"Do you know anything about this door Mr. Peterson? Why is there dirt on the carpet?" Roger waited for him to come up with a plausible reason for the concealed doorway in the floor under the shelf unit.

"I have never seen that door before, so no, I don't have any idea what it means. The dirt got there the other day when I was trying to move a large plant from the room. The container fell over, and I stepped in the dirt." Boyd came over and inspected the door. "You never know what you'll find in these old houses, do you?"

"Then you won't mind if we take a look behind the door." Roger saw the fleeting look of nervousness pass across the man's face then the mask was back in place again. "If you would stand over there, please."

"Very well." He didn't look very happy.

Peter approached the small wooden door, grabbing the brass doorknob. With a sharp upward pull on the handle, the door opened with a squeak from the worn, rusted hinges. It fell back against the floor with a loud bang. Both men looked into the dark tunnel that was exposed. The long narrow steps led downward into the darkness of the cliff. Lanterns were situated along the length of the exposed tunnel to act as a guide to anyone inside. The faint sound of surf could be heard in the distance, somewhere below them.

"Let's take a look inside. I've heard stories about these old tunnels, but I've always wondered if there were any around here." As Roger moved down the steps into the interior, the air felt cooler, almost damp. Water seeped from the wall to his left. Moving a bit further down the steps cut into the gentle slope, he noticed a dark alcove off to his right. "Peter, does that look like boxes to you?"

"It's boxes, all right." Peter pulled a small LED flashlight from his pocket, shining the bright beam on the stack of crates that nestled against the wall. "Take a look at the addresses on these boxes. They're all pharmacies in Avonvale. I'd like to see Boyd Peterson explain his way out of this one." As he continued to examine the drugs, he saw several boxes of prescription drugs. Some of the drugs had been opened, obviously for someone's use. It was obvious that this was the destination for the missing drugs. Near the stash, he could see an old steel safe.

"It looks like we have grounds to take Boyd in for questioning. There's a whole series of prints leading into the house." Roger turned, coming face-to-face with Boyd Peterson. Boyd looked upset enough to chew nails.

"What's all this stuff?"

"I think you can drop the innocent act. These are stolen drugs from local drugstores. As of now, you can consider yourself under arrest. Let's go back to the house." Once inside the house again, Roger looked at Boyd as well as his girlfriend and went on. "Boyd Peterson, you are under arrest for hiding stolen drugs, for the purpose of trafficking. As of now all of your assets will be frozen. This house is considered a crime scene, so will be taped off. You may remain silent." He recited the rest of the declaration, while the man in front of him paled.

"I have nothing to say. I'm calling my lawyer. This is a setup. I don't have any idea how the drugs came to be there You have no right to shut down my trucking company."

"You're making a big mistake, officer. One that you'll live to regret! Boyd hasn't done anything wrong." Sara was very upset, her mouth drawn into a thin line. She moved quickly to her boyfriend's side. Turning toward Roger, she raised her hand to strike his face.

Peter grabbed her arm, whispering in her ear, "I wouldn't do that, unless you want to be charged with assaulting a police officer." His voice apparently got through to her, for she lowered her arm to her side. However, she was seething inside.

"Sara, let it go. Call my lawyer and Sam. He'll know what to do." He seemed to be very calm on the outside, but Roger knew he was angry. He was also very dangerous.

Sara disappeared into the office under the pretense of getting some money for transportation. However, as she opened the desk drawer, she smiled at what lay on the bottom of the compartment. With a quick movement, she grabbed the small black revolver, hiding it in her pocket. In only a moment she was back next to Boyd and the others.

While Roger called for some help to recover the stolen drugs, Peter led Boyd out of the house. Sara was told she could not stay in the house, so she was forced to go stay at a friend's place. She followed, tears spilling from her eyes. She looked sad, but there was something else there too.

Determination.

CHAPTER NINETEEN

Once Boyd Peterson was in custody, he was charged with multiple crimes. Added to the drugs that Roger had found, the men at the transfer company had located drugs hidden in some electronics. Because of the seriousness of the acts, and because he was a flight risk, bail would probably be denied. Boyd's lawyer monitored their questions, occasionally advising his client to say nothing. The next couple of hours were spent doing up reports, interrogating Boyd Peterson, and planning their next move. It was an exhausting schedule, but Roger felt vindicated now that Boyd was in the slammer.

The rest of the day was filled with the usual things that police in a cruiser did. After the excitement of the morning, the rest of the day dragged. The next couple of days were also rather boring.

Roger had Wednesday to Saturday off, so he decided to see Janice. Luckily she was also off on Thursday, so he planned to take her for a drive to Lawrencetown Beach. The first week in August was proving to be very hot, so a trip to the beach was the perfect answer. It would also give them both some down time. He didn't know if he could handle another month of the jitters. No doubt, Janice was feeling the same way. He smiled when he thought of her.

On Thursday, he drove into the city to pick Janice up for their 10:00 a.m. date. He had packed a small lunch for later in the afternoon. As he swung into the subdivision, he saw a cluster of teens playing street hockey just up from the Peterson home. Somewhere nearby, a lawnmower could be heard, its engine sounding like a hive of buzzing bees. Pulling up behind a silver Lexus, Roger slid from the hot leather seat.

Before he had even reached the house, the door swung open and he was face-to-face with Janice. Her beauty stalled his breath in his chest. Dressed in a pair of blue designer jeans, a yellow blouse, with hoop earrings, she looked stunning.

"Wow. You look wonderful." Roger leaned in and kissed her cheek. She smelled like citrus. Her eyes held his, the deep violet drawing him in.

"Thanks. You don't look so bad yourself. What's on the agenda for today? I heard about my uncle. I'm glad you were able to arrest him. Now Amy can relax when she goes to school. Dad will be okay, although I know he was really worried about his brother. And just for the record, Roger, I never doubted that you would eventually catch Uncle Boyd."

"I'm glad Boyd and his men are off the street too. There are still a few of them to nab, but in the next day or two, we'll have it all covered. I know you've been worried about your niece. She'll be okay, I'm sure. She's a smart girl." He paused for a moment then continued, "Thought we'd take a little trip out to Lawrencetown. Maybe walk along the beach. Okay?"

"I'd like that. My nerves are on edge, maybe that will help me relax."

Roger gave her a shrewd glance, aware of the things she didn't say. It didn't take a rocket scientist to figure out that she was nervous about the coming wedding. They were more alike than he had originally thought.

"Prewedding jitters, eh?"

She gave him a searching look then said, "How did you know that."

A burst of laughter escaped him, "Because I have the exact same problem. Let's go. I can't wait to feel the coolness of sand between my toes." He moved past her to say goodbye to her father who stood just inside the door. His face was radiant as he glanced from him to his daughter.

"Have fun, you two. Janice, did you pack sunscreen?"

"Yes, dad. I've got everything except the kitchen sink in this purse. I'll be back around 4:00 p.m." She gave him a quick hug then turned to join Roger on the sidewalk.

"The idea of running barefoot through the sand sounds heavenly. Let's do it."

"I've got some food in the hamper, blankets, and a couple of frisbees. We can plan some, if you want." He tried to help her forget her nervousness. Hopefully, he could forget his own.

"Lots of time. I want to get rid of these butterflies, if I can. Betty told me she was the same way then she told me when she saw Roy, the nerves disappeared. I just have to survive the next month."

"Uncle George told me the same thing last night when I was talking to him. We're going to have a good time and forget all the other stuff. Just the sand and surf."

After pulling open the door for her, he helped her get settled in the seat. Then he went around to his side. Once behind the wheel, he pulled out into the street and headed for Cole Harbour. The traffic was light, the trip made in about ten minutes. As they moved along the old highway on their way to Lawrencetown, he turned the stereo on. A song by Taylor Swift filled the interior of the car, and Roger began to hum along.

"That sounds good to me. And," she added, "you have a really nice voice. Very relaxing." She leaned back against the seat, enjoying the drive and his soothing voice.

They wouldn't have been so relaxed if they had taken the time to look in the rearview mirror. A large black luxury car was following a discreet distance behind them. When Roger pulled off to get gas at a small service station, the car passed. Once they were on the road again, it pulled out of a driveway and began to follow them again. They were now on the old highway that would take them to the beach. The car behind them was about four car lengths back, so Roger didn't pay any special attention to it.

With his window rolled down, he could feel the cool ocean breeze blowing into the car. The smell of the salt air was invigorating. He looked over at Janice, who was watching him. "That breeze feels nice. I can't wait to have a run down the beach. Maybe I'll give you a race." Her voice held a definite challenge.

"Do I feel a challenge from the lady? You've got yourself a deal as soon as we get to the beach." He smiled at her, knowing his gaze would get her heart racing.

While they were bantering back and forth, the car behind them began to speed up. It was now only a car length back of them. Roger glanced in the rearview mirror a split second before the other car rammed them from behind. Their car jerked with the impact, throwing Roger against the back of the seat.

"What does that guy think he's doing? If he wants to pass, why doesn't he just go around us?" As Roger looked in the mirror, he motioned to Janice, "Does that car look familiar to you? Large Town Car, tinted windows. I've had a few run-ins with it myself, so I'd like to know who owns it."

When she looked over the backseat, her face went white.

"It's the same car that followed me a while ago. When Dad had to take me to my aunt's place. Roger, I'm scared. This means my uncle is trying to get rid of us. Even in jail, he still has the power to terrorize us. How are we going to outrun a car that powerful? What if they have guns?" Her face was pinched, her eyes wide with fear.

Both of them were thinking of the accidents four years ago.

"I've been trying to figure out a way to outsmart them. We need to stay as calm as possible. We sure can't outrun them. Their car is a lot more powerful than this one. Hold on, here they come again." He concentrated on driving, his body slammed hard against the seat as the other car hit them from behind. He could hear the scraping sound as the two cars collided.

While Janice had her hands braced against the dash, he gripped the wheel, trying to hold the car on the road. They swerved closer to the gravel at the side. She was keeping a very close eye on the bank. He was watching the road ahead of him. The other car pulled out and moved alongside them. It was useless trying to identify anyone, the windows were tinted. There was no plate on the front of the vehicle. Out of the corner of his eye he saw the car make its move. Almost in slow motion, it swung close to his Chevy, striking the front fender. He held the wheel tight, fighting the pressure as the larger vehicle tried to force them off the road. It took all his strength to keep the wheel from being jerked out of his hands.

Janice screamed.

His muscles burned from the effort required to hold the car in place.

With his window rolled down, he could hear the roar of the cars' engines, the low humming sound of the tires on the pavement. As the two cars moved along, he also heard the sound of metal grinding against metal. It reminded him of chalk being dragged across a blackboard.

Finally, the car dropped behind them again. He looked over at her, trying to convey his love through his tender expression, when he would have preferred to put an arm around her. "Are you okay? I know, I'm scared too, but I'm not going down without a fight." When she gave him a nod, he said in a terse voice, "Grab the cell phone from my belt and call 911. Give them our location. We're near the hill leading up to the beach in Lawrencetown and need police backup. Tell them the men might be armed and could work for Boyd Peterson. Okay?"

Janice answered, her voice trembling, "I trust you and know that if there's a way out of this, you'll find it." She then reached over, removing the small phone from the clip at Roger's waist. While she dialed, he formulated a plan of escape for them. Time was running out. His old car wouldn't take many more of these assaults. He could feel his arms aching from the strain of holding the steering wheel so tight.

Ahead of them was a steep hill with a large house off to the right. The road passed a salt marsh, with a small inlet on the left, and a small beach to the right of them. He didn't like the look of the embankment on that side, or the telephone poles. This section of highway had several large potholes that could pose a problem.

As they approached that section of the highway, the car behind them made its move. The driver again pulled out and moved up parallel to his Chevy. He could see the Lincoln starting its swing toward them. Time for him to try the plan he had been forming in his mind.

"What are you planning Roger? I'm really scared we're going to end up in the ditch, or worse!" She didn't voice the words that he himself had in the back of his mind.

"If I time this right, and that's a big if, when I hit overdrive, the car should pull ahead of Boyd's car. Hold on, Janice, here they come again!"

If this didn't work, they were in big trouble!

As the Lincoln swerved toward them, Roger began to put his foot down on the accelerator. When the other car was several feet from his fender, he tramped down hard on the gas pedal. Somehow, he managed to avoid the holes in the cracked pavement.

Would the car have enough power?

The Chevy suddenly lunged forward as overdrive kicked in. Both of them were pressed hard against the seat as the car shot ahead. Out of the corner of his eye, he could see the bigger car almost against their rear fender.

It was going to be very close.

He could see the tears in Janice's violet eyes, the strained look on her face. She was trembling. Forcing himself back to the task at hand, he gripped the steering wheel so hard his knuckles turned white. A slight bump indicated the other car had grazed the back of his car.

He felt the back of the sedan slide toward the ditch. The back right tire dropped into the gravel shoulder and rocks spewed out, clattering against the bottom of the car. They continued to skid until he was able to regain control. It had been a very narrow escape.

"We did it. Take a look to see if they have been able to correct their steering, Janice." Roger began to breathe a bit easier. He took a quick look in the rearview mirror.

"Their car is heading toward the ditch. Your plan was brilliant. I can hear sirens in the distance, so we should have help soon." Her voice sounded faint.

After slowing down, he pulled over to the side of the road to watch the car behind them. The larger, heavier Lincoln was a lot harder to steer away from the side of the road. He could see the driver frantically trying to correct his mistake. For a minute, it appeared he would be successful then the front right tire hit a hole in the pavement.

It seemed that the steering wheel was almost wrenched from his hands as the car's movement carried it into the gravel shoulder of the road. The front dropped into the scrub grass at the edge of the embankment then it slid slowly down the slope, hitting the bottom.

After the car stopped, the only thing that could be heard was the soft background sounds of surf on the nearby beach.

With blue and red lights flashing, an RCMP cruiser came toward them from the beach, while a second car pulled up next to the accident scene behind them. As Roger climbed from the car, an officer approached the disabled car. His legs were a bit shaky, so he had to take a deep breath and lean against his sedan.

"What happened here?" An RCMP officer from the car near them addressed him in curt tones. "Someone called to report a car chase, is that correct?"

"My fiancé called it in. My name is Roger Abbott. I'm with the police in Avonvale and am involved in the apprehension of a drug ring near Sheet Harbour. Apparently some of his men that are still free decided to force us off the road."

"That's what she said. I remember the drug ring, we helped with some of the arrests." The middle-aged man had a thin moustache, thick gray eyebrows, and dark glasses. His name tag said his name was Fred Summers. He looked toward the other car. "Who are the two in the Lincoln?"

"Never seen them before, Officer Summers."

By now, the two had crawled out of the car and were scrambling up the slope to the shoulder of the road. An officer was waiting for them, his gun drawn. That police cruiser was sitting on the shoulder nearby, red and blue lights flashing on the roof's light bar. He could see the anxious expression pass across the face of the younger man. The thugs had weapons which were quickly taken from them.

Janice had slowly emerged from the car, and he looked over the top of the roof at her. His heart nearly stalled when he saw the tears in her eyes, the shaking of her body as shock set in.

"Excuse me, I need to see to my fiancé, I think she's in shock." Without another word, he rounded the car and took her into his arms. This was what he had wanted to do earlier, but couldn't.

"Hey, I'm here, it's going to be okay. Just take a couple of deep breaths. I'm sorry you had to go through this, honey, really sorry. It's over now, they're in custody." He could feel her shaking as he held her then he felt the wetness of her tears against his face. "I love you, Janice, and would do anything to protect you."

"I know you would, and you did just now. I was so scared. Even though I know in my heart we're okay, I can't stop shaking. Just hold me for a few minutes until I get under control."

"As long as you need me to." His own voice sounded strained, his eyes suddenly burned with unshed tears.

Their little interlude was interrupted when Officer Summers came around the front of the sedan. "Sorry to barge in, but I need you to identify the car. It was obvious they tried to force you off the road, there's black paint and dents all along the front fender of your vehicle." He noticed that Janice was shaking. "Is she going to be okay? Maybe you should take her to the hospital and have her checked out after."

"That might not be a bad idea. I'll be right with you." Looking at Janice, he asked in a soft worried voice, "Are you up to staying for a few more minutes? We have to identify the car as belonging to Boyd Peterson."

"I can stay for a few more minutes, yes. What I'd really like is a few pills to settle my nerves then a rest. This has been a rather hair-raising trip." Somehow, she managed to give him a slight smile. She could get through this. "It's okay. I'll survive."

As they walked along the gravel shoulder together, she looked at the two men standing next to the police officer. Both had their backs to them and were being read their rights. When they heard their footsteps, they turned.

Janice gasped.

"What is it, Janice? Do you know these men?" Roger noticed by her expression that she had recognized one of them.

"The younger one with blonde hair is Peter Boyce, my ex-boyfriend. I sure didn't expect to run into him again."

By now they were at the site with the men, and Peter Boyce's eyes widened when he saw Janice standing in front of him. "Janice, what are you doing here? You were in that car we were chasing?" He looked shocked that he had put her life in danger. "Looks like you have moved on." He gave Roger a quick assessment, his eyes narrowing. He recognized him as well.

"Yes. I see you haven't improved your choice of friends since I last saw you. This is my fiancé, Roger Abbott. Do you realize you almost killed us, Peter? You work for my uncle Boyd, don't you?" Her expression hardened as she waited for her ex-boyfriend to answer.

"Yeah, I work for your uncle. He put out a hit on your boyfriend here. We meet again, Roger. Seems like you are a very worthy opponent. Where did you learn to drive like that? Touché, Roger, I'm impressed." Here he offered a mock bow. "I hope you will both be very happy." The last words were laced with sarcasm.

"Enough chitchat. Both of you are under arrest, so let's go. Mr. Abbott, we need you to come to the station in Cole Harbour to fill out some paperwork. You'd best take your fiancé to the hospital before she passes out." With that, the officers loaded the two thugs into a waiting cruiser.

As he looked over at Janice, she seemed to wilt and sag against him.

"Come on, we've got to get you to a doctor. Just lean against me." Roger's concern escalated when he noticed her washed out face and pinched lips.

After getting her settled in the car, he turned around and headed back to Dartmouth. As he passed the police cruisers, one of the officers gave him a wave. A quick peek at Janice showed she was resting, her head turned toward the window. Despite her strength, he knew the ordeal of the past half hour had taken a toll on her. If he was being honest with himself, he was a little shaky too.

It took a couple of trying hours before they got in to see a doctor in emergency. While there was nothing serious, the man had given Janice some pills to help relax her.

"Let's get you home so you can forget all about this afternoon. I know I'd like to forget about it and your uncle for a while. I'll support you if you feel faint."

"A nap should help, although I think it will be a while before I can forget the whole ordeal. I was scared, Roger."

"Me too. I was doing a lot of praying, I can tell you. We're almost home, honey." Boy, he liked calling her that.

As he pulled into the driveway at the Peterson home, he noticed that they had company. A small car sat just behind her father's Lexus, leaving a bit of space off to the side for his vehicle. He had just moved around to open her door when someone called out to them from the house. Turning, he saw Janice's sister Betty in the entrance. Concern was etched into her face as she saw her sister's ashen face.

"What's wrong with her, Roger? Did something happen when you two were at the beach? You look like you could use a hand." She came forward, taking her sister's arm. "Janice, it's okay, I've got you."

"I'll tell you when we get her inside. What she needs is a good rest. It's been an afternoon that I'd just as soon forget." He gave Betty a grim look, revealing just how upsetting the past hour had been for both of them.

Between the two of them, they succeeded in getting her to the couch in the living room. As soon as her head hit one of the flowered pillows, she sighed and turned on her side. In a matter of minutes, Janice was asleep.

"She's out like a light. Now, what happened out there? She looked so pale that I thought she was sick." Betty gazed down at her sister, concern showing on her face. Her frown brought Roger's attention back to her.

"We were almost forced off the road in Lawrencetown." He stopped when he heard Betty's sharp intake of breath. "One of Boyd's men tried to put us in the ditch, but I managed to outwit them. It's been a traumatic experience for her, so I took her to the hospital for something to help with the shock. She should sleep for a couple of hours. Betty, I was so scared we were going to end up in an accident. The police have the guys in custody, and I have to go in later to file against them."

"It seems like Uncle Boyd has a lot of friends on the outside. Is there any more danger to Janice, or to the rest of us, Roger? I knew he was into drugs, but I didn't think he would stoop to murdering his own family! I'm glad he's behind bars. Thank you for your dedication to seeing that justice is done. And for taking care of my sister." She had tears in her eyes, the drops hanging on her long lashes. She left the sentence unfinished.

"I'd give my life for your sister. She's the most precious thing in my life." He hesitated for a moment then added, "Is it okay to talk about this stuff? Are the kids around? I don't want to alarm them with talk of our ordeal this afternoon."

She saw the intensity of his feelings for Janice reflected in his eyes, in his fervent words. "Don't worry about the children. They are watching a pirate movie downstairs. They'll be busy for at least an hour. So what about my uncle?" Betty wanted some answers to calm her concerns about further danger to her family.

CHAPTER TWENTY

"Boyd won't be in any position to hurt anyone again, and neither will his so-called friends. They are all going to become very well acquainted with their prison cells pretty soon. As far as I'm concerned, it's too good for them!"

Betty looked into his eyes, seeing the fierce passion in their depths as well as evidence of the stress of the past couple of hours. He looked like he could use a good rest himself. Before she could comment further, her father came out of his study. When he saw Janice asleep on the couch and the pinched look in Roger's face, he knew something was very wrong.

"Why are you home so early and why is Janice asleep on the couch at two o'clock? And you son, look like you've been hit by a Mack truck. What happened?" He went over and gently brushed back some stray strands of hair from his daughter's face. When he straightened up, his eyebrows were raised as he waited for an answer.

When Roger had finished relating the experiences of the past couple of hours, he saw the tight line of Frank Peterson's mouth, the hard glint in his eyes. For a moment, he wondered if the anger would be directed at him then the doctor gave a disgusted remark about his wayward brother.

"I knew my brother was into drugs in a big way, but I didn't think he'd try to harm us. Although if I think back to the encounter we had several months ago, it shouldn't surprise me. He's always been a loner, tested the boundaries of decency. As sad as this makes me, I'm glad he's behind bars. It looks like his bad choices have finally caught up with him. I hope now he will have time to see what he's missed by being involved with drugs." His eyes told of the sadness he felt.

"One of his men implicated him in the drug smuggling ring. Other than rounding up a few strays, all of them are now behind bars. I should be going, I really need to unwind a bit." He saw the tears run down Betty's cheeks as he turned to look at her. The emotion in the room was so powerful, it could have been cut with a knife.

He moved to where Janice was still curled up on the couch. Bending over her still form, he brushed a couple of stray hairs away from her face, and then dropped a soft kiss on her cheek. Several seconds slipped past as he gazed down at her. It seemed like they were the only people in the room.

Betty's voice seemed to jar him from his private thoughts.

"She'll sleep for quite a while yet, Roger."

Turning, he looked into eyes that were wet with tears. "I was so scared that I was going to lose her today. I'd give up my career in a minute if I figured it would put her in danger." His voice had a note of resignation in it that Betty didn't miss.

"I know you love my sister very much, and I don't doubt for a minute that what you said is true. But you shouldn't have to make that choice. Life is full of insecurity as well as pain. All we can do is enjoy the moment and hold on to each other. Believe me, with Roy in the army, I know firsthand what it's like. So you don't need to feel guilty." Her compassion was written on her tear-stained face. "And by the look on your face, I think you should go home and get a good night's sleep. You look like you're going to pass out."

"Thank you. I think that's an excellent idea. I can't seem to stop my hands from shaking, so I won't be going home. I have to stop at the RCMP station to file against the guys who tried to force us off the road. Then I'll go to my uncle's place and crash on the bed in my old loft."

Roger didn't hear the others come up until Frank cleared his throat. "Listen to her, son. You've been through a harrowing experience, so get a good night's sleep. Do you work tomorrow?"

"No, sir." He heard Janice moan then she let out a soft cry. His heart seemed to cry out along with her. "What's wrong with her?"

"She's probably dreaming." Betty went over and draped a light blanket over her sister's body. She was still making those soft crying sounds. "The incident today probably made her remember the accident when our mom was killed."

"I'm sorry about today. Will she be okay?" Frankly, he was worried about her mental state after what Betty had just revealed.

"She doesn't talk to anyone about it. She'll be fine. We'll watch her, so you can go get some rest. We'll talk later."

Reluctantly, he said goodbye then left for his uncle's place. He was really worried about Janice. There wasn't much he could do but pray for her recovery at this point. Looking down at his hands as he clutched the steering wheel, he saw that they were still shaking. The incident with the Town Car as well as his worry over Janice were starting to show. It was a good thing that he had tomorrow off.

The incident at Lawencetown was forgotten as the month of August slipped by. He managed to do some work on his novel, but he was kept busy preparing for the coming trial of Boyd Peterson and his cohorts. A hearing was held to determine if Peterson and Cox would get bail. The answer was *no* because of the flight risk. Boyd remained defiant, although he was mostly bluster. It was very obvious now that he knew he would be spending a lot of time behind bars. He began to relax as the whole bunch of them had been rounded up and were now cooling their heels in various jail cells. When he thought about his coming wedding, a tender smile crossed his face. Both of them had decided they didn't want to wait another year. Because of their experiences together, and because their hearts were so in tune, they set the date of the wedding for September. Still, he was jittery, his nerves taut as he thought about the coming commitment. His uncle was going to take him to a clothing store so he could purchase his attire as well as plan for the coming honeymoon. To save time and gas, he decided to stay in the old loft above his uncle's garage.

Janice had recovered from her ordeal and was now kept busy preparing for the coming wedding. With encouragement from her family, she was able to move forward. The harrowing experience on the road to Lawrencetown was now just a faint memory. There were more important things to attend to. She didn't realize all the things one had to do to be ready for the big day. There were fittings, purchasing of clothes, and a myriad of other things. She was thankful Betty had the experience and could help her through the wedding maze. Despite all the advice and reassurances, Janice was still very nervous. As yet she hadn't talked to Roger about where they would go for their honeymoon. They had a week. All she knew was that his uncle George was arranging things. She hoped she could settle some of the butterflies that were taking up residence in her stomach.

She was sure it was going to be a long nerve-racking month.

Actually, the month went by quickly as the two of them made final preparations for the ceremony on September 15. The wedding was to be held at the Peterson's church, with the reception in the church hall. Caterers were in place, the guest list sent out, and the dresses were hanging in the closet in Janice's bedroom. Roger told her that his uncle had purchased tickets for a trip to Hawaii. Both of them were looking forward to spending time relaxing on the beach.

The morning of September 15 brought with it the promise of a perfect day for the wedding. Roger woke to birds singing in the trees outside, while the sun shone through the open curtains of the loft. Quickly, he headed into his uncle's house. Boy, was he nervous.

A short distance away at the Peterson's place, Janice, along with Betty and the children, were having a family gathering over breakfast. Despite all the assurances by her sister and support from Amy, she couldn't seem to banish those butterflies from her stomach. Her palms were sweaty, her pulse racing.

"How come your face is all flushed Aunt Janice? You look like you ran all the way down the street." Amy was very observant, her eyes showing concern as she looked at her.

"I'm not sick, honey. I'm nervous about the wedding, that's all." She gave her niece a hug.

"You don't need to be nervous. I know Roger will take really good care of you. You always have a big smile on your face whenever he's around." Amy glanced down at the engagement ring that glittered on the third finger of Janice's left hand. "And he looks really happy when you guys are together."

"Thanks for the advice. I'm looking forward to seeing you as my flower girl. I know that you will do a good job, Amy."

"It's going to be awesome. And you know what's really neat, Aunt Janice?"

"What's so neat about being flower girl, sweetie?"

"I get to see you and Uncle Roger get married. You guys were meant to be together. You'll look really pretty in your wedding dress."

"And you'll look beautiful in your pink dress. Ready?" Janice put an arm around the girl's shoulder, a tender expression on her face.

She nodded, "I'm ready."

They cleared away the dishes then Betty and Janice went down to the bedrooms to dress for the wedding at 11:00 a.m. at St. James church. Amy and Ben went to other rooms to get their clothes on. As Frank finished tidying up, there was a knock on the door. When he swung the heavy door open, two young women stood in front of him.

"You must be Jane and Marne. The women are all hidden in the second bedroom on your left. Just down that hall. While you get yourselves prettied up, I'll go pick up my tuxedo. I'll be back in about a half hour." Frank gave them a bright smile then grabbed his car keys. He was very pleased that his daughter had found a special young man. For the first time in months, he felt like whistling. With his brother in jail, he let himself relax. When he went outside, he found that his car was blocked in. A quick trip to see his daughter Betty produced her car keys.

In Janice's bedroom, there was a flurry of activity as the women prepared for the service a mere two hours away. The pink dresses were all laid out on the four-poster bed. The pink bridesmaids' dresses were long, with lace sleeves and white sashes at the waist. As Jane Peters and Marne French picked up their gowns, Betty moved to help her sister into the white satin wedding gown.

"You can relax, Janice. This will be one of the most special days in your life. Roger is head over heels in love with you, and I know once you see him you won't be nervous anymore. Trust me. I was just the same."

Janice gave her sister a faint grin, trying to cover her jitters. "I know I'm being silly. Oh, sis, this dress will knock Roger for a loop. It's so beautiful." As she went to stand in front of the floor length mirror, she turned around, "Can you help me with the zipper?"

With a lump in her throat, Betty's voice was barely a whisper "It's not just the dress. You are absolutely glowing. You will be a beautiful bride." Once the gown was fastened, she turned her sister to face the mirror once more. She hardly recognized the vision that stared back at her.

The only thing she could say was, "Wow."

The white satin dress had full sleeves, a lace overlay, and the gown just touching the floor. The fifteen-foot train was lace and curled around her feet. As she adjusted her hair, Betty came to her with the veil. Once it was in position, she put the white baby's breath along the edge of the headband. The effect was stunning.

"Perfect. Now, let's get the rest of the girls ready." Betty quickly helped Janice's friends from work with their pink gowns then slipped her own on. "I think I should check on Amy and Ben. Dad said he would get them ready. Amy was so excited when she heard she could wear a pink dress."

"I couldn't have a better flower girl, Betty."

The women grabbed their purses, checked their makeup, and then went out into the living room. Amy and Ben were waiting for them.

"Aunt Janice, you sure look pretty. Do you like my dress?" She twirled around in front of her aunt, the skirt of the pink gown billowing out around her.

"You look lovely, Amy. Pink suits you. Do you have the package with the rose petals in it? When I start up the aisle, you sprinkle the petals on the carpet in front of me. All set?"

"I'm ready. It's going to be so cool."

When Janice turned and saw her father, she stared at the transformation. He wore black slacks, a black jacket with satin edging. With a crisp white shirt and pink tie, he looked quite handsome. "You look great, Dad. I'm going to have to watch you around all those widows at the wedding today." She was impressed with how he had changed and couldn't help teasing him about it.

Frank actually blushed.

While the Petersons were preparing across the lake, Roger was making an effort to change into his tuxedo. With Peter Butler for best man and his uncle as the MC for the reception, he felt as ready as could be expected. Now that the day had arrived, he fought his ongoing battle with nerves. Besides his stomach being in knots, his palms were sweaty. And he didn't like wearing suits. The ties always seemed to choke him. He would be more comfortable in a T-shirt and a pair of faded blue jeans. He smiled at the reaction he would get if he showed up wearing that getup.

"That will definitely get Janice's attention. You look good in a black tux, son." Uncle George was very aware of his bad case of nerves. He thought of his own wedding, eons ago now, and smiled. "Relax. It's not every day a man gets to marry the girl of his dreams. And just so that you don't think you're alone, I was the same way when I got hitched to your aunt. It's perfectly normal, and when you see Janice, all the jitters will go away."

"I hope so, Uncle."

The three men moved out into the living room. All three wore black tuxedos with white shirts and pink ties. As they moved to the door, Peter gave his friend a quick glance, "Did you bring the rings? They were sitting on the top of your dresser."

Roger's face turned red, and he gave them a sheepish grin, "Thanks for reminding me. My mind seems to be somewhere else today. If my head wasn't fastened on, I'd probably forget it too. They're still on the dresser. I'll be right back." He turned and disappeared into the bedroom.

"I thought I was a nervous wreck when I got married. Roger definitely needs a best man. He takes nervousness to a whole new level, George." He chuckled as he thought of his friend and partner. As a cop, he was unflappable, as a groom, no. He was amused by Roger's feelings of unease.

"A few nerves never hurt anybody, Peter. It will disappear when he sees his bride. And he always was a bit forgetful. You'll do fine, you're a good friend. I'm so glad you were able to solve the drug gang problem. He's been stewing over that for months now. Thank goodness he doesn't have that distraction anymore. This is going to be the most special day of his life. Janice is a special woman, just what he needs." George spoke with passion, his love for Roger shining in his weathered face.

"I'm glad that's all behind us too. He's been worried about Janice because it was her uncle who was the gang leader. I'm happy for him. He deserves a break in his life." He glanced down at his silver watch. "Well, I guess we better head out, it's less than an hour until the wedding."

Peter made sure his friend had all that he would need then the men headed out into the bright September sun. It was a warm Indian summer day, a slight breeze blew, and birds chirped happily in the nearby maple trees. Those trees were just starting to turn orange. They approached Roger's red Chevy. It had been freshly waxed and gleamed brightly in the morning sun.

"Could you drive, Uncle? My hands won't stop shaking. My mind definitely won't be on my driving, that's for sure." He handed the keys to his uncle, who gave his shoulder a gentle squeeze. When Peter clasped his shoulder in a show of support, he turned and grinned at his friend.

"And I wonder what your mind will be on. Probably a certain blonde waiting at church."

"Yeah." It was only one word, but it spoke volumes.

As they drove the short distance to the church, Roger lay back against the head rest, hoping to relax a bit. That lasted until they pulled into the church parking lot. The side lot was almost full, with several people milling about outside. He felt his pulse flutter. His uncle parked the car in front of the church, in the place of honor, they scrambled out, and then went inside the building.

Roger stared in awe at the interior of the Gothic architecture of the church. Red carpet ran the length of the pews, across the front, and then up the steps leading to the altar. He took in the special decorations someone had set up for his wedding. Large white bows with pink hung from the front two rows where the wedding party would sit. Colorful flowers on pedestals sat at the front on opposite sides of the center aisle, while a tall lit candle stood on a wooden pedestal near the brass pulpit. Sunlight streamed through the side stained glass windows that ran the length of the wall to his right. The riot of colors cascading into the sanctuary was breathtaking.

"Quite stunning isn't it, son? As much as I'd like to admire the décor, we need to get ourselves to the dressing room for a quick meeting with the minister. How are you holding up? Still got the butterflies?" His uncle gave him a tender smile.

"The church is beautiful. I'm still nervous, but I'm not worried anymore. I can't wait to see what Janice is wearing. It really doesn't matter. She'd look good in anything." As his uncle gave him a knowing look, he walked down the aisle with Peter and his uncle to some dark stained doors that were set into the wall at the far side of the choir loft.

As he disappeared into the small room, Janice, with her bridesmaids, prepared in the hall nearby. She felt a flutter of nerves, but the butterflies seemed to have left. Her sister was kept busy trying to settle her two children. Amy was almost as excited as she was, and Ben was learning how to hold the red pillow level. That pillow would hold the two gold wedding bands that had mysteriously appeared a minute ago. She felt a few tears run down her cheeks as she watched her family.

"Hey, no tears allowed, sis. You don't want to ruin all that makeup, do you?" Betty glanced over at her, giving her a tender look.

"I'm just so happy, and the kids are adorable in their outfits. And you're right. The last thing I want is smeared mascara. Otherwise, I'll end up looking like a raccoon." She laughed at that thought.

The women and two children made final preparations for the service. A quick look at her watch told Betty that the service would start in about fifteen minutes. She could hear the pipe organ music as the organist played the prelude music. The clear sound of the organ wafted to them as they prepared to walk the short distance to the church.

Once inside the church, Janice got in line behind her bridesmaids with Amy and Ben. Her father appeared, taking up his position next to her. Smiling at him, she took his extended arm for the short walk up the aisle. She could see into the sanctuary of the church, could see all the special flowers. However, it wasn't the decorations that had her attention. It was the sight of Roger standing to the right side of the pews, waiting for her. Her jitters faded away at the sight of him. He was so handsome.

"Ready, sweetheart? Your young man is waiting for you. As much as I hate to be giving you away, I know you'll be in good hands. Roger is a fine man." He looked down at her, his love for her shining in his eyes.

"Thanks for everything, Dad. I feel more relaxed now. And I can't wait to become Roger's wife. I've dreamt of this day for months. I can't believe it's actually happening." She hesitated for a moment, smiling up at him, "I'm ready."

Frank whispered in her ear, "So am I, honey."

The organist changed the prelude music to the "Wedding March." It was their cue to start moving down the aisle. Betty and her friends preceded her, followed by Amy. As the procession moved slowly down the narrow aisle, Amy began to sprinkle pink rose petals on the thick red carpet. Ben was next, with the plump pillow holding the two precious gold rings.

Janice felt like she was gliding across the carpet. Before she knew it, she was at Roger's side. She couldn't take her eyes off his face. His eyes shone with his love for her. She felt calm, her heart full.

When Roger saw Janice for the first time, his breath caught. He had to make a conscious effort to breathe again. She looked like an angel in the white wedding dress. The material seemed to shimmer from the light cascading into the room. One of the neighbor's girls had been assigned the task of holding the train of Janice's wedding dress. A sense of awe overtook him as he thought about the fact they were to be married in a few short minutes. The butterflies had finally left; his palms were no longer sweaty. A sense of peace settled over him, much like a warm blanket. Everything felt so right. A slight smile crossed his face when he thought of his uncle's comment that his bad case of nerves would disappear when he saw her at the altar. He had been right all along.

Janice's father gave her away. Roger saw the sheen of tears in the older man's eyes.

When it came time to exchange vows and rings, his voice was firm and confident. After she recited her own vows, he reverently lifted the lacy veil and kissed his new wife.

While things were calm inside the church, outside something sinister was moving up the street. A black VW Jetta drove to the end of the road, turned, and pulled into the open spot behind the wedding car. Sara Martin wore a tight expression as she stopped the car and turned the engine off. Her hands were trembling slightly, her pulse racing. She was very aware of the cold metal of the small gun that she held cradled in her right hand. It was a stroke of luck that she had overheard Roger Abbott when she was in the grocery store in Avondale. He had been inviting some of his friends to his wedding. As she listened she found out where and when he was to be married.

Sara didn't know how long weddings took, but she hoped they would hurry. Now that the moment was here, she was anxious for the whole thing to be over so she could even the score. Then she would disappear until things died down. Vengeance had been on her mind constantly ever since Boyd's arrest. It ate at her like acid. Her frequent emotional visits to him in jail had only added fuel to the slowly building fire. At times he seemed almost cold toward her, but she figured it was because of his imprisonment.

Roger Abbott would pay!

Her gaze was fixed on the two massive oak doors of the cathedral. She hardly noticed the decorated car behind her, the call of birds from the nearby trees. The trembling in her hands increased. "Come on. How long does it take to say *I do* anyway?" She gritted her teeth in frustration.

It seemed to take forever, but finally, the doors were swung open and people began to spill out into the lawn. A couple of them took up their positions on either side of the entrance. She could see they held bags of some sort. As more families moved out into the autumn afternoon, she caught a flash of white just inside the door. A sinister smile stole across her face as Janice and Roger stepped out into the bright sun. They both looked radiant. At that moment, the two with the bags released their contents. Confetti showered down on the wedding couple, and she heard Roger cough a couple of times as he got some of the stuff in his mouth. The shower ended as suddenly as it had begun.

Sara watched impatiently as they chatted with several of their friends. She saw the bridesmaids in their pink gowns, a small boy in a black suit, and a young girl in a pink dress. Her hand gripped the gun more tightly. It wasn't supposed to be this complicated. Her hand was now trembling so much that she had to rest the gun on the side of the car door frame.

Finally, Roger and his new bride moved further down the walk, closer to Sara. They continued to chat with friends and well-wishers. In another couple of minutes, they would be in just the right position. She saw the two children directly behind the newlyweds and several men off to one side. She didn't like the idea of children being around. One of the men looked vaguely familiar. She forgot about him as she positioned the gun against the door. Doubts began to assail her. Would this solve her anger? Would it really bring closure to the whole mess?

Her shaking continued as Roger stepped down onto the first step.

He was now directly in her sights.

As distracted as he was by all the excitement, Roger didn't realize the danger he was in as he chatted with Janice. It never occurred to him that someone would be out to seek revenge. "Janice, you look wonderful. It's been such a special day. One I'll cherish for the rest of my life." His smile tugged at her heart.

"You don't look so bad yourself. I couldn't take my eyes off you in that tux. It felt like I was actually floating up the aisle." She gave the two children behind her a bright smile of encouragement. "Amy and Ben did great too."

"They were perfect. I guess we'd best get over to the hall for the reception, seeing everyone is waiting for us," he observed, as he glanced at the groups of friends heading for the nearby brick building.

As they stepped down onto the bottom step, Sara slid her finger into position against the trigger of the small semiautomatic pistol.

CHAPTER TWENTY-ONE

It would all be over in a nanosecond, and she could be out of here. However, she hadn't counted on the flashes of conscience that kept creeping into her mind. For the first time, she wondered if this was the right way to handle her hatred. And she hadn't counted on her past to suddenly spill its pain into the foreground.

In that instant, Sara had a sudden blinding moment of clarity as to the impact of her decision. It was like looking in a mirror, into who she had become. It hit her with the force of a two by four. She was no better than Boyd. As she looked at the newlyweds, she saw a new bride's life destroyed, she saw her own life in shambles, and then she thought of Boyd sitting in a jail cell in Avonvale. She now realized he had never loved her. It had all been play acting on his part.

Unfortunately for her, it had been very real. She had been blind, and she had let Boyd use her. She had been so starved for love that she had made a very unwise decision. Bitter tears consumed her.

She moaned, her whole body shaking so hard, she had to set the gun down. As she looked down at it, she felt the sting of guilt at what this small instrument could have done. Her eyes burned then the tears came. It was like a dam had burst as the tears ran unchecked down her cheeks.

While Sara was starting to come to grips with some serious soul-searching, Amy had been watching the dark car for several minutes. When she saw the gun pointed at them, she tugged at the sleeve of her mother's pink gown.

"Mom, there's a woman in that black car with a gun pointed at Uncle Roger." When her mother gave her a curt look, she added more earnestly, "Honest Mom. I'm not kidding. She's going to shoot him!"

"Amy, what are you talking about? What did I tell you about making up stuff?"

Amy grabbed at her mother's dress, making her turn toward her daughter. "She's in that black car just behind Uncle Roger's red one. And she looks real mean."

Betty looked past Roger to where Amy was pointing, her throat going dry when she realized that Amy had not been joking. There was no mistaking the gun in the brunette's hand. "You're right, honey. I'm sorry I doubted you. Now we need to get you and your brother to the safety of these trees."

Quickly, she ushered her two children behind her, close to the large oak on the lawn. Then she got Peter's attention. As a fellow police officer, he would know what to do. Within seconds, he used his cell phone to call the local police, and then he, along with another invited officer, were running toward the Jetta. She went to watch her children as the scene unfolded before her.

As the two men ran toward the car, they saw the woman lower the gun. They saw her body begin to shake. Something was going on, and they were going to get to the bottom of it. By the time they reached the car, they could hear her crying.

"Could you get out of the car, ma'am? Now, please!" Peter stepped into his police officer persona and used his sternest voice. "Is it true you have a gun and intend to harm someone in this group?"

While his companion pulled the door open, Peter watched as the distraught woman reluctantly climbed out of her car. She looked familiar. With long brown hair and a heart-shaped face, he was sure he had seen her in the past few months. "Up against the car, please."

"W-who are you anyway? If y-you're not a c-cop, I d-don't have to do a-anything you say." She was still shaking, tears still ran freely down her face.

Peter reached into his pocket, producing his wallet. When he flipped it open and she saw the police ID, she grew very quiet. Her eyes widened as she recognized him. It looked like she would pay for her bad decision to come here.

As Peter looked more intently at her, he remembered where he had seen her. "Well, well, Miss. Martin, we meet again. It seems you feel you have a score to settle." His eyes narrowed, his lips forming a thin line when his friend reached into the car, producing the small black handgun. "If you figured you could use violence to settle things, you're mistaken."

"I-I remember you n-now. You're that c-cop that was with Officer A-Abbott a couple of months ago. When you c-came and a-arrested Boyd." Her voice held a note of quiet acceptance. She found it hard to speak as emotions flooded to the surface. "Y-Yes, I d-did come to e-even the score, and I k-know I am in s-serious trouble. I couldn't do it. I-I'm n-not a k-killer." The last words were ended on a sob. Fresh tears again began to flow.

Sirens could be heard in the distance. As the shrill sound grew closer, several others began to mill about, wondering what was happening. With blue and red lights flashing, the police cruiser pulled up next to the wedding car. A dark clothed man jumped from the vehicle.

"Someone called the police. What's the problem here?" A young officer in a dark blue uniform came up to Peter. When appraised of the situation, he turned to a grief-stricken Sara. "It looks like you're in a lot of trouble, Miss Martin. Could you get your ID out of the car, please?"

Reluctantly, she reached in and produced a permit that she had forgotten would be in the glove compartment. "Here." She almost threw it at him.

"This is not your name here. I'm sure you have a good explanation for that?" The officer raised his eyebrows slightly as he stared at her.

"I stole the car." Sara's voice had a flat defeated tone that the men did not miss.

By now, Roger and Janice were standing nearby, watching things unfold. As he looked more closely at the woman being questioned by the authorities, his expression changed. Janice noticed the hard look pass across his face.

"Do you know what's going on, Roger? I don't know the woman with your best man." She glanced quickly at the brunette and saw tears in her eyes. Something was very wrong here.

"Janice, remember when I told you Boyd had a girlfriend?" He held her hand and pulled her to him.

"I recall you mentioned it. Why, is that her? Why is she here?" Her curiosity was now piqued.

"As far as I have been able to figure out, she came here today to seek some sort of revenge. I'm going to talk to Peter." When he saw her stricken expression, he tightened his grip on her hand. "She's not a threat, honey. She's shaking like a leaf." He could see Sara standing with Peter and the uniformed officer. By her appearance, it was very obvious she was in no condition to harm anyone.

When he confronted her, Sara's face crumpled, "Mr. A-Abbott. I-I'm s-sorry. I k-know I made a m-mistake c-coming here t-today. I couldn't h-hurt y-you or your b-beautiful bride. P-please f-forgive me." Fresh tears made their way down her cheeks. Her eyes were red, her face flushed.

Roger wasn't sure he could just shrug this off. The gun in the young officer's hand was pretty incriminating. Before he had a chance to form some sort of reply, Janice whispered in his ear, "She needs help Roger, not condemnation. Look at her, she can't hurt anyone. I forgive her, it's what God would want us to do. I really hope that you can find it in your heart to forgive her too. Please say you can let go of all the hate. If we hold onto the hurt, we let her win." She looked up at him, hoping he would understand. "We have a whole life ahead of us, can't we leave all the hurt and pain behind?" She gave the trembling woman a somber look. "It looks like she will have enough problems forgiving herself." Her compassion for this woman, who was an adversary, humbled him. Because of his wife's tender heart and forgiving spirit, he nodded.

By now, Sara had been read her rights, the gun had been placed in a plastic evidence bag, and the policeman had handcuffed her. As she was led away, she turned one last time and looked at them. Her face revealed the depth of her sorrow.

"It's over. I think I can forgive her. And you're right, it's not worth the hassle of holding on to past wrongs. Actually, I feel sorry for her. She was unwise to get involved with your uncle. I'm grateful she saw the light before she made an even worse choice."

"Me too. What will happen to her, Roger? I hope she can find some sort of peace. She looks utterly devastated." Janice was still looking at the retreating police cruiser as it turned and headed into the city.

"She'll be taken to a hospital and have a psychiatric assessment to see if she is mentally accountable for her actions. She may get a suspended sentence. Anyway, it's out of our hands now. Let's forget about it. Now, what were we going to do when all this came down on us? Seems like we were in the process of having a wedding reception." Glancing over her shoulder, he noted that almost everyone had disappeared into the brick hall across the parking lot. That left the two of them, Peter and the other friend.

Someone had been busy when they were being married. For the first time, he saw all the decorations on his car. White and pink pompoms were stuck to the sides of the vehicle, while a huge sign across the trunk proclaimed **Just Married** in bold black script. To complete the effect, cords hung from the back bumper, with tin cans at the ends. He smiled for the first time since the interruption.

Peter called out, "Hey, you guys, are you coming to the reception? It might be a good idea. If I'm not mistaken, you're the guests of honor." His face held a look of amusement. His broad grin brought the two newlyweds back to reality.

"Be right there." Both of them said in unison. He grabbed Janice's hand, and together, they walked across the lot to the reception. As long as he had her by his side, everything would be all right.

Later, after changing into their travel clothes, they emerged from the hall, moving to their car. People followed, throwing confetti in the air around them. There was a lot of cheering along with yells of congratulations. After a couple of final handshakes from family, they climbed into the red Chevy and pulled away from the curb. As they drove down the street, the rattle of tin cans could be heard as they bounced along behind the car.

Janice and Roger felt at peace as they drove away. After a while, they pulled into the driveway of their new home in Avonvale. All the improvements were complete, and both of them loved the place. Roger went around to the passenger's door, gently helping his wife from the car. Wife. His heart swelled with love as he looked at her. He swept her into his arms then carried her over the threshold. They were home and were about to begin their lives together.

EPILOGUE

Two years later.

Roger and Janice were relaxing in their new home in Avonvale. Since they both liked the quietness of the small town, and Roger worked on the local force, it was a natural fit for them.

He sat in the armchair next to the flowered couch. Although the news was on, he was watching Janice. She was relaxed and seemed to be asleep. He didn't doubt she was tired after a busy day looking after their daughter. In his mind, he replayed the events of the past couple of years. Now that the dust had settled, they both could relax and move on with the knowledge the danger was over. Boyd was in jail for at least thirty years, while Jason Cox got life for the murders of Ballantyne and the man in the hospital. It turned out that Boyd set up the fire on Spooner's Island. The others were in for lesser sentences. The big surprise was Sara Martin's confession. After her arrest for her attempt on his life, she admitted that she was the woman who had been involved in the drugstore robberies. Officer Simms got five years for conspiracy. He came back from his musing, looking at the soft features of his wife. Boyd Peterson and his gang faded into the background. This was what was important to him now. His family. Being a mother definitely agreed with her.

She must have sensed his stare, for she turned slightly and looked at him. "Sorry, I must have dozed off. What time is it, Roger?"

"It's four o'clock. And I was just sitting here thinking how beautiful you look when you're asleep. What's the white book next to you?" His gaze went to the large white photo album lying on the couch.

"It's our wedding album. You're such a romantic. You're always saying how pretty I look. The other day I had curlers in my hair and you said the same thing." She thought about his tender comments then smiled. "I guess it's true what they say, that beauty is in the eye of the beholder. I know I'll never get tired of hearing you say it."

"And I'll never get tired of telling you. We've got some time, let's take a look at that album." He moved to sit next to her on the couch. "That's much better."

After flipping open the large hard-covered book, they enjoyed looking at the many pictures taken at their wedding. Janice whispered, "It's hard to believe we've been married two years already. Here's one of you with your best man. Both of you looked great. The photographer got some great shots of us." She got a wistful look on her face when she turned the page and the photos of her and her bridesmaids came up.

"You looked like an angel in that wedding dress. You seemed to float up the aisle. And the kids were adorable." Roger turned another page, and both of them looked down at the images of Ben and Amy. "Ben was so proud to be carrying the rings. He did a good job of keeping that pillow level. And Amy. She had this smile that revealed just how happy she was for us." He reached over and gave her arm a gentle squeeze.

"I don't remember all the things that happened that day. I remember our vows, that kiss at the altar, the clanging of glasses at the reception. I don't know who came up with the idea of kissing every time a glass tinkled. I think I had chapped lips by the time we left."

"I didn't mind that part at all." After she gave him a nudge, he gave her a tender smile. "Here's one of your Aunt Audrey catching the bouquet. She had this silly grin on her face, like she had some big secret."

"She did have a secret, Roger. I don't know if you noticed, but your uncle danced with my aunt a lot during the reception. And later, I saw them together at one of the tables."

"My uncle did seem a bit preoccupied. So do I sense romance for the two of them? I know they've been seeing each other the past year." Roger's expression hinted that he thought that would be a great idea.

"From what Aunt Audrey told me later, I think they like each other a lot. Maybe that bouquet will bring her good luck." At this point, she laughed. "Amy told me she thought the whole idea with the flowers was kind of dumb."

"Maybe she'll change her mind when she gets a bit older. Her turn will come someday." His face took on a wry look when he saw the picture of her feeding him wedding cake. "I think I wore more of that cake on my face. Somebody missed my mouth." Here he raised his eyebrows at her.

"When I was feeding you the cake, you moved your head at the wrong time, so I missed your mouth. It was pretty funny, honey. Dad took the pictures of us eating the cake. I think Betty got the shot of Amy chasing her brother around. She was pretty excited to be in the wedding. I know she told Betty she thought I was the prettiest bride she had ever seen. She definitely had stars in her eyes."

"You've been a good example for her. She wants to be like you when she grows up."

"I hope she stays just the way she is now. She's a precious little girl. I guess she's not so little anymore."

She grew quiet then, and he looked into her eyes. He saw the tears that shimmered, hanging on her long lashes. She sniffed a few times then offered him a watery smile. "My emotions are pretty close to the surface right now. Hormones, I guess." Flipping through the photo album, she stopped when she came to the pictures of their daughter. "Speaking of precious, here's some pictures I took of Rebecca. She has your chin. With that tuft of hair sticking up, she looks just like a pixie. And here's a shot of Amy holding her. Looks like we have a ready-made babysitter."

"We couldn't ask for a better one, Janice." As Roger leaned over to admire the pictures of his daughter, he chuckled, "Do you remember the night you went into labor and I had to rush you to the hospital?

"You were a nervous wreck. If I hadn't yelled, you probably would have left for the hospital without me." She grinned at him. Then her expression softened, "When you saw her for the first time, you had such a look of awe on your face."

"She was so beautiful, just like her mother." He listened to a faint sound coming from down the hall. "Speaking of our daughter, do I hear her calling for you?"

She listened to a faint sound. "It sounds like someone is just waking up, and wants to be fed. I really appreciate how you have taken your share of looking after Rebecca. She adores you." With a louder wail coming from down the hall, she got up and headed to the baby's room.

By the time Roger joined her, she was sitting in the large wooden rocking chair in the corner of the small nursery. They had decorated the room in pink when they found out they would be having a girl. The small crib was white with pink frills, while a series of colorful mobiles hung from a hanger. The bright colors would keep the baby entertained most of the time. Except when she was hungry.

Again, his attention returned to Janice as she nursed their daughter, Rebecca Louise. Rebecca had been his grandmother's first name, and Louise was Janice's mother's first name. Both of them had agreed that it was the perfect name. The sight of mother and daughter squeezed his heart. If she had been beautiful before, now she was radiant. Motherhood gave her face a special glow. It seemed to come from somewhere deep inside her. When she looked up, their eyes met. She gave him one of her brilliant smiles. His breath stopped, for the moment was charged with feeling. His own eyes became misty. Seeing her with their three-month-old daughter, Rebecca, made him realize that he was the luckiest man in the world.

No, not lucky. Blessed. "Janice, you're so beautiful."

While he watched, their daughter drew away from her mother's breast. When the baby turned at the sound of his voice, he stared in awe and joy seemed to explode inside him. His heart melted when he looked at Rebecca. She was the spitting image of Janice, right down to the perky nose and deep violet eyes. Her lashes were long and curved up on the ends. As she looked up at him, she gave him one of her full dazzling smiles.

He thanked God that he had turned the corner and had been able to move on with his life. He had made mistakes, had even blamed God for them. Years had been wasted while he had wallowed in self-pity. With the help of a kindly minister, friends, and a spunky nine-year-old, he had moved forward. The best choice he ever made was to give his heart to the beautiful woman sitting in the old rocking chair in front of him. She was his soul mate, his other half. Through all of this, he learned that choices determine destiny. And he now knew that his destiny was to spend the rest of his life loving Janice. When she moved forward to fasten her blouse, she cradled their tiny daughter on her lap.

"Would you like to hold her, Roger?"

"I'd love to. Come on, sweetheart, come to Daddy." He cooed as he reached for the baby.

As soon as he held Rebecca against his chest, he felt his heart melt. She smelled of baby powder and that new baby smell. She grabbed at his shirt with tiny hands. Then as he patted her back, she gave a very unladylike burp. Looking over the top of her small clump of blonde hair, his eyes met Janice's. "I guess that means she's full. She can make a lot of noise for such a little thing." He looked down at the tiny face of his daughter. She seemed quite content to snuggle against his chest.

She gave him a tender look, happy tears filling her eyes. "She's beautiful, and I wouldn't change a thing about her. Or you, Roger."

She stood and gave him a quick tender kiss. With the two of them in his arms, his world was complete.

Edwards Brothers Malloy
Thorofare, NJ USA
March 25, 2013